Key
to
Love

by

Judy Ann Davis

This is a work of fiction. Names, characters, places, and incidents are either the product of the author's imagination or are used fictitiously, and any resemblance to actual persons living or dead, business establishments, events, or locales, is entirely coincidental.

Key to Love

Cover Art by *Kim Mendoza*

The Wild Rose Press, Inc.
PO Box 708
Adams Basin, NY 14410-0708
Visit us at www.thewildrosepress.com

Publishing History
First Crimson Rose Edition, 2013
Print ISBN 978-1-61217-927-8
Digital ISBN 978-1-61217-928-5

Published in the United States of America

"You still haven't told me about your nephew, Todd."

The luster in Lucas's face faded. "There's not much to tell. He lost his mother and father and has been tossed into foster care with the Johnsons. I'm trying to get temporary custody, but I'm not hopeful anything can be done until the investigation of Mike's death is completed. I guess it's standard procedure when a cop gets killed. I've been lucky enough the Johnsons let me have him on weekends."

"Is that allowed?" Elise opened the bread drawer and withdrew a half loaf of bread.

Lucas rose and walked to where she was working. "Well, it's bending rules a little, but they trust your father, and the Johnsons need a break. In case you haven't noticed, they're elderly, not in shape for chasing a child Todd's age."

He slapped a palm against the refrigerator. "Damn it, Liz, it's not fair. The kid is the one being punished, taking the brunt of things he had no part of. He's so lonely he cries himself to sleep at night. He doesn't understand what's happening. He doesn't even know where he belongs."

"So we spring him."

"It's not that easy!"

"Of course, it's not going to be easy." Elise forced herself not to shout back, "but that doesn't mean it's impossible, Lucas. Sit down, will you? I'm cooking this morning." She waved the half loaf of bread at him, then withdrew four slices and dropped them into the toaster slots.

He blinked. "Toast? You call that cooking?"

Dedication

Dedicated to my sons, Justin and Jeffrey,
and all my friends who understand the passion to write
and the need for creativity in our lives.

Chapter One

Scranton Wilkes-Barre International Airport was doing a brisk business for a Monday afternoon when Lucas Fisher arrived late because of heavy traffic on Interstate 81. He scanned the electronic arrivals board and instantly realized the early arrival of the San Francisco flight via a Detroit connection and his own tardiness meant one thing. He had already lost Elise Springer, sister of his best friend, Fritz. He'd bet all the money in his wallet she was impatiently wandering around the airport in search of him. Now he'd have to track her down or have her paged. Lucas sighed. He should have never washed his cell phone.

Before he left, Fritz Springer had given him explicit instructions. "Elise will be tired, and when she's tired, you know what she's like. Even at thirty years old, she hasn't outgrown being scrappy."

"Define scrappy." Lucas had looked at him with knitted eyebrows.

"Argumentative. Strong-willed."

"Cranky?"

"Yeah, downright cranky. So for your personal sanity and safety, please refrain from arguing with her. You will lose. Don't let her sidetrack you and be prepared for a ton of luggage and electronic paraphernalia. Just bring her out to the hospital where Thomas and I will be waiting for Dad to come out of surgery."

Collecting his thoughts, Lucas looked around the terminal with hopes of finding an attendant to direct him to a place where he could have scrappy Elise Springer paged. Finding none, he set out in search of her himself. After all, even if he hadn't seen her in ten years, and even if he hadn't seen the latest magazine clippings of her, he was sure he could recognize her from her brother's final parting words and stellar description: "a five-foot-five techno-nerd loaded down with enough electronic hardware she'll look like she ripped off the plane's control panel."

He caught up to the electronic wonder as she strode past a passengers' waiting area beside Gate Three. She wore a stunning, red silk suit with a gold designer purse hanging from her right shoulder and she held a smartphone to her ear. A laptop computer in a soft black leather case was slung over the opposite shoulder. He'd bet his life she had an iPod and graphing calculator hidden somewhere on her as well. He wondered how she ever made it through security without being detained for hours.

"Lizzie!" he shouted, closing the distance between them in long strides. She whirled, showing shapely, well-defined legs.

"Lucas? Dear Lord, Lucas! I can't believe it's you." She set her computer case on a chair beside her and threw her arms around him, enveloping him in hearty bear hug. Her perfume was exotic, expensive, with a hint of jasmine, and smelled as sensually exciting as she looked.

She pulled away, smiling, her eyes the same devilish blue he remembered and had always adored.

"You haven't changed," she said.

"You have." He studied her at arm's length and made a mental note to berate Fritz for neglecting to include "dynamite-looking" in his hasty description. But then, she had always been a beauty, even as a child when she tagged along behind her brothers, begging to be included in their every activity. Later, in high school, she'd been surrounded by swarms of adoring males, but it had been well known the Springer brothers' sister was off limits to anyone who didn't pass muster or whose intentions were anything but honorable. As the poor waif down the road, Lucas had resigned himself to the fact he would never have a chance with her, but he noticed her. Oh yeah, he had noticed all right.

Releasing her, Lucas paused long enough to scoop up her case from the chair before shepherding her toward the luggage area at the other end of the concourse. "I'm sorry I'm late. I didn't think Monday traffic would be this bad."

"How's Dad?" she asked as they hurried along.

"In surgery as we speak. Fritz is with him. Thomas should be there shortly as well. That's why you got me." He and Fritz had mutually conspired not to tell her father she was arriving. Lucas couldn't wait to see Anton Springer's face. He would think he was dreaming when he awoke and saw her. The old man deserved a slice of happiness. He was one of those rare persons who gave much more than he received.

"For God's sake, how could he break an ankle *and* a leg?" she asked. "He's usually so careful. I keep telling him he needs to slow down now that he's turned sixty-eight."

Lucas's mouth tightened into a grimace. "Actually

3

he stepped backward into a deep rut while repairing a tire on that decrepit thing he calls a hay wagon. I found him this morning. He made me promise I wouldn't call an ambulance, so I had to haul him into the hospital in his truck." Plowing down the long corridor, Lucas quickened his pace and was amazed she neither complained nor struggled to keep stride. "Listen, if we beat the five o'clock rush, we can be back before he gets out of recovery. He'll be so pleased to see you, Lizzie."

Elise rarely made it to the East Coast anymore. Her very impressive job as an architect with Winston and Sanders Architectural Designs in San Francisco didn't allow for much time off or long vacations.

"How's he taking it? Not just the leg and ankle, but the surgery, I mean?" Her voice was natural and steady, not showing the least sign of strain as they hurried along. With a body like hers, Lucas would bet his life she worked out on a regular basis in one of those posh fitness clubs—the kind where the personnel had weird, funny names and brought you ice chips, bottled water, and towels on tidy little silver trays.

"He seemed okay with the busted parts. He was churning out orders about the farm right up to the minute they wheeled him into the operating room. The surgery he wasn't too keen on. He wanted them to wrap everything up, but the doctors convinced him without surgery he might never walk again." Lucas threw the words over his shoulder, mentally gauging the time and distance to reach the luggage area. "I stopped by the house to take care of the dog before I came over here. Your father had Fritz in a tailspin. He was torn between following his orders and staying close by in the waiting room. I thought I was going to have to beat him on the head with a pitchfork and chain him to a chair in the waiting room."

Elise laughed. "Sounds like Dad and Fritz." She tapped Lucas on his shoulder. "We have to find a place around here to rent a car."

"Rent a car?" He whirled to face her, walking backwards as he spoke. "That's why I'm here, kid, remember?"

"Uh-uh." She waved a perfect oval-shaped, red fingernail at him, shaking her head sideways in unison. "I refuse to bump around in a pick-up old enough to legally drink. I need something reliable to get to the hospital and to grocery shop. A real car, Lucas, with comfortable adjustable seats, a sound system and A/C. Equipped. Dependable. You know what I mean?"

"Piece of cake. I can scare up something without any problem. You can drive mine until then." He turned back around.

"Oh, no. I couldn't possibly impose."

"No problem, I have a garage full."

"If my memory from high school is correct, you liked to piece together cars from odds and ends of other vehicles. Tell me, are any of these so called vintage cars road worthy yet?"

"Sure." Lucas grinned, thinking of his restoration and auto body business. He could do everything from rebuilding an antique Ford sedan to repairing a tiny scratch on the door of a sleek Lamborghini Roadster. "But I have some real gems in pieces, too."

"Ah, just as I thought. I want a rental, Lucas, not a pieced-together pile of metal, rubber, and plastic. Where's the rental booth located?"

At first he thought she was joking. Then he looked at her, *really* looked at her. Her huge pool-blue eyes were dead serious. He pulled her aside, away from the bustling hallway crowds and raised a hand, palm out. Fritz had warned him she could be a handful. Independent and strong-willed. Hadn't those been his exact words?

"Okay, just stop right there. Here's your highly organized plan as I see it. We wait in line for a half hour to rent a car you don't need, another fifteen minutes to pick up the luggage, which is probably more than you'll need...then let's say fifteen more minutes to drag all of it to the parking lot, and guess what?"

"What?" She stared at him like he should be institutionalized.

"We're smack in the middle of rush hour and still the same distance away from the hospital because you don't want to impose." He watched her face turn from confusion to anger.

"You need to get a pair of glasses, Lucas," she said.

"Glasses?"

"Yes, so you can see better. I'm not the Springer brothers' silly little sister anymore, so you can dispense with the hostile tone. Don't call me kid. Ditto for babe, sweetie, honey, princess or any derivatives thereof. I'm also now capable of making my own decisions including deciding what I want to drive."

"Okay, my mistake," he said, conceding. He had no desire to make a scene they both might regret. "Does Liz or Lizzie push your buttons the wrong way?" He was surprised to see her lips turn upward into a smile.

"No, it's obvious everyone around here is going to

call me Lizzie. I can handle the nicknames. Now, what about the car?"

Lucas's gaze slid over to the rental car booth several yards away where businessmen, singles, and a trio of boisterous children with chocolate ice cream cones were waiting in line to talk to an agent.

"Be my guest, Miss Springer. Give it your best shot. I'll wait." He gestured to a row of nearby seats. "Hell, I could use a thirty-minute break. Word of caution about the suit you're wearing—I'd be inclined to tread lightly around those sticky little munchkins with the ice cream cones. Give me a high sign if you get lucky, and I'll head out."

He dropped onto a chair, crossed his arms, and fell silent. Lord, he had almost forgotten how bull-headed she could be. And Fritz had the audacity to call her scrappy? He snorted. Scrappy hardly made a dent in defining her. But if she wanted to burn up valuable time at a rinky-dink car rental booth when he owned a whole flipping fleet of cars, why should he care?

Chapter Two

Elise Springer scrutinized the crowd at the booth and winced as threads of guilt pulled at her sense of logic. At best, she would waste a half hour inching her way to the front of the line. She turned back to meet Lucas's gaze and found him staring appreciatively at her backside and legs. That he was doing it on purpose made her blood boil. She was tired and hungry, and she prayed she'd never have to walk a hundred steps more in the new shoes she was wearing. She stomped back to where he sat.

"Are you getting an eyeful?"

"Yeah, are you getting a car?" His smile quickly turned to a grin. A lazy grin. One she had almost forgotten. He stretched out his booted feet, crossing them at the ankles. Facing off, they stared at each other.

Though she hated to admit it, he was outrageously good-looking, even in his worn jeans, faded black tee-shirt, and boots that had seen better days. He had changed considerably since she had last seen him, over ten years ago, during her second year in college when he was home on leave from the Army. Age had chiseled his face even more and taken away any hint of boyish features. But he had the same thick crop of ebony hair and a trademark dark scowl that seemed to reinforce his devil-may-care demeanor. His body, lean and trim, was a hardened mass of muscle. He had been raised by his grandmother just a few miles up the road from Elise's house and had spent more of his high school years swiping leftovers from her parents' refrigerator than from his own. All through childhood and high school, he and her brother, Fritz, had been loyal, inseparable friends. Elise wondered what his car restoration business actually entailed, but she didn't think it would be polite to start grilling him within ten minutes of meeting him.

"Listen, I have an idea." He stood, rolling his shoulders to dislodge the kinks. He scrubbed his eyes with his fingertips. "Let's put the rental on hold for the time being."

"How long have you been up?" she asked.

"Since about five this morning."

"Oh, Lucas, I'm sorry. I had no idea."

"No, it's all right. Five wouldn't have been so bad if your dad, Fritz, and I hadn't stayed up until one this morning playing poker. Anton and I had high hopes of cleaning your brother's clock."

"And did you?"

He laughed. "Fritz? Get real. He bluffed the money right out of our pockets." He glanced again at the long line leading to the rental cars. "If you're all fired up about renting a car, how about I bring you back later? We're on a tight schedule here."

"Sounds reasonable." She glanced again at the line where two new people had already taken her place. "Sorry, I'm not thinking straight." She watched his smoke-colored eyes narrow. She rubbed her forehead where a headache was threatening and wondered why on earth she was taking the time to validate herself.

"A day of surprises, huh?" he asked softly.

Elise sighed. "Complicated," she admitted. She wasn't about to tell him she had almost gotten herself fired. For the first time in her life, she had told their most valuable client, Mort Levinson, what she really was thinking when he decided to change all the plans for a new hotel they were building together, along with the lead contractor and dozens of subcontractors. Luckily, the eccentric old man, a multi-millionaire and genius businessman to boot, had taken a shine to Elise and her work a long time ago. Also luckily, he had a sense of humor. She was also fortunate Chuck Sanders, one of the senior partners, was a jovial and forgiving sort, especially since they had clinched the deal and averted a crisis with Levinson who, it was rumored, was planning a series of new hotels in five major cities across the United States. Paul "Mr. Personality" Winston, the other half of the firm, was another matter. The pompous, cold-hearted dimwit didn't even want to give her time off for a family emergency, even when she pleaded and promised she'd use her vacation days.

They set out again, and she felt the heat of his fingers on her arm as he guided her around an airport shuttle car. "So just what do you do in your swanky California office besides drive people nuts?" His breath was a soft whisper near her ear.

"I design structures of all sorts, complete with parking lots and landscaping. I coordinate the interior decorating, if the client chooses. I oversee the construction and handle details and difficult clients. I work hard at the last two, especially in-house mediating."

The last remark made him chuckle.

"I'm serious, Lucas, it's what I do best. Hold up."

She skidded to a halt near a small alcove where a vendor sold books and magazines. She slipped off a shoe, pretending to shake out some irritating piece of grit. It was as good a time as any to give her feet a much-needed break. Why had she ever decided to wear a new pair of shoes on a trip across country? Italian leather be damned. Her feet were cramped and swollen, and were turning red and blue. She'd choke on her tongue, she decided, rather than admit her shoe dilemma to him, or to any living male. "You don't believe me, do you?"

"Sure I believe you. You should be an expert by now." He nodded and watched her, his hand shoved into the back pocket of his jeans. Elise wondered whether he was thinking back to when she used to twirl her brothers around her little finger throughout high school. For that matter, middle and elementary school, too. "So what happens when you get unyielding ones?" he asked.

"I poison the coffee of those dudes."

For the first time, Elise heard him laugh. Really laugh. It was rich, deep and smooth, all sensually male.

"I suppose that's just as humane as running them down with four thousand pounds of metal and rubber, which would have been my first instinct."

They entered the luggage area, and she was relieved to find her two suitcases already waiting and spinning slowly around the carousel.

Easing the case from his grip, she pointed out her luggage. "We'd better get a cart or porter," she suggested.

He swung the luggage off the belt, shoulder muscles bunching beneath his tee-shirt screen printed with a blurb about enjoying speed behind a 350-cubic-inch V8 engine. He set both down and pulled the handles out. "Got them. Through there." He jerked his head toward an exit.

In the parking lot, Lucas hustled her quickly between rows of cars bearing colorful license plates from around the country, and stopped beside a glistening, black Pontiac.

"A '77 Trans Am? *This* is yours?" Elise moved past him to get a better view while she slipped a foot out of the worse-offending shoe, balancing a toe on the warm concrete. She had been trained to have an eye for detail, and the Trans Am was sleek, its lines highlighted by the flawless finish. It was polished to a brilliant shine and sparkled like glass in sunlight. She remembered he had always loved to tinker with mechanical things. Growing up, he and Fritz had spent endless hours under the hood of Fritz's jeep. They had watched *Smokey and the Bandit* so many times, they had worn out the VCR tape and had to buy another one.

"For the next thirty days." He tossed the bags into the trunk. "Then she's headed to a buyer in Atlanta."

"You restored this?"

"Yeah, it's sort of a hobby and business all rolled into one." The shoe trick didn't get by him. Gray eyes peered at her naked foot. "Hurt yourself?"

She hurriedly stepped into the shoe. "No, my shoes hurt. They pinch my toes."

"Why don't you buy ones that fit?"

"I thought I did."

He shook his head, as if he had heard the same line a dozen times and probably from a dozen females. A tattered blanket lay inside the trunk and he tossed it aside. Two children's books tumbled out.

He's married, or has been, Elise thought, and there's a child involved.

Following her gaze, Lucas straightened. "Long story, Liz."

She glanced at him long enough to see his eyes cloud over. Was it sadness? Or despair? The curtain fell quickly, blocking any emotion as his scowl returned.

"So what's the deal?" he asked.

"Deal? What deal?"

He gestured to her arms where she was unconsciously cradling the computer in a protective embrace. "Are you intimately attached to that heap of leather?"

She blushed. "I get a little overprotective with my gear."

"Smuggling data, huh?"

"No, nothing that exciting." Elise handed it to him and waited until he stashed it in the corner of the trunk, wedging it in with the blanket. Rounding the car, she reached for the door handle only to feel the warmth of his hand as it covered hers. Startled, she peered up, pulling her hand away.

"Don't be too astonished, Lizzie. I did manage to pick up a few finer points over the last few years, though I don't make them a habit. I can't afford to ruin my bad boy image."

Determined not to start another war, Elise slid into the soft leather seat that wrapped around her like a second skin as she buckled her seat belt. She ditched the shoes again. It felt glorious to free her cramped toes. "I always wondered why men referred to these machines as female."

Lucas settled himself in the driver's seat. "Because they're soft, sleek, fickle, and my, oh my, can they purr under the right touch." His hands lovingly caressed the steering wheel. Grinning, he turned the key in the ignition and artfully maneuvered the car through the mazelike parking garage.

She had no doubt the remark and gesture were meant to get a rise from her, but before she could make a retort, the alarm on her watch triggered. Irritating bleeps swamped the Pontiac's interior. The car screeched to a halt, brakes grabbing and propelling her against the shoulder harness.

Lucas turned to face her. "What the hell is that?"

"My watch." She pushed her sleeve up and fumbled with the buttons on her wrist. "It's my daily four o'clock reminder to check my client list before I leave the office."

"You have a wristwatch with an alarm *and* a cell phone?"

She worked frantically, toying with the button to no avail. "Just my dumb luck, it doesn't want to turn off." She felt her face grow hot and tore the watch from her wrist, all but slamming it against the door frame. Inside the closed car, the steady beeping grew increasingly annoying.

"Oh, for the love of Pete!" Lucas reached over and snatched it out of her shaking hands. Cutting the engine, he opened the door and slid out.

In the rear view mirror, Elise watched the trunk fly up and then slam shut. Seconds later, he settled himself behind the wheel again. He raised an eyebrow. "Any other distractions we need to dispense with?"

She tried to sound contrite. "I only have the phone

left."

She withdrew the phone from her purse, fiddled with a setting, and slipped it back inside. She stole a peek at his face, which was hard to read. It was less than an hour and already they were at each other's throats, just like when they were kids.

A pair of low-heeled shoes appeared under her nose.

"Put these on while you're at it."

Shoes. Her shoes. Her old, black leather flats. From her luggage. "Where did you get these?"

"I ran out to a 7-Eleven and scarfed them up. Where do you think I got them?"

"You went through my suitcases?" Her voice rose an octave. The thought of him rummaging through her personal belongings without permission made her blood boil. "How dare you?"

He took a deep breath as if he was summoning his last ounce of patience. "You needed shoes, Liz." He gestured to the shoes on the floor. "Those three-inch stilts weren't cutting it. The other alternative was a drag rope."

"I can't believe you rifled through my clothing!"

He popped the clutch, leaving rubber on the smooth concrete. "If you're fired up I might divulge any of your sizes, rest assured, it'll never happen. I only talk"—he paused to concentrate on maneuvering the car through the exit and onto the highway, darting easily between slower moving vehicles to access the fast lane—"under torture."

Tired from the flight, she leaned back in the seat and let silence settle around them. She was too tired to quibble over the watch or shoes and was content to let the landscape fly by in a whirling multitude of colors. Through the half-open window, she could smell the light, earthy scent of spring. She had been in the city so long she had almost forgotten how glorious clean air smelled. Pennsylvania was lush green now, bearing up to the soft spring rains. Soon cows with swollen, round bellies would be grazing in brilliant emerald pastures, awaiting calving and motherhood. Late-blooming tulips would be bursting into colorful mounds of yellows and reds, and the farm's lilacs into shades of rose, lavender, and white.

Several minutes later, Lucas looked over at her as he reached to turn on the radio. "Tell me, have you ever forgotten one of those fancy gadgets and had withdrawal symptoms?"

She glared at him as the clear, clipped voice of Taylor Swift wailed from the stereo speakers. "No. Have you ever learned to drive below seventy miles per hour?"

He laughed, and Elise felt the car surge forward even faster as he applied gentle pressure on the accelerator. She settled back in the seat again, allowing the speed and music to carry her away, toward center city Scranton and the hospital. At least if they were going to wreck, she decided, they were headed in the right direction.

Chapter Three

Community Medical was quiet and antiseptic-smelling, like most hospitals in every city of every state. Elise tried not to dwell on the cold, sterile feelings it invoked as she and Lucas made their way to the small, third-floor waiting room, sprinkled with padded vinyl seats a shade darker than the blue, nondescript wallpaper.

"Wake up, Fritz, she's here." Thomas' voice, perfectly timed with his elbow, awakened the sleeping man beside him. He rose and grabbed Elise in a warm brotherly embrace.

Yawning, Fritz squinted up at Lucas. "Easy deal or tricky maneuver? Elise, I mean." He stood and waited patiently for his older brother to release his sister.

"It was touch and go," Lucas admitted in a weary drawl. "I considered commando tactics at one point. A drag rope was mentioned in our conversation."

Fritz winced. "You made good time."

"You're kidding, right?" Elise turned and enveloped her younger brother in a hug. He lifted her off her feet like so many times before and jiggled her as if she was little more than a rag doll. "With Bandit at the wheel, we could have outrun a cop. Put me down, you big goon."

She landed on her feet and took time to fill her eyes with both of them. They were so opposite in

17

temperament and looks it was hard to believe they were related. Thomas was tall, methodical, reserved, and without a particle of lint on his finely tailored suit; and Fritz, dressed in khaki slacks and a comfortable plaid shirt, was the comic, sporting a wicked grin that made women's hearts melt. He could sell life insurance to a corpse.

"How's Dad?" she asked.

"He's out of recovery. We should get to see him in a few minutes, as soon as the nursing staff gets him settled for the evening." Fritz jammed his hand into his pocket to fiddle with loose change. "Breezed through it. Got a plate in the ankle, a pin in the fibula, and should recover nicely if he stays away from large magnets."

"Hold on, Fritz, it's a little more complicated," Thomas countered.

Now she was going to get something closer to the truth. Thomas was the one who lived his life on a more cautious, serious note, so typical for someone who practiced law. "Yes, he came through with flying colors, but it could mean a week's stay or more in the hospital, physical therapy, and a long recovery. Then we'll have to make arrangements for him to adjust and recover comfortably at home."

A stocky nurse appeared in the doorway. "You can go in now, but it might be best if you keep your visit short."

Anton Springer looked old and tired and fragile against the white sheets and bleak surroundings. Elise felt a sting of remorse. It had been over a year and a half since she had last paid a visit home to see him. Since her mother had passed away, she had found it harder and harder to sandwich in even a yearly trip to

Pennsylvania.

"Dad." She kissed him gently on his weathered, wrinkled cheek.

"Elise?" He opened his eyes, still sharp and luminous, but clearly pain-filled, and automatically reached for her hand. A weak smile spread across his face. "When did you get here?"

"Two minutes ago."

He tried to push himself upright while he searched the room. "So it takes an old man with a busted leg to get you all together again?" Fitfully, he toyed with the buttons on the bed rail until the mattress rose. "Gosh darn mechanical beds. You need a PhD to be able to run them." Anton waved his hand toward the door. "Don't try to hide, Lucas. You're as much a part of this family as these other rascals. Get in here before the nurses get cranky and toss you all out on your backsides."

The next half hour was like a family reunion as they talked, clowned around, and teased each other, rehashing the accident, and recalling old times and tales until excitement finally took its toll.

It was Elise who noticed her father's weariness first. She rose. "I don't know about these dudes, but I need some rest. It's been an exhausting flight and a long day." As if on cue, her brothers and Lucas stood and headed for the door.

"Don't leave yet," Anton said to her as the men silently filed out. "How long can you stay?"

"However long you need me." She decided this was no time to tell the truth. Paul Winston had begrudgingly allowed her two weeks of vacation days with an underlying inference to get back earlier if possible.

"It's not just me." Wincing, Anton struggled with a pillow behind his back. "It's Lucas."

"Lucas?" She moved to help him, meticulously fluffing and positioning his pillow until he was comfortable.

"He came back over two weeks ago, claiming he's going to settle here for good. His brother died a few months ago in a car accident and left some loose ends behind. Now rumor has it that it might not have been an accident, maybe a drug bust gone bad or maybe someone had a vendetta. He was a state trooper."

"I didn't know Lucas had a brother."

"Not many people did. Mike Fisher was raised in a foster home in upstate New York. It's too complicated to sort out now, and it's not my place to say, but Lucas is chasing lots of ghosts. Work with him, will you, Lizzie? I promised him I would, but I can't now, not with this dad-burned busted leg."

Elise watched her father's grizzled face become agitated, more upset because he could not fulfill a promise than because he was worried about his health.

"I'll see what I can do." She hoped her voice sounded more reassuring than she felt. Lucas Fisher had never been the type of person who wanted anyone to meddle in his affairs. She pecked her father on the cheek again and stifled a yawn. "I'll stop by tomorrow. We'll talk. You can fill me in. You need to rest, Dad."

"Look who's talking," the old man muttered. His voice held more amusement than chastisement.

Outside in the hall, the three men, their heads bent, were huddled near a wall, speaking in hushed whispers. As soon as she approached, they fell silent and looked up at her with guilty expressions.

"We can transfer my things to Fritz's car," she suggested, at a loss for something to say. "Thomas, you're coming back to the house for a few minutes, right?"

He nodded, looking anything but pleased. "Elise, we need to talk."

She glanced at Fritz, who looked like he was about to squirm out of his clothes. Through a careful breath, she said, "So what's up? Somebody fill me in."

"She hasn't eaten," Lucas interrupted in a voice so calm it unnerved her. He pushed himself upright from where he had been leaning against the wall and uncrossed his arms. His expression was brooding but controlled, his eyes a cloudy gray. He glanced at her, then looked over at Fritz. "Why don't you pick up some pizzas? Lizzie and I will meet you at home. Thomas can take his car, too."

"Good idea," Fritz agreed, visibly relieved.

"I can go with Thomas," she offered. "It's been a long day, for you, too, Lucas. You have to be exhausted."

Three pair of eyes darted cautiously back and forth among each other.

"We need to talk," Lucas said in a low voice, coming to stand beside her. "Just you and me." She could feel the heat of his body so close to hers. "I'll drive you home."

"Okay." She nodded, wondering what could be so important it couldn't wait a while longer.

Minutes later, seated inside the car in a half empty parking lot, she waited for him to start the engine. The scent of warm tar from freshly laid blacktop filtered in through the open windows. After what seemed like an eternity of silence, she leveled a glance his way. He sat still, his hands gripping the steering wheel.

"All right, Lucas, spit it out. You guys were acting like baboons back there. In triplicate." She felt her mental energy waning. The disagreements with Levinson, Winston, and Sanders, and the flight out were beginning to wear on her.

"We have a problem." He returned her stare. "I've been staying at the farm with your father for the last few weeks."

She studied him a moment. His jaw, now rigid, gave him an almost defiant appearance in a handsome sort of way. "That's the problem?" Actually, it was, she thought, as she saw all hopes of an uninterrupted, peaceful evening fly out the window.

"It's not a big deal with me, but your brothers seem to think it might be with you."

"Hey, I don't own the place."

"So you're not concerned?"

"About what?"

Lucas scowled. "Your reputation, I imagine."

This time she laughed a musical laugh. It rippled outward into the car and night air. "Lucas, the only reputation I'm concerned about is becoming a noted architect before my hair turns gray, or God forbid, falls out."

"Don't you want to ask why?"

"Why what?"

"Why I decided to come back to the area?" he asked.

"No, it would be prying."

His face split into a grin. "It's never stopped you before, Miss Curiosity."

"Okay, what are you doing back in the Scranton area?" Elise smiled.

"I'm moving here and opening a specialty restoration and auto center in Scranton, a spin off from my business in Atlanta. I'll be selling and leasing high-end used vehicles combined with a restoration facility for collector cars. I've hired a manager to run my Chevy dealership in Atlanta." The engine came to life, and he shifted the car into reverse and eased out of the parking place. "I would have stayed at my grandmother's house, but it needs lots of work and the utilities haven't been turned on yet."

"That's a pretty big undertaking. Why here?" She remembered his grandmother's house. It was more a cottage than a house. She had been inside it only once, her first summer back from college, but she had barely noticed any of the details, except it was quaint and situated in a magnificent rural setting with its own little lake.

Lucas shrugged, frowned, and gripped the wheel tighter while he concentrated on the road ahead.

Elise had learned many things working with people. It wasn't always what was said, but sometimes what wasn't said. A subtle body movement, a certain look, a slight hitch of a shoulder often revealed more than what the ear heard.

"It's...it's..." He groped for the right word. "It's complicated. Very complicated." His face was grim, and she could see he was struggling with something. Inner demons, perhaps.

Elise leaned back, resting her head against the seat and closed her eyes. She sighed. "Hey, we can talk about it later. After all, it's not like we're going to have to make an appointment to see each other."

"True enough," he agreed in an exhausted but appreciative tone.

****

Lucas wrapped his fingers around the steering wheel and gave his full attention to the road, listening to the soothing hum of the motor. He loved the sense of control an automobile provided. The speed. The motion. It was all part of a glorious, cleansing experience.

Monique, unfortunately, had not shared his love and interest in cars. Monique DuBois. The name tumbled in his head like some ancient dream, flimsy and without substance. Hell, he and Monique had not shared much, except her perfect body on occasion, when she was between modeling engagements. How had he ever believed he could sustain a lasting relationship with someone whose most important concern each day was selecting which outfit to wear?

Bile rose in his throat when he thought about the day his brother had died. He had been chasing after Monique in the Caribbean, and it had taken the authorities four days to track him down.

He had flown directly to Scranton where Mike had been assigned to work undercover—where the body was on ice, waiting to be claimed. Monique had not joined him, begging off with the lame excuse she was under contract and would meet him for the funeral, a few days later. She never arrived.

In the end, it was Anton Springer, Fritz, and Thomas who stood by him through the whole ordeal. Gently, the old man had guided him through the chaos that followed, including the flowers, casket selection, even the service arrangements and music for the viewing. Afterward, when he had gone on a four-day drinking spree, it was Anton who had sent Fritz out to gather him up, bring him home, and help him while he spewed his guts into the porcelain bowl.

Later, sober and harboring a headache to match his heartaches, he learned the old man had saved his hide without his knowledge. Todd, Mike's four-year-old son, had been placed in a foster home nearby, but only because Anton Springer had intervened, climbing on the backs of the Children and Youth Services Agency and pulling strings when he discovered their plans were to ship the kid back across the state to New Castle, Pennsylvania.

Orphans. Foster brats.

Lucas despised those words. They were worse than the most hideous swear words. Adults whispered them in pitying sighs, behind your back as they sent slanted, curious looks your way. Did they honestly believe children could help it that their parents were dead or couldn't take care of them? Did they honestly think children really wanted to wear hand-me-down clothes that didn't fit properly? So kids could taunt and stare at them as if they were freaks?

Well, if Lucas had anything to say about it, Mike Fisher's son was not going to be subjected to any sort of humiliation. He would take the boy and raise him, single-handedly if necessary. Todd was not going to become a foster brat, not if Lucas could help it. The Fisher name was finally going to crawl out of the slimy hole of nobodies. In addition, the petty Moniques of the world and anyone else who tried to stand in his way could go straight to hell. Clenching his teeth, he squinted at the road in front of him, irritated his thoughts had wandered out of control. Again.

He looked over at the passenger's seat. The dainty techno-wonder had dozed off. She even slept neatly and organized, rolled into a tiny ball, on her side, hands clasped at her waist. He wondered whether she would be upset if they took a slight detour. Deciding it was best not to wake her, he swung onto the exit ramp, heading southeast of the farm and turning into a small country lane where a sun-faded maroon house with peeling white shutters sat along the road. He pulled into the drive and cut the engine.

Elise roused, sat up, and yawned. "What time is it?" Her voice was thick, still husky from sleep.

"Around eight," he said. How in hell could the mere sound of her voice make him catch his breath and send his stomach into a dive?

Elise pushed up her sleeve to check her watch. Frowning as soon as she realized it was in the trunk, she yanked the sleeve back into place. "Thank heavens, we're home." She peered out the window. Her brow wrinkled. "Oh, no, don't tell me we're lost."

"Not exactly," Lucas said. He had hoped she would continue to doze. It would have made everything easier. "I needed to make a small detour and see someone. Can you spare a few minutes?"

"Sure. Want me to wait in the car?"

He started to say, "Yes," and then changed his mind, heaving a sigh. "No. Hell, why not? My life's an open book lately. This is just another page in a chapter."

He reached over, unlocked the glove compartment and took out a small bag.

"Is it a mystery, adventure, or comedy?" she asked with an amused look.

A damned tragedy, he wanted to say. Instead, he said, "You decide."

Chapter Four

"You came. I knew you would!"

The small voice at the top of the stairs halted the conversation before Elise was properly introduced to the elderly couple standing in the lighted entranceway.

A little boy, barefoot and wearing too-large, green pajamas that puddled around his tiny ankles, peered down at them. He held a battered storybook protectively against his chest, partially obscuring a picture of a dog she recognized as Copper from *The Fox and the Hound.*

Taking the stairs two steps at a time, Lucas reached the boy and stopped. "Slight problem, Todd. Mr. Springer was hurt, and I had to take him to the hospital."

"Is he going to die?" The child's eyes grew large and wary.

"No, no, of course not. He's fine," Lucas assured him. He handed him the bag. "Here's the animal crackers I promised you, but you must promise me you won't eat them until tomorrow." He scooped up the child and, with a little arm locked around his neck, returned to the entryway. "I'd like you to meet an old friend of mine."

"Come, sit down," said the elderly woman, whose last name Elise remembered was Johnson. "Can I get you something to drink? Miss—?"

"Elise. Elise Springer. No, I'm fine, thank you." Elise smiled.

The small living room they entered was tidy and clean and reminded Elise of the Fifties. Square, dark tweed chairs and a sofa with walnut end tables lined the room's perimeter and were strategically situated to face the television atop a metal stand in a corner. Through an opposite archway, she could see a well-kept kitchen with a red and white Formica table and vinyl-padded chrome chairs.

"He's been peppering us all day with questions, ever since I told him you might not be coming today," Mrs. Johnson said to Lucas, and turned to her white-haired husband standing beside her. "Hasn't he, Hank?" She motioned for Elise to take a seat.

Elise chose a chair beside the sofa, its back draped with a colorful ripple afghan. Lucas, carrying Todd, buckled down onto the sofa beside Mrs. Johnson.

"I'm sorry," Lucas said, settling the boy on his lap. "I hope he wasn't too much of a bother."

"No need to be sorry," the elderly woman replied. "Accidents happen. Lord knows we've had our share of them over the years. Right, Hank?"

Her husband nodded and peered at Elise through wire-rimmed glasses. "So you're Anton's daughter? The architect?" When she nodded, he asked, "How's your father doing?"

"Fine. Much better than I expected."

"Good. Good to hear," Mr. Johnson said, sounding genuinely concerned.

The uncomfortable silence that might have followed was punctuated, as if on cue, by the muffled sound of a phone.

"Her purse rings!" With a powerful leap for someone so little, Todd flew off Lucas's lap, sending the box of animal crackers and his book skidding across the floor. He rushed over to stand a wary foot away from Elise's knees.

"My cell phone," she explained, feeling foolish under the stares of everyone present. She reached for her purse and withdrew the phone. "Elise Springer." Relieved, she heard her youngest brother's voice.

"I thought you shut it off?" Lucas interrupted.

She turned from the phone. "No, Lucas, you assumed I did." She spoke into the phone and then turned back again to Lucas. "Fritz wants to know where we are."

"Mulberry Road," Mrs. Johnson supplied with a smile. "Just tell him the Johnsons' place. He's our insurance agent, so he'll know. Such a nice young man."

Elise relayed the information and then glanced at Lucas again. Beneath his visible air of calmness, she sensed irritation. "Fritz and Thomas are at the farm. They have the pizzas and want to know how long we'll be."

"Fifteen minutes." The answer came out with a tired sigh. "Tell them to start without us."

Elise repeated Lucas's reply and disconnected, glancing up in time to see Todd curiously regarding her with huge gray eyes, the same color as Lucas's.

"Can I see it?" Todd asked shyly. He inched his way toward her. He was a little charmer, Elise decided, with his cherub-like face and fine, flyaway blonde hair cut in a tattered bowl style.

"It's not a toy, sport," Lucas said.

"I just want to see it. It's flat." His tiny lower lip ballooned outward. "It's not like Mrs. Johnson's Jitterbug and it isn't like the phone you washed, Uncle Lucas."

"Washed?" Elise raised a quizzical eyebrow at Lucas and smirked. "Here, Todd, come and take a look." She motioned to him, and he scrambled up into her lap. She resettled his needle-like elbow lodged against her ribcage and cupped his soft hands around the rectangular cell. The delicate scent of baby shampoo from his hair, still damp from a bath, reached her nostrils.

"How does it work?" he asked.

"It's called a smartphone. I'll show you. Do you know your numbers?"

When he nodded, she took his finger and positioned it over the on-screen number pad. "What's the phone number here?" she asked Mrs. Johnson, memorizing them as the elderly woman spoke.

Elise repeated them slowly to the child, helping him locate the correct ones. He giggled each time a number chirped beneath his touch.

In the kitchen, the Johnson's phone rang.

She glanced up to find Lucas intently watching them.

The phone sounded again.

"Okay, Lucas, snap out of it," she admonished, nodding toward the wall phone. "You're supposed to be the guy on the other end. We need a second party here."

"What?" Lucas looked at her with baffled eyes.

"The phone. Pick up the Johnsons' wall phone."

"Oh, yeah, right." He strode to the kitchen and plucked the receiver from the phone beside the refrigerator.

"Now say hello," she whispered to Todd.

Warily, the boy put the phone to his ear. "Hello?"

"Hello, is this Todd?" she heard Lucas ask from the kitchen.

"Uncle Lucas!" he said, beaming. He turned to her, his eyes bright. "It's Uncle Lucas!"

"Well, talk to him," she coaxed. *Uncle*? The boy had said uncle three times since they arrived. So this must be Mike Fisher's son.

"What should I say?"

She smiled and snuggled the child closer. "Tell him, he has a nice car and a cute nephew."

"Eee-lise says you have a nice car and a cute nephew."

"Am I the cute nephew?" Todd asked in a whisper, swiveling and peering up into her face. A soft, tiny hand came up to brush her cheek.

"Yes, absolutely," she whispered and saw him beam.

"Well, tell her thank you and say good-bye," she heard Lucas say seconds later. From the kitchen, he stared at her through the archway. His eyes, a penetrating black from a distance, seemed to probe her very soul. She felt a tug at her heart as if the phone had strings.

"We have to hang up now, Todd. It's way past your bedtime," Lucas said.

"Bye. Oh, wait, did you find Ranger yet?" the little boy asked.

"No. Sorry, Todd, I'm still looking for him. There are a lot of boxes left at the cottage."

"Okay." Todd reluctantly relinquished the phone.

"Can you come back? Tomorrow? With your phone?"

Lucas's tall frame filled the archway. "Elise will be very busy the next few days, Todd."

"For just a few minutes?" he pleaded. Disappointed, he pouted, hung his head, and stared at his bare toes.

"Sure. I'll try," Elise said. "Now, do what your Uncle Lucas says."

"Okay." Happy now, he slid off her lap, picked up his box of animal crackers and his book and padded to the bottom of the steps with Lucas behind him. Strong arms reached down and swung him up into them.

"Good night, Todd." Elise waved at him.

"Night, Elise." He waved back, twisting his little body in pretzel fashion to get a better view. The two disappeared from view, but not before she heard their puzzling exchange.

"Is Ee-lise a possum's ability, Uncle Lucas?"

"No, sport, she lives too far away."

****

The farm hadn't changed much, from what Elise could see in the soft moonlit night when she arrived. The solid weathered gray barn stood peacefully in the wide yard with its twin silos guarding it like sentinels. Rosy warm lights flooded from the two-story house with a wraparound porch complete with a white wicker swing and colorful, floral-cushioned wicker chairs. Off to the right, a spacious farmhouse kitchen ran the full depth of the house. The entrance gave way to a solid oak staircase climbing up to four bedrooms and a glorious bath with an oversized bathtub.

Elise sank lower in the steaming water, listening to the loud antics of Lucas and her brothers below in the kitchen as they finished off the pizza and what she hoped was no more than a few beers. Beside the tub, Bess, her father's Dalmatian, was stretched out on a blue throw carpet, patiently waiting for her to finish. The dog had become permanently attached to her the minute she walked through the door, and Elise surmised she was just simply missing her father. Anton had bought the pup eight years ago when Elise was in her third year at the university.

She heard the front door slam shut and a car roar to life. It would be Thomas, returning to his house in Wilkes-Barre fifteen minutes away. Earlier, he had given her a list of Home Health numbers to call to arrange for in-home help once her father was released from the hospital. In his usual efficient way, he had already enlisted a farmer down the road to tend to her father's beef cattle. Anton Springer had given up his dairy cows six years ago, when he reached sixty-two. Elise at first thought the transition would be difficult, but he seemed to enjoy the freedom from the strict hours needed to manage milkers.

Drying herself quickly, Elise pulled on a navy sweat suit and headed for the now-quiet kitchen. Fritz had obviously headed for town as well. Beer can in hand, Lucas stood by the sink and was staring out the window at the inky blackness.

He turned to face her. "I thought you'd turned in for the night."

She went to the counter beside him and pulled out the carafe from the coffee maker. If the number of beer cans littering the counters and table was an indication of how much he had downed, there wouldn't be enough aspirin in the house to relieve his headache in the morning.

"If you're fixing that for me, forget it." He took a sip of beer, leaning against the refrigerator to watch her work.

"No, actually, it's for me," she said. It was partially true. When she worked late, she often enjoyed having a cup.

"Caffeine will keep you wired all night."

She shook her head. "As a rule, it doesn't." In fact, she could guzzle coffee by the cupful and still fall into bed and be instantly asleep. Removing a can of coffee from the cupboard, she measured some coffee grounds into a filter. "So what have you been doing the last twelve years, Lucas?"

"Did my stint in the army, wandered a few years doing odd jobs, and then settled in Atlanta. I've been there ever since."

"Why Atlanta?"

He shrugged. "It was as good a place as any. I picked up a job in a small garage and got hooked on cars." The barest of smiles crossed his face. "Not that I hadn't been hooked before, mind you. I got bored with bars and blind dates and took a few night courses at Georgia State."

"And?" she prompted.

"I finally got a degree in business administration."

Elise's head shot up.

"You seem surprised, Liz. It doesn't fit the picture, does it? The poor little waif, abandoned by his parents and living with his grandmother, getting a college degree?" His smoke-colored eyes blurred with a trace of bitterness or maybe anger.

She looked away, steadying her nerves. If he was

looking for a fight, she was not about to tangle with someone plied with beer.

"No, not at all," she said evenly. She turned on the faucet and filled the carafe with water. "I'm surprised you chose business administration. I guess I always pictured you as the environmental or mechanical type." She poured the water into the well and snapped the coffee machine to the "on" position. Within seconds, the aroma of coffee filled the kitchen.

"Then you weren't far off target, kid." His voice softened. "I ended up full circle to find out I was still addicted to cars. When a unique opportunity popped up, I bought into a small dealership, enlarged it, added a separate specialty body shop which catered to restoring antiques and classics, and finally bought my partner out."

"And you want to relocate here? Won't it be tough, trying to run two businesses in two different states?"

"No, I'm going to put a manager in the south and start a spin-off here." He twisted the can in his hands. "I don't have a choice."

She saw it again. The veiled look of desperation and despair. Somehow his brother's child was playing a vital part in his decision.

"Anyway, I have this college kid who worked for me part-time for four years while he was getting his mechanical engineering degree. He's a real whiz with automobiles, computers, and finances. He's agreed to manage my dealership and operations in Atlanta, once I get the restoration garage with its showroom in motion in Scranton."

"So the business is succeeding?" She wondered just how large an operation it was. She would ask Fritz about it the first time they had some private moments together. If the way Lucas dressed was any indication of his monetary success, he could ill afford to sink a bundle of cash into a new venture in Scranton, unless he was knee-deep in loans. Buying a house would only add more strain. No wonder he was staying with her father.

"It pays the bills," he said matter-of-factly.

Removing a cup from the cupboard, Elise turned and studied the coffee machine. "I love these gadgets that let you get coffee before the carafe is filled and without spilling a single drop."

"Only you would." He shook his head in disbelief.

That made her chuckle. She poured herself a cup. "Sure you don't want some?"

He held up the beer can in mock salute. "No, you go ahead, I'm fine."

"Yes, so I see." She stepped toward the refrigerator. "I need the milk."

He pushed himself away with a lazy motion, but she could feel his gaze riveted on her as she retrieved the carton. She walked to the counter and poured some into her cup. He was leaning against the door again when she turned to replace it. She stared at him, watching his gray eyes darken to charcoal, as she stood awkwardly wondering what to do next. He took a long swig of beer, his gaze never lifting from her face. The look was sensual, too intimate for her liking. Lowering the can and shifting it to his left hand, he reached out, taking the carton from her grip. She felt his fingers touch hers. She pulled away quickly, spinning and putting distance between them as she moved to her coffee at the far counter. Trembling inside, she took a sip, her back still turned away from him. She heard the refrigerator door slam.

"Lucas, maybe we ought to establish some rules." She swiveled to confront him.

"Rules?" He scowled at her.

"Yes, house rules." She felt her senses return to normal as she took control. This is what she did best, orchestrating situations, managing details, maintaining order. "Listen, we have ten days together under the same roof, and we need to have mutual working guidelines."

"Mutual working guidelines?" He set the can aside and reached into the refrigerator to take out another. "What the hell are those?"

"I wish you wouldn't drink so much," she said.

"Is that a guideline, too?" He wandered over to the window on the other side of the room and pulled the curtain aside. "Never mind," he said, peering out.

"First rule, are you listening?"

He popped the tab on the can. "How can I not?"

She sighed. "First person up in the morning makes the coffee."

"Okay."

"I want first dibs on the upstairs bath in the evening. You can shower downstairs, morning or night, or use the upstairs bath in the morning, if you do not mind maneuvering around in a trashed bathroom. Be forewarned, I prefer to leave all my things handy and within reach. Bath salts, make-up, toiletries, even lingerie. My one vice is soaking in the tub after dinner."

"Only one, Liz? Only *one* vice?" he asked.

"Stuff it, will you, Fisher?" She started tidying up the kitchen, pitching beer cans and paper plates into the garbage. "You also need to know I don't cook."

"Don't or can't?" she heard him ask over the dull metallic clank of the cans.

"I guess a little of both."

"Your mother was a wonderful cook," he said. "She could make the most fabulous cinnamon rolls. I remember when she baked me a chocolate birthday cake for my sixteenth birthday. I was so angry when Fritz ate half of it that she baked another the next day—just for me."

Elise smiled, remembering the incident. Her mother always had a soft spot for guys and chocolate cakes. She picked up the empty pizza boxes. "So it's either fast food, order in, or TV dinners, unless we can convince Fritz to come over for a few evenings and cook."

"Fritz can cook?" Lucas asked, totally surprised by Elise's words.

"Yes, somehow the insurance salesman got a double dip of mother's Julia Child gene. Go figure."

She finished cleaning up and wiped the counters. She was rinsing her cup when she heard him come up behind her. She whirled around. He stood inches from her.

"Any more rules?" His eyes met hers as he slid his beer can onto the counter. He reached up and smoothed a tendril of hair from her face. "It's as soft as it looks. Kiss me, Liz."

"Lucas, this isn't a good idea," she whispered. "You've been drinking. Too much. Much too much."

"Not enough," he said and bent his head, touching her lips with his. She staggered back against the counter, but he grabbed her, sweeping her into his arms and devouring her with his mouth. She felt his body vibrate against her, hot and hungry.

For a moment she froze, her head reeling as she remembered a time four years ago when she had refused to comply, refused to yield to a strength she couldn't match.

Philip had come to her apartment in a drunken stupor, refusing to acknowledge their three-year engagement was over. She could no longer continue to innocently turn her head the other way to all the females who demanded his time and his body.

When she had told him they were finished and handed him the ring, he had gone berserk. He had tried to kiss her and when she refused, the force of his backhand had sent her flying backwards, stumbling over a chair in the living room. She had tried to reason with him, but it had only made him more furious. He had lunged at her again, and she had struggled and screamed, scratching at his dark, angry face, but the blows had only come harder then, faster, until she lay on the carpet in a ball, begging for blackness to descend upon her and take the pain away.

She had awakened later with the tinny taste of blood in her mouth. Her eye was swollen shut, her face and lips battered, and her clothes torn. She knew then that the body and the hands of a lover who had once gently caressed and made love to her was capable of violence and revenge when scorned.

She felt the pressure of hard, demanding lips pressed against hers. This was not Philip Cullington, she told herself. This was Lucas Fisher. Lucas who had been like a brother to her. Regaining her senses, she pushed hard against him. Immediately he released her and stepped backward.

"For the love of God, Lucas, don't do this! My life is complicated enough. And after what's happened today. My father—"

Her words were like splashing ice water on him. He took another step backward, away from her, as his face registered reality and his gaze locked with hers. "Liz, I'm sorry. Please believe me, I'm really sorry. I don't know what came over me." He pushed his hand through his hair. "I didn't hurt you, did I?"

"No. No, I'm fine." Elise swallowed and steadied her trembling hands. "Let's just call it a night, all right?"

He started to say something, but thought better of it as she stepped around him and walked to the stairs.

"Get the lights and locks, will you?" She halted at the bottom step. Her heart was beating wildly. She glanced through the wide archway and saw him standing by the refrigerator, one arm braced flat against the door, his head bent, disappointment shadowing his face. She knew she should go to him and explain. Reassure him. Help him chase away the demons he was battling.

Instead, she turned and headed for her room. She had her own demons to deal with.

Chapter Five

Fresh from the shower, Lucas gazed out the kitchen window at the early morning sky speckled in the same shades of gray as one of Springer's barn cats. He had taken time only to pull on an old pair of Levi's, hoping to dispel the grinding pain in his head with some stout caffeine and several ibuprofen tablets. His head pounded as if someone had beaten him with a tire iron, and his stomach felt as if he had swallowed a handful of lug nuts.

He had made a total fool of himself last night. Why hadn't he kept his hands to himself? Elise Springer was not the kind of woman to be manhandled in her father's kitchen. What in heaven's name was he thinking? She was no Monique. Hell, she was nothing close to Monique. He remembered how she didn't blink when Todd leaped in her lap the other night. Monique would have never allowed him to wrinkle her precious silk suit, let alone take the time to show him how a cell phone operated.

His mind replayed their encounter the night before like a tape in slow motion. He had seen fear, close to terror, in her eyes when he had released her and she skidded away from him like a trapped animal set free. He wondered what or who had been responsible for her fright. Who had hurt her?

"I see you remembered rule one."

Wearing a pair of black running shorts and a pale pink tee-shirt, she stood in the doorway with Bess beside her. She held a new-fangled, wireless and programmable telephone, complete with speakerphone capability and an answering machine, in her hands. Running shoes, laces knotted, dangled from around her neck.

"I thought you'd be sleeping in." He was hoping to have a few minutes to dress and collect his thoughts before he had to face her. "Are you always up this early?"

Crossing the room, she brushed past him and dumped the phone and cords on the counter and the shoes on the floor. She poured herself a half cup of coffee. He gave her credit—either she was good at acting the little tough girl part or she had decided to dismiss last night's incident entirely. Maybe she was being tactfully gracious. He dismissed his last flash of insight as quickly as it occurred. The Liz Springer he grew up with was the kind of woman who'd have no qualms about ripping you wide open when she had the urge to set things straight.

"Most of the time," she replied. "I try to pick up lost sleep on weekends. Then I sleep until seven or eight." She brought the cup to her lips, took a quick swallow, and glanced at him from the corner of her eye. "Wow, you look like you drank drain cleaner."

He winced, stifling a groan as his stomach did a push-up. "You know, Liz, that's what I always liked about you—your gracious compassion for the sick and dying."

Her lips curved. "I always thought it was my honesty. Hey, it's your vice, you big goon, so don't blame me for the repercussions. I gave up heavy drinking a long time ago." She cocked her head and studied him for a moment. "You still run?"

"Not much anymore, not like I used to," he admitted. He wished she'd just get it over with, stop the polite bantering, and sternly berate him. Even a flying object would help, although at the moment, he questioned his strength to duck.

But Elise Springer wasn't a predictable woman.

She smiled a whimsical smile instead. "I remember when Fritz and you ran track in high school."

He squinted at her. God, it even hurt to see. "It was Fritz's wild idea. He thought it would be a good way to meet girls. You can see where it got us." He paused a moment, trying to gather his thoughts. "Elise, about last night."

"What about it?" She flopped to the floor, untied the laces of her sneakers, and shoved a foot into one. Positioned advantageously above her, he could see she had fashioned her hair into some kind of fancy braid to keep it from falling into her eyes. The shorts she wore were so deprived of cloth, he wondered how she ever found them on the clothes rack. She was all legs, the kind men would kill each other for.

Easy, Fisher, a little voice inside his head warned. This is Anton Springer's daughter. His *only* daughter. Those very same legs got you into the mess you're in now.

He cleared his throat. "I don't know what to say, except I'm sorry. It'll never happen again." He rubbed his temples to try to dispel the thumping sensation. "My behavior was inexcusable. I was a complete jerk."

"Got that right!" She fired off her response so fast

44

he flinched. Finishing the lace on the first shoe, she double knotted it, and moved to the other. "You're a pinhead, too."

He sighed. "You're going to make me grovel, aren't you?"

"No." She finished her task, stood and did a little jumping dance to settle into her shoes. "I was thinking more along the lines of torture. You're going running with me."

"Running?" He groaned again. "Lizzie, I can't. Do you want to kill me? My eyes are going to pop out of my goddamned head."

She grinned. "Come on, Lucas. It's the best medicine I know to clear a fuzzy brain. Anyway, your life insurance is paid up, right?" She reached out and swiped the coffee cup from his hands, dumping the remainder down the drain. "Quit drinking that stuff, will you? I'm not going to stop every five minutes while you sneak behind a tree to water the roots."

He swallowed uncomfortably. "This is a joke, right? *Please* tell me you're kidding?"

"Do I look like I'm kidding?" Her voice was alarmingly quiet, and her pool-blue eyes were calm and serious. She folded her arms across her petal pink chest.

Swearing under his breath, Lucas stared at her. The woman actually thought he was insane enough to agree. Frantically, he searched his mind for a plausible excuse. Any excuse. "I can't, Liz, I have to be at the garage this morning to meet a contractor about some renovations. I'll have to take a rain check."

"It'll only take a half hour."

He thought about just telling her to go to hell, but then remembered he was already a drowning man, up to his ears in troubled waters. In addition, drowning men knew better than to aggravate the alligators. He decided to change tactics. "I'm not even dressed for running."

She shrugged. "I'll wait."

"If I refuse?"

She gave him an obviously fake smile. "Either you run, or my mouth runs. Remember those two thugs I call brothers? Take your choice, pal. You've got ten minutes to get out of those shrink-wrap jeans and find a pair of decent shoes."

Annoyed, he was about to inform her blackmail was illegal, but she had turned away to eliminate any further conversation. She picked up the phone from the counter. "It should give me enough time to hook this up and program in a message. I'll just identify Dad's number, so both of us can get messages when we're out."

Squatting by the baseboard, Elise unplugged the old phone from the jack.

Now desperate, Lucas felt sweat begin to drip down his back. He decided to make one last appeal to her compassion. "Seriously, Liz, I don't know if I can even make it to the mailbox."

He thought she didn't hear him at first. Eyes glued to her work, she gnawed on her lower lip, concentrating on untangling the cords. They looked like a heap of spaghetti to him.

He was wrong.

"Nine minutes, Fisher. You're wasting precious time. Keep talking and you'll be running barefoot."

****

Much to Elise's surprise, Lucas returned shortly, dressed in a pair of sweat shorts, tee-shirt and a worn pair of running shoes. His face was as gray as the shorts he wore.

"Take it easy, okay?" he begged, coming to stand beside her where she was fiddling with the buttons on the answering machine.

She smiled. Little did he know she had already decided to cut him a break whether he deserved it or not. She remembered how sore her muscles used to get when she didn't run on a regular basis. As for the hangover, she couldn't quite recall what he was feeling. She hadn't had one of those in years. But then, she hadn't had dinner or drinks with anyone significant from the male species for so long she'd forgotten what alcohol tasted like.

The trail Elise selected ran along the edge of a pasture and up a small hill into the woods, circling the house and ending at the back door. With Bess trotting merrily ahead of her, she took off, choosing a pace slower than she normally ran.

"So this is how you keep in shape?" Lucas asked through a painful groan. "I thought you were one of those fitness club freaks."

"With my job? Get real. I'm in the office six days a week, sometimes seven." She ventured a glance at him. For someone whose face now matched the greening pastures, he was making a valiant effort to keep up with her. "I finally did buy a treadmill for those days when I can't get outside or when I get home late and still want to exercise."

She stopped at the edge of a lower field to open an iron gate, shooing Lucas and the dog through. "So tell me about Todd."

"You're going to make me talk and run?" His voice

rose an octave in disbelief.

"I never said torture would be easy, Fisher."

The gate clicked shut and she trotted off again. She smiled when she heard a stream of expletives follow her. Glancing back, she watched him stubbornly fighting to force his unsteady legs into action.

"When did Todd's mother die?" she asked when he finally caught up and was running beside her.

"When Todd was two. She had a fatal heart attack. Mike and Carol had him later in life. She was thirty-five or so. Carol had been warned against getting pregnant, since she'd had heart problems as a kid. But they wanted a child so desperately, she decided it was worth the chance."

"Mike was a cop?" She slackened her pace.

He geared down to match it. "Yeah, he was doing undercover work in New Castle. After Carol's death, he played the single parent role for about a year, and then hooked up with his second wife, Clarisse. It was a match made in hell."

"Clarisse?" She pushed a tendril of hair from her eyes that had come loose from the braid.

"I don't know if it's her real name or one she just decided to use. Anyhow, Clarisse despised the time Mike was away from home. She liked her nightlife, and Todd was always in her way. Mike came home one night unexpectedly and found some sleazebag in his bed and the rest is history. He filed for a divorce, asked for a transfer, and moved here with Todd. He'd been here less than a year when he was killed in a car accident. Hey, can we take a breather before I pass out?"

She stopped beside a stone wall separating the field

from a long, narrow pasture with a trail leading to the wooded knoll above the house. "All right, we have to cross here anyhow." She scrambled up and sat down on a flat, lichen-covered rock. He hoisted himself up and sat beside her, dangling his long, athletic legs over the edge. Color had begun to come back to his face.

"So you moved here to get the child," she said matter-of-factly.

He wiped the beads of sweat from his forehead with the back of his hand. "It's a little more complicated. You see, Clarisse has resurfaced and is trying to get custody of Todd, too."

"Why, that's crazy! The divorce was granted?"

He pulled a well-muscled thigh to his chest and retied his shoelace. "I believe so, but there are some insurance policies still unresolved, and Clarisse can smell money a mile away."

"There was no will?"

"None I can seem to locate, which isn't like Mike. The insurance money will naturally go to Todd, but if Clarisse gets guardianship, she has control of it. There is enough to pay for her nightlife without her having to be a cocktail waitress for a while. Not that she would abandon the job. I'm told she likes her customers a lot, a whole lot."

"She'll never get guardianship, not with a blood relation standing in the wings." Staring over the pasture, Elise scowled. The sun was coming up, changing the horizon to gold. Far off, beef cattle grazed in the early light, their coats a rich red. Until now, she had not realized how much she actually missed the farm where the clear, clean-smelling mornings were blissfully peaceful and the rolling hills so exquisite.

Stands of light green, just-budding maples made the darker lush green of spring look dazzling.

"I have to prove myself a fit guardian as well, Liz. Why would the courts want to give the kid to a guy who lives in Atlanta, drives fast cars, and hasn't had a meaningful relationship with anyone in his life?"

His hand went to his stomach. He slid onto the other side of the wall and stretched. Wincing, he bent forward and placed his hand on his thighs.

"Are you all right?" She was beside him instantly, one hand on his shoulder, the other reaching for the pulse at his neck. Satisfied his heart rate wasn't erratic, she withdrew her hand. "Jeez, Lucas, you're not going to recycle that coffee, are you?"

He shook his head. "No, it's just stomach cramps. I'm not as young as I used to be."

"Here, sit down," she said gently. Noting his shallow breathing, she didn't think age had anything to do with what he was feeling at the moment.

Lucas slumped down onto the grass, and she knelt on one knee, facing him. Pushing aside a shock of hair, she felt his forehead.

"Breathe deeply. You're overheated."

"Of course I'm hot, Clara Barton. The putrid alcohol in my system is having a toxic reaction with this clean country air." Lucas sucked in a slow, cleansing breath. "There's more. When Mike was working here, he was working undercover on drug deals. Supposedly, he had access to a hundred thousand dollars never recovered after his death. As his only family member, it puts me in a tight place, under suspicion."

"So what do you think happened to it? Was he a

gambler?" While he talked, her hand came up to the back of his head and stroked it gently. His dark unruly hair, in need of a cut, curled over the back of his shirt and had the barest threads of gray below his temples, only noticeable on close inspection.

"No, I think things got hot with a deal, and he stashed it somewhere for safe keeping. The biggest gambling Mike ever indulged in was a few hands of poker with his friends every so often. I didn't know my brother for very long. We just started communicating a few years before his first wife died, but from what others tell me, he was one of the most honest, untainted cops on the force."

"Debts?"

"None I can find." He swiped a hand over his face and pushed out a lengthy breath of air.

"Can you stand up?" Elise asked worriedly.

"Keep caressing me like a lap dog and everything will stand up."

"Just concentrate on the feet first, Rover." She removed her hand and stood. "Come, we can just walk the rest of the way."

She could see the suggestion was heaven to his ears. He grinned, lips curving upward from both corners. She tried not to think of those lips, solid and demanding against hers the night before.

Lucas stood, and they circled the house ending up at the back steps to the kitchen. As soon as they entered, he headed straight for a chair and collapsed. Bess dropped to her rug behind the door.

"See," she said. "You didn't die."

"Yeah, well, just because I'm talking doesn't mean I'm not on my deathbed." He gestured to Bess. "Look, even the poor dog is frazzled. Dear Lord, now I can better understand the term 'dog-tired.'"

"You'll feel better after a shower. You still haven't told me about Todd."

The luster in his face faded. "There's not much to tell. He lost his mother and father and has been tossed into foster care with the Johnsons. I'm trying to get temporary custody. Thomas is working on it, but he's not hopeful anything can be done until the investigation of Mike's death is completed. I guess it's standard procedure when a cop gets killed working under cover. I've been lucky enough the Johnsons let me have him on weekends."

"Is it allowed?" Elise opened the bread drawer and withdrew a half loaf of bread.

Lucas rose and walked to where she was working. "Well, it's bending the rules a little. Someone is supposed to be with him at all times, but they trust your father, and God knows the Johnsons need a break. In case you haven't noticed, they're not in shape for chasing a child Todd's age."

He slapped a palm against the refrigerator. "Damn it, Liz, it's not fair. The kid is the one being punished, taking the brunt of things he had no part of. He's so lonely he cries himself to sleep at night. He doesn't understand what's happening. He doesn't even know where he belongs."

"So we spring him."

"It's not that easy!" He gave her a disgusted look.

"Of course, it's not going to be *easy*." Elise forced herself not to shout back. "But it doesn't mean it's impossible, Lucas. Sit down, will you? I'm cooking this morning." She waved the half loaf of bread at him, then withdrew four slices and dropped them into the toaster slots.

He blinked. "Toast? You call making toast cooking?"

She blew out an exasperated breath. "Okay, so name something you want to eat. I'll try to cook it, but the question will be...will you eat it?"

She saw his face blanch as he considered the thought. He waved her away and then gestured at the toaster. "Good God, just don't burn it."

When the toast popped up, Elise buttered the slices, and they sat at the table, sharing the meager feast in silence.

Elise could still see the turmoil clouding his face. He was probably hurting as much as the kid. Lucas had always been the champion of the underdog, the downtrodden, even when they were kids. She remembered the many times when they used to choose teams in a game of pickup baseball in the neighborhood. Lucas was always the one who selected the less experienced, less skilled players first. Initially, she thought it was only an act of kindness, but later she realized he wanted them to win, wanted them to know how glorious it felt to be anything but last all the time.

"Dad knows a few people down at Children and Youth Services, Lucas. I could see if there's anything we could do, maybe to hurry things along," she said.

His gaze found hers. "I don't want to get you involved. You have your hands full already."

"I don't mind. I can't spend every minute at the hospital."

He shrugged. "Have a go at it. Nothing can hurt, that's for sure."

"I'll need a car."

He motioned to the top of the refrigerator. "Take the Trans Am. I've been using your Dad's truck for the last two weeks to haul materials for renovating an old garage I bought."

"What's Dad been driving?"

"The Trans Am."

"My father's been driving the Bandit's car? You're kidding?"

Lucas smiled. His eyes were bright and clear now, like polished silver. "Yeah, it makes him look kind of cool and funky. He was a fan of *Smokey and the Bandit*, just like Fritz and me." He finished his toast and glanced at the phone. "I'm glad we have the answering machine. I have some shipments coming up this weekend from Atlanta. Although I'm far from getting the restoration garage up and running, I figure if I put some cars on the lot, it'll look like there's at least some leasing activity about to start. Sort of like advance advertising. I'll get you something new from Atlanta to drive once I get the lot set up."

"One more thing. Who's this Ranger Todd was talking about the other night?" she asked.

"It's a tiny beanbag dog, golden brown in color, and about five inches tall. Mike gave it to Todd when he was younger. For some reason, it was like a security blanket or lucky charm at one time in the kid's life. From what I can gather, he used to take it everywhere with him. During the move or commotion of Mike's death, it was somehow misplaced or lost. He keeps asking me to look for it among the boxes at the cottage where I stashed Mike's belongings. I was hoping to sort them someday."

She nodded, and they rose together and carried their plates to the sink.

"First dibs on the upstairs bath," she announced and inched her way backwards across the floor.

"It wasn't the original deal. Nights only, remember?"

"I modified the rules for today." She made a mad dash for the stairs, but he was quick for someone who claimed he was on the brink of death. He grabbed her around the waist with one arm just as she flew through the archway. He lifted her off the floor, her feet pedaling in thin air.

She laughed. "I give up. Put me down!" She wished he'd stop touching her. A series of lightning shivers coursed through her.

"If I forfeit the upstairs bath, am I forgiven?" His breath was hot in her ear.

"I was never mad, Lucas," she admitted truthfully. "Maybe just a little ticked off. Put me down, I'm all sweaty."

With an agile motion, he set her on her feet, but not before his lips lightly brushed against the side of her neck. "I'd never hurt you, kid, I promise," he said with brutal honesty. "With everything that's happening I feel like I'm inside a speeding car and can't get control of the wheel."

She skidded out of his reach and started for the stairs. "I know," she agreed, taking the steps two at a time, but halting long enough half way up to turn and look down at him, "but remember, out-of-control cars have been known to crash and burn."

Chapter Six

"I'm sorry, Miss Springer, but Mr. Morrison is a busy man. If you care to make an appointment, I can check his schedule."

The secretary from Children and Youth Services tapped the upended pencil on her desk and spoke in a clipped voice. She had been schooled by the very best to run interference for her employer. With pursed, no-nonsense lips, she peered over slim bifocals magnifying the pores on her aging, late-forties face.

Elise had met her type before, on the telephone, in boardrooms and offices, at conventions—any place where industry and service-related businesses scratched out their daily profits. They were the secretaries from hell, meagerly paid, but loyal as guerrilla soldiers to their bosses.

"We're old friends, and I'm just in town for a short time," Elise said, trying the first thought to cross her mind.

"Hmm, is that so?" The woman laid down the pencil and opened her planning book. "Mr. Morrison specifically insisted he wanted no interruptions. His time is very valuable, you understand. Let's see, he does have an opening on Friday."

"I don't."

The secretary's eyebrow shot up. "How unfortunate."

Elise smiled. So she wanted to play hardball. She had won imaginary blue ribbons against secretaries more hostile than this one. "I'm sorry, your name is?"

"Linda."

"And your last name, Linda?" Elise prompted.

"Cook."

"Well, Ms. Cook, would it be possible to slip a note under Mr. Morrison's nose?" She lowered her voice to a near whisper. "I'd hate to see my relationship with Jack...or maybe yours...jeopardized because I wasn't able to connect. You know what I mean?"

From her purse, Elise withdrew a pen and small tablet. "Have you known Jack long?" she asked, scribbling away. She could feel Linda Cook's eyes burning holes through her.

"A little over a year."

"Well, Jack's a great guy. A real charmer, isn't he?" Elise mused aloud as she finished the note with a flourish. She folded the paper into neat quarters. Rising, she brazenly reached across Linda Cook's desk, snapped off a piece of tape, and sealed the note from prying eyes.

"I have another meeting across town in a half hour. I'd hate to keep my client waiting. Could you... ?" Elise nudged the paper toward her and glanced at the clock on the wall.

Frowning, the woman accepted it, and with a back stiff as a telephone pole, she strode toward a door across the room. A minute later, she emerged, clearly displeased. "Mr. Morrison will see you, Ms. Springer."

Elise smiled a phony, beguiling smile. "Thank you."

Jack Morrison rose from behind a large oak desk

entirely devoid of paperwork. The shelves behind his desk held books, all categorized in alphabetical order with no folders intermixed with them. Everything looked like it had been organized with serious thought and never touched again. Beside him, a chair held a stack of golf and fishing magazines. In the corner of the room was a golf bag with clubs.

"Lizzie Springer, I did not break your nose," he uttered, defensively, almost irritably. He crossed the space between them. "I can't believe you still remember that silly little incident. What was it? Sixth grade pickup baseball?"

She laughed. "You bloodied it, Jack, and it was eighth grade. I hope you've learned to drop the bat when you get a hit, or better yet, have given up baseball completely. How've you been?"

She extended her hand, and he shook it. Then he pulled her close and gave her an unexpected giant hug. "How are you?"

"I couldn't be better," she replied and stepped away quickly. "What about you?"

"Fine, fine." His eyes did an undisguised perusal of her, and she was glad she had decided to change into a black business suit at the last minute. "Well, well, no one mentioned you were back in town."

The last ten years had not looked favorably on Jack Morrison. He had lost a lot of hair and gained weight. Once bright brown eyes were now marked with crow's feet, and his hawk-like nose only seemed more prominent with age. His clothes, though well-made, lacked a crisp, put-together look. Or maybe it was just his blinding tie in swirls of reds, blues, and yellows, she decided.

"Here, here, sit down," he said. "Back in town, huh? Everyone eventually gravitates home, it seems."

"I guess." She chose a chair in front of his desk. To her right, she noticed his computer screen held a game of solitaire before a swirling screen saver flashed on to obscure it.

"What brings you here?" Morrison asked.

"A little of everything. Dad injured an ankle and leg, so I'm taking time to be with him. I'm looking up old friends and helping some others out. Dad and I are especially interested in a foster child with your agency."

"What's the name?"

"Todd Fisher."

"Todd Fisher?" He leaned back in his chair and linked his fingers on his stomach. "Yes, I vaguely remember him. His parents are deceased. His dad was a cop. No will has been found stating who the father wanted for custodian of the child. It's a sad story."

"I need to know what it takes to get temporary custody."

"Who wants it? You, your dad, or his uncle?"

Vaguely remember? Right, she thought. "Actually, Dad and I've taken a shine to him. He's been staying down the road from our farm with the Johnsons."

"There may be extenuating circumstances to prevent it, you know," he said, hedging. "If it's a special case, you'll have to go through the department head, Mrs. Pedmo. You'll have to go through her anyway to become eligible as a foster parent."

Elise sighed. "Do I have to go through Miss Congeniality out there to get an appointment?"

Rubbing his jaw, he chuckled. "I suppose I can see

what I can do."

The words were like the harps of heaven singing out to her. She wanted to ask *when*, but dismissed the urge, not wanting to appear too eager. She caught him checking her hands, obviously looking for a ring. She hoped he wouldn't stray too far from the subject at hand. She had promised Lucas she'd meet him at the garage at noon, and she was already a half hour late. Luckily, she had already visited her father at the hospital, but she still had to pick up a list of names of private duty nurses from the local Home Health office.

"I see Fritz once in a while," Jack said. "He handles my insurance. He told me you were a big shot architect in San Francisco. How's it going?"

"It keeps me busy."

"It seems like it's agreeing with you. You look wonderful, simply stunning, Liz."

"Thank you." Pinned by his leering gaze, she squirmed in her seat, wondering how much longer she could keep up the endless chitchat. "So how long have you been with Children and Youth Services?" she asked.

"For a couple of years. It works for me. Benefits are good and all that jazz."

She gave him a killer smile. "I'm sure you're excellent at it. Listen, I hate to rush off, but I have a luncheon engagement." She started to rise.

He moved quickly from his seat to round the desk, adjusting his god-awful tie flapping at his stomach like a huge tongue. "Elise, if you're free Saturday, maybe we could have dinner and discuss old times? It's so good seeing you again."

He moved close to her, much too close.

"That might be nice, Jack. Maybe if you can squeeze in an appointment for me with Mrs. Pedmo in the next few days, we could figure out the details for the weekend?" She patted his tie. "Nice tie."

"Sure, sure, thanks." He grinned. "How about I call you later today?"

She rested her hand on the doorknob. "If I happen to be out, leave a message on the answering machine at the farm, will you? I wouldn't want to miss it." She forced out another of her killer smiles.

He nodded, not hiding his pleasure, and she left quickly, heading straight to the parking lot where she slumped against the gleaming car. She blew out a puff of air, scattering tendrils of hair around her face. "Well, Springer, not a bad day's work," she mumbled to herself. "One caseworker down, one to go."

****

Lucas stood outside the office of the old garage and felt the warm April sun beat down on his back. Somewhere lilacs scented the soft afternoon breeze swirling around the parking lot. Elise was already an hour late, and he was beginning to worry. She had promised him she'd meet him as soon as she finished at Home Health. He heard the hum of the motor before he saw the Trans Am's sleek black finish. He lifted his gaze toward the highway. Seconds later, she barreled down the road and tore into the parking lot, tires squealing in alarm. The car slid to a stop, and she jumped out. In a black suit with a white blouse and three-inch heels, she could have passed for the Flying Nun on stilts. She crossed the lot toward him in quick, efficient strides, trampling the weeds growing through the cracked cement.

"Christ almighty, Liz, who taught you how to drive?"

"I'm a little rusty with standard." Her voice was clipped and irritated. She removed her sunglasses, slipped them on top of her head and squinted up at him. "How's the head?"

"Fine. How'd you make out?"

"Fine."

"What took you so long?"

"Traffic and sadistic secretaries."

"Who won?"

They were firing conversation like bullets from a machine gun.

"I did, of course."

"So what did they say?"

"Who?"

"Children and Youth Services."

"Later, I'm starved." She pushed the door to the office open and stepped inside. "Where'd you stash the food?"

"I picked up a pizza, but it's cold by now." He followed her into the office and rubbed his forehead, certain it was about to explode if they didn't gear down to a slower speed.

"We really are going to die if we keep eating pizza, Lucas." She whirled and looked around. Her eyes flitted from floor to ceiling, wall to wall. "So this is it?"

He shoved his hands into his back pockets and looked at the dirty gray concrete floor, grease-stained fly-speckled windows, and yellowed water-stained ceiling. "Yeah, not much to look at, huh?"

"It depends on your perspective. The cracked window and broken ceiling light panels give it a bit of a worn, nostalgic feeling."

Like a starving dog homing in on a bone, she headed straight for a battered steel desk in a corner of the room where he had earlier deposited the pizza. A shabby vinyl-padded chair, its tears bandaged with duct tape, stood nearby. She pulled the chair close, sat on the desktop and kicked off her shoes, resting her feet on the seat cushion. The top on the pizza box flew up under her eager hands.

Glad for the brief lull, Lucas dragged another chair from a corner and slumped down opposite her. He propped his feet on the desk.

"Another shoe malfunction?" he asked as he reached for a piece of pizza.

"Don't start, Fisher," she said through a mouthful and wiped sauce from her lip with her finger.

"I guess when women say they've discovered a pair of shoes to die for, they really mean it."

"I'm so thrilled my feet amuse you."

He grinned, leaned forward, pulled some napkins from beneath the box, and handed one to her. His gaze slid over her lips to her face. She had twisted her hair into some kind of fancy knot at the back of her head, leaving wispy strands to dangle seductively over her forehead and cheeks. Tiny earlobes flashed with gold earrings and a small gold chain pendant hung between the soft folds of her white blouse crisscrossing in a V above her bra. He didn't have to guess what was underneath it. Her bra was lace. Hell, everything beneath that sophisticated black suit was lace. Why, oh why, had he ever pawed through her suitcases at the airport?

"You're staring, Lucas," she said.

Her words startled him. "Huh? No, just thinking." He reached into his chest pocket and withdrew a paper. "There were three messages on the answering machine when I stopped by the house. You're supposed to call some guy named Paul Winston. Linda Cook set up an appointment for tomorrow morning at ten with a Mrs. Pedmo of Children and Youth Services. And Chuck phoned. The last guy sounded pretty desperate, like he was being held hostage by bloodthirsty aliens."

"He probably is," Elise said, chuckling. "He's doing my share of the work while I'm away."

Lucas leaned forward and reached for another piece of pizza. He caught the whiff of her perfume. It was delicate, almost rose-like and sensual, different from the one at the airport.

"What's the scent you're wearing?"

She shrugged. "I don't know. Chuck bought it for my birthday. Do you know it takes five hundred pounds of flower petals to make a single drop of perfume?"

"No, it must've been part of some trivia quiz I missed." Lucas leaned back in his chair, eyeing her. "Tell me, is this Chuck fellow in the habit of killing flowers for you?" For some reason he didn't like the idea.

"Chuck always gives me expensive perfume on special occasions," she said. "It's kind of a tradition since I've been with the company. Charles is..." She paused pensively. "Chuck is a sensitive, special, comical, somewhat bizarre guy. I don't think I would have stayed as long as I have if it weren't for him."

He was about to ask how special when the door opened and Fritz Springer sauntered in. "Anybody home?" he called out.

"Over here," Lucas said. So, now the second big brother was making his rounds and checking up on the little sister. Earlier, Thomas had phoned him with some silly questions regarding the paperwork he was finalizing for the real estate transaction. It was an excuse, Lucas darned well knew, to learn whether Elise was comfortable with his presence at the house. If there was one thing he knew about the Springer brothers, it was they had a deep sense of loyalty to each other and an overprotective nature where their little sister was concerned.

Crossing the room, Fritz grabbed the back of his Elise's neck and shook her gently. "Hey, good-looking, who are you trying to schmooze in those funeral director's duds?"

"Morrison."

Lucas shot off the chair like a cork from a champagne bottle. "Morrison? Why that idiot? You didn't say you were talking with Jack Morrison."

Elise's pizza stopped midway to her mouth.

"Lucas, enough," Fritz said sharply turning to him. There was no denying his anger. "Just because Dad and you have a total dislike for the man, doesn't mean we all have to share your views. He was only doing his job. Some of us have to do business in this town, as you'll soon find out."

The two men exchanged murderous looks.

"No, but if the swine has his life insurance with your company, I hope to God someone gets to collect. Sooner rather than later wouldn't bother me either."

Fritz snorted. "Glad to see you don't hold any grudges." Setting aside his differences with the natural ease of a sales person, he asked in a calmer tone, "Got anything to drink that wasn't here when this place was built?"

"There's some Coke and Dew in the refrigerator in the showroom. I just bought it. Get me a can, too." Lucas looked at Elise. "What'll you have?"

"Just a sip of Fritz's," she said and swiveled toward the showroom. She watched Fritz disappear and turned back to Lucas. "All right, give up the goods. What's the problem with Morrison?"

Lucas ran a hand through his unruly hair. "When Mike was killed, your Dad initially appealed to Morrison to try to keep Todd here, instead of sending him back to New Castle. When he got no results, he went over his head. He later found out Morrison had recommended Todd be returned, even though he denied it."

"Why would he do that?"

"I don't know." Lucas shrugged.

Fritz had strolled back, handing a can of Coke to Lucas and popping the top of his can. He had obviously overheard their conversation. He grinned. "Probably because he still remembers how Lucas used to beat the pants off him in sandlot baseball. Or was it the time you two tangled at the field over a call and Jack ended up on the ground eating dirt?"

"So what?" Elise pursed her lips. "I still get angry when I think how Mary Jo beat me out as homecoming queen."

"Mary Jo was your best friend," Fritz said.

"I know, but I still hated to lose."

Fritz laid a hand on her shoulder. "Give it up, Liz, you didn't have a chance in hell. You had beauty *and* brains. Mary Jo... Well, she had beauty and a body." He whistled under his breath and made an hourglass figure with his hands. "There was no way in hell your classmates would vote for someone who took advanced calculus and could outrun the high school's quarterback. If it's any consolation, you'd beat Mary Jo out now with a hand tied behind your back."

"Is she married?" Lucas asked.

"Yeah, to Ted Meyer. He's a city cop now. Hey, I have to go. Insurance does not sell itself. How about I stop by tonight and whip something up for dinner?"

Both Elise and Lucas grinned openly at each other. Elise gave two thumbs up and uttered gleefully, "Make it Chinese, brother, and you're on!"

Lucas watched them. He had never known what it was like to have a relationship with a sibling, a bonding of blood and family love so strong one family member would kill to defend and protect the other. In addition, he had no doubts Fritz Springer would annihilate anyone who tried to harm his sister. He felt her eyes on him.

"Is Chinese okay with you?" she asked.

"It's fine with me. Anything but pizza." He nodded and offered Elise his Coke. She took a quick sip, not in the least concerned he had already downed half the can. She was the most uninhibited person he knew. Monique would have never touched her lips to the rim of a can, and never, even in dire thirst, if someone had taken the first drink from it.

When Fritz disappeared, she stood and slipped her feet into her shoes. Catching Lucas off guard again, she asked, "Do I get a guided tour of this place, or do I snoop around by myself?" Her eyes were curious, and her smile so infectious it astounded him. He never expected she'd have any interest in a greasy old garage, long abandoned and crumbling under the weight of years gone by.

"You really want to see this graveyard of steel and old blocks?"

"Sure, I'm into anything made of concrete, steel, wood or mortar."

"What about men?" he asked casually as he led her outside toward the two, steel storage buildings out back.

"They just don't seem to fit into my blueprints at the moment," she said.

They doubled back through the two-bay garage into the showroom he planned to enlarge and remodel. He found himself stopping to explain his many ideas while she listened attentively. Her eyes seemed to drink in the structure, as if she was analyzing every stud, rafter, even the blocks in the walls. When they reached the office again, he gave her a baffled look.

"You really dig this stuff, don't you?"

She looked at him and smiled. "Lucas, I'm an architect. This is what I do. We create, we build, we remodel." Her hands flew out in animation as she spoke. "I look at a structure like this and try to envision what it was like when it was new and ponder what drove the mind of the person who created it. Why did the builder choose certain materials and not others? How did he utilize space? Why did he choose certain lighting or colors?"

"You are a just a tad demented, you know?"

She only laughed, the sound lilting and melodic.

"Well, if you come up with any grand ideas for remodeling, I'd appreciate them," he admitted. He knew the showroom was much too small and he needed something larger which would adequately display older restored vehicles along with newer models.

"Are you serious?" The look on her face matched that of a kid just handed a fistful of candy. "You'd actually consider any ideas I have?"

"Why not? Hell, you're the architect, Lizzie."

Her eyes circled the office. "Yeah, this needs work, too," he admitted, following her gaze. "I have a rough floor plan with dimensions at the farm. I'll dig them out and make copies for you."

She walked to the back of the office where a door led to the parts and storage room. Her hand reached for the knob. "No," he said sharply, "you don't have to worry about this room. Don't go in there; it's filthy and stacked full of junk."

However, it was too late, she was already pushing the door open.

He groaned.

She peered in and then stepped inside. On a long service counter, six huge unopened boxes sat side by side.

"Lucas Fisher, you devil," she whispered in awe as soon as she recognized their contents. "You've been holding out on me, haven't you?"

Chapter Seven

"Computers."

The word rolled off her lips in what sounded like reverence, wonder, and delight.

"Six, to be exact." Lucas slouched against the doorjamb. "Another is on its way."

She stepped farther inside and glided her hands over the first two boxes. Her eyes lit up like beacons on a lighthouse. "Sixteen hundred megahertz processors with one terabyte hard drives," she whispered, still awestruck.

"You're losing me, Liz. Is this good or bad?"

She laughed a low, throaty chuckle. "Lucas, with these machines you can launch a rocket ship."

"I don't want to launch a damn rocket, just a garage with lots of power tools and machines."

"How much do you know about computers?" Her pool-blue gaze danced back and forth between the boxes, then found his face.

"Very little," he admitted reluctantly. He didn't want to tell her the extent of his knowledge was to use email, surf the net, and find the car parts he needed from the company's database. Bryan, his mechanical engineer, had ordered the computers and was planning to set them up. One was to be linked to inventory, another to billing, one for the accountant, one for sales, one in the office, and the last one was to be set up at home so he could have access to both the Atlanta and Scranton sites.

"I honestly don't know how they are supposed to be tied together," he admitted. If the truth were known, he didn't have a clue.

"Network, it's called a network." Elise moved from box to box, reading the outside of each one with the intensity of someone on a very serious scavenger hunt. "How long have they been sitting here?"

"Over a week or more."

"Over a week? Oh, no, you're serious, aren't you?" She gave him a sunny, infectious smile. "Oh, Lucas, let's take one home, set it up, and put it through the paces, just to see what it can do."

He angled his head, considering. It was exactly what he was afraid of when he tried to stop her from seeing them. He had never considered himself a high-tech person. Mechanical, yes, but certainly not high tech. It wasn't as if he was opposed to learning about computers, but with all he had to accomplish to get the garage and leasing business on its feet, learning computer jargon was not part of his immediate plans. It was the old cars, the reliable ones with powerful engines and sleek lines—and with understandable parts—he loved the most, above everything else in the business. However, seeing Elise so enraptured with a heap of boxes, he knew he was a lost man.

"I'm agreeable, but I want no part of this. I refuse to spend days tangled in cables, or with my nose in some technical manual that reads like a crash course in Greek. I mean it, Lizzie. I have a shipment of cars arriving. I have to get the garage bays ready and this place up and running as fast as possible. In order to get custody of Todd, I need to prove my permanence and stability to Children and Youth Services and quite possibly to a judge, if our petition goes that far." Frowning, he reached for the largest box. "Okay, Whiz Kid, let's put them into the back of the truck."

She made a gleeful squeal as she reached for a smaller box, chattering like a frenzied squirrel as she hoisted it in her arms. "We can hook it up in the spare bedroom. Fritz's old room. There's a second phone line coming in. Dad had it installed when we were in high school. I'll call the phone company and get DSL, or maybe I'll try the cable company and get us the super speed we need. Wait until you see this thing purr. I can have you linked to the whole world in matter of a few hours!"

"What fun," Lucas said with a cynical drawl. "Linked to 6.8 billion people on the globe." Like he needed or even wanted to converse with the whole world. He was having enough trouble with the Scranton area.

Undeterred, Elise said, "You'll change your mind, you just wait." She trotted to the truck with a wide smile on her face.

Minutes later, they stood in the parking lot, both with keys in hand. The smell of oil, grease, and gasoline, heightened by the unseasonably high temperatures, wafted from the pavement and open bay doors beyond. No matter how long he was away from it, the scent never ceased to comfort Lucas. Cars were the one thing he knew, the one thing that gave him security.

"It's going to be easier to get guardianship of Todd if you can prove stability by having a home for him,"

Elise said, interrupting his thoughts.

He shoved his hand into his back pocket and looked over the battered parking lot. He would have to get it resurfaced. One more thing to do. "Yeah, I know. I was hoping to get my grandmother's cottage in order. Hell, it's a disaster. Mike stashed a lot of his belongings there when he shut down his house in New Castle and moved into an apartment here. I piled the remainder of his things in the shed out back."

"Maybe there's something lying around that might help us get a handle on where his will is located, or where the money disappeared."

He shook his head. "If there is, I couldn't find it."

"We should go back to the farm, so I can change into jeans," she suggested, "and we'll take a run up."

Lucas looked at his watch and rubbed his temple. Ever since Elise had stepped off the plane, he felt as if his life was a video tape playing in fast forward. She moved through life filling each minute with purpose and motion, like a spinning top. "Fritz is coming in a few hours. Why don't we take a break?"

"No time." She headed toward the Pontiac. "I'll meet you back at the farm. I'll change clothes, and we'll go together. A few hours is better than none, and without electricity, we need daylight, right?"

He nodded and moved toward the truck, pausing until she was safe inside the car and had it running. She peeled out of the lot like a high-powered jet taking flight. He grimaced as the tires squealed against the pavement, laying rubber. He'd have to ask Fritz what it would take to get her out of overdrive. He'd also have to check where he could lay his hands on a new set of tires. The car would need them before it was shipped to

Atlanta.

The cottage was quaint and picturesque, straight from a storybook, Elise decided, the moment they parked the car in driveway. It was larger than she recalled. The outside was fashioned of mortar and gray fieldstone. A rock garden, now growing wild, but blooming with spring flowers of daffodils and grape hyacinths, bordered both sides of a winding, yellow brick sidewalk leading to the faded blue front door. A small white garage on one side allowed access to it from the side as well. Beside the garage, Elise saw a new doghouse had been built. It must have been Mike's handiwork. She couldn't imagine Lucas having time to construct a doghouse, and for what purpose?

Lucas motioned her around to the back of the house and up a flagstone walk. He pushed open the back entrance door leading directly into the kitchen.

Elise stepped inside. Immediately her eyes were drawn to the hand built, high cupboards climbing to the ceiling and the hewn beams above that lent structural support. Dusty gingham curtains, once a bright green but now mottled and faded in sections from the sun, hung limply from the leaded glass windows. An old wooden table with white chairs, nicked and yellowed, sat in the corner of the room.

"Jeez, I wonder how old this place is? It looks like mid-eighteenth century construction. It's exquisite. Absolutely exquisite."

"I didn't think so when I was growing up," Lucas said bluntly. "Everyone else had the most modern conveniences, dishwashers, fancy televisions, you name it. Your house seemed like a temple of the gods compared to this."

She could hear a tinge of sadness in his voice. She remembered when he was growing up he had never invited anyone to his grandmother's house, except Fritz on rare occasions. He had been too embarrassed to let anyone see he had so little.

She followed him to two rooms at the back of the kitchen. The smaller one held laundry appliances and looked like it had once been a sewing room. The other, a huge walk-in pantry with wooden counters and cupboards on both sides, was stacked to the ceiling with boxes.

"See what I mean?" he said, gesturing at the boxes.

He led her to the cozy living room with its matching fieldstone fireplace and honey-colored oak floor. Beyond were two more bedrooms of ample size, also piled with boxes. The rooms smelled musty and damp from lack of heat. "I'd do better to rent an apartment in Scranton until I can fix this up or buy a suitable house. I wonder why Mike even considered living here?"

"You'd sell this?" she asked incredibly.

"Liz, there are no memories here I can't live without." His eyes were dark and clouded. She watched him put up the hard shield that surrounded him like a steel cage.

"But then you'd never have met the Springers," she pointed out cheerfully.

"True." He smiled faintly, slouched down into an old wicker rocker, and peered at the water-stained ceiling. "You know, I tracked down my father when I was still in the army. He was working on a rig up in Alaska."

"Did you see him?" she asked with curious interest.

"Yeah, I saw the bastard. I made it a point to. Guess what?"

Elise shrugged.

"We had nothing to say to each other. Absolutely nothing! He had no remorse for leaving my mother. He said the marriage just wasn't working, so he lit out. He was badly injured about ten years ago when the braces gave way from a rig he was working on. I was stationed overseas in Germany at the time and given family release time if I wanted it. I saw no need to rush to the side of someone I hardly remembered. Hell, he's probably dead now, for all I know. Not that it really matters."

"Oh, Lucas." She tried to imagine the pain he must have felt. How could a father just walk away from his children and never look back?

"Don't feel sorry, Liz. Your dad was more of a father to me than my old man." He slapped both hands on the side of the rocker and started to get up.

"And your mom?" Elise asked.

"Mom died a couple of years ago." He slumped back down in the chair.

"I'm sorry. But you were able to see her?"

"Yeah, occasionally. Every Christmas and birthday while I was growing up, a present arrived to help relieve the guilt she felt for abandoning me with Grandmother—and Mike with strangers in New York."

"Lucas, maybe she wanted to get you both together, but just couldn't." Elise's heart cried out to him. Her entire life, she had never known anything but a warm, loving family.

He laughed bitterly and his eyes had a wounded

look to them. "Oh, sure, Liz, an alcoholic's first thought is her children and their welfare. Get real."

He stood, his face hardening as he scowled and crawled behind that protective cover of his again. "So what's your take on this place?"

"It looks really sound. The location is fabulous. I'd even add on a huge sunroom someday. It'll take some money though."

"I didn't ask about money." He waved his hand around the room. "Can it be repaired...to livable? In a reasonable amount of time?"

"Lucas, anyone can make a castle out of a cave, given the right resources. I'm merely trying to figure out how much you really want to spend to set it right. Without a budget, I have no basis for giving an opinion." She turned and started to walk toward the side door. If he was going to grouch at her, she had no desire to give him her two cents, let alone her creative ideas.

"Don't walk away from me," she heard him say. "Elise, please."

He caught up with her in the kitchen. "Wait just a damn minute. I didn't mean to anger you." He grabbed her by the arm. "My, you get testy and bent out of shape easily."

She spun and glared at his hand on her arm. He removed it.

"Testy? Bent out of shape? Listen, Lucas, I wasn't trying to pry into your finances, if that was what you were thinking. I was just looking for some guidelines here. Contractors and materials cost money."

"I know, I know." He ran a hand absently through his hair, than looked around the kitchen. "It's just there's so much to do, only so much I can do."

Elise heard the frustration in his voice and sighed. "Lucas, give me some figures to work with, and I'll do what I can. This is a piece of cake. You're talking to the paint and wallpaper diva of Winston and Sanders." She peered at the ceiling and frowned at the water marks. "It may need a new slate roof. Roofs can be costly."

"You're leaving in less than two weeks," he reminded her.

"Maybe, maybe not. Depends upon how well Dad is doing. I can always plead for a few extra weeks, though not without repercussions. But with a proper crew, I can have most of this laid out and taken care of in a reasonable time schedule. We'll have to check the structural integrity and hire a contractor. Basically, we're only talking repairs, paint and wallpaper, a few new furnishings and carpeting. Besides the roof, you'll need to replace the flooring and linoleum in the kitchen and entranceways. We'll need to get a dishwasher, certainly new appliances. A lot of the time will be consumed sorting through and removing those boxes."

"That's the least of my problems. We'll just throw all of them in the shed with the others until I have time," Lucas said.

"No, I think it might be best if we at least took a quick look through them to see if there's anything important."

"If you insist," he replied, agreeably, looking relieved. "Tell you what, I'll pay you whatever you charge at Winston and Sanders. You can be my personal general contractor and decorator, okay?"

She stepped back and felt her jaw drop. "I can't take your money."

"Of course you can."

She sighed again. "I'm not going to stand here knocking heads with you. Think about costs and give me a budget. I'll work with whatever you give me."

He cracked the barest of smiles. "You'll do it then?"

"Yes, and God only knows why." She shook her head wearily. "Let's go see if Fritz is back yet. His cooking is to die for."

"You just ate barely two hours ago," he pointed out, coming up behind her. He slapped her playfully on the backside. "You're going to get fat."

"Keep up the compliments, pal, and see how fast this cottage gets finished." She heard a snicker as he locked the door behind them.

They climbed back into the car and rode back to the farm in silence. Elise suspected Lucas was struggling with memories from the past elicited by the visit. She silently questioned whether repairing the place would prove to be a solution to his problems or whether it would complicate them. She wondered what Todd would think of the cottage. It was comfortable and quaint, and once some modern appliances were installed, perfect for raising a child. The woods surrounding it, the huge lawn, and the small lake behind it only added to its appeal.

Minutes later when she entered the kitchen at her parent's house, the phone was blasting out an endless series of shrill rings. Lucas had forgotten to turn the answering machine back on. She picked up the receiver, not at all surprised Chuck Sanders's frantic voice was on the other end. She tapped the button for the speakerphone and went directly to the refrigerator for something to drink.

"Elise? Thank God, I finally reached you," Chuck Sanders said in an exhausted tone. "Paul is laying eggs in his office."

"Gold ones, I hope." Opening the refrigerator, she searched the shelves.

"Don't be cute. We lost the files for the hotel Simson and Associates backed out on. I've torn the office apart looking for them. I want to take a closer look at the lay-out."

"Chuck, we filed them under new numbers when the deal fell through. Look in the dead files, last drawer from the bottom. The number starts with a six-two something."

She heard him shuffle across the floor and open a drawer. It slammed shut seconds later. Chuck Sanders came back on the line. "You're a lifesaver. How's everything going in Pennsylvania?"

"Fine. If Dad keeps recovering as fast as he appears to be, we can bring him home next week. Of course, there will be weeks of therapy. He'll have to be in a wheelchair and will have to keep the leg immobilized. I'm going to interview some nurses for in-home help."

"We really miss you, Elise. How long do you think you'll stay?"

"Come on, Chuck, I haven't even been away for forty-eight hours. It's only Wednesday. You guys promised me parole until the end of next week."

"I know, I know, don't remind me. It was a silly, impetuous question."

She laughed. "And you don't miss me, Chuck, you miss my organizational skills."

"Of course, I miss you, but I won't deny things are

falling apart here. No one can seem to find anything. Levinson called today. He asked about you. It looks like the five-city hotel plan will become operational after all, once the investors are lined up."

"Has Paul forgiven me for my act of insanity with Levinson before I left?" Elise poured herself a glass of orange juice, smelled it, and turned the carton slowly in her hands, looking for the sell date, hoping it was fairly recent.

"Right now, since Levinson affirmed our position in the deal, Paul is ready to nominate you for architectural sainthood."

"Tell him I want a raise instead." A partnership would be a real thrill, she thought, but bit back the words. She heard silence for a moment, then a soft chuckle.

"Sure, I'll give it a whirl. Nothing like putting the squeeze on, eh?"

"You got it. I figure he owes me."

"Listen, Elise, I have to go. It's really not the same around here. I miss your voice, your perfume, your laughter—"

She scoffed. "Yeah, yeah, yeah, Sanders. Then there's my efficiency and the way I organize your notes and make your coffee. I get the drift of where you're headed. Bye, Chuck." She pushed the button on the phone and stood near the kitchen window in silence. Through the open window, she watched a pair of swallows dart through the sky playing air tag, and far off, she heard a calf calling for its mother. Two years ago, she would have felt homesick for the office and its hectic schedule that attracted her like a human magnet. So why wasn't she feeling it now?

Maybe it was because she finally realized she was trapped, like a pathetic hamster inside an exercise wheel. She was racing to nowhere. She had been smoothing everyone's feathers since her arrival at Winston and Sanders without one mention of a senior partnership even slipping past anyone's lips. Efficient people, she had learned, were always rewarded; unfortunately, with more work. Well, she was fed up with correcting other people's errors, acting as company gofer, and playing nursemaid to cranky clients. She was tired of choosing wallpaper and carpet colors and designing landscape and parking lot patterns. If her career was stuck in neutral, it was her own fault. She had only herself to blame. She had let it happen. She had become too efficient.

Elise looked through the archway and saw Lucas sitting on the steps, chatting with Fritz. Bags of groceries were scattered at their feet. He reached down and took out a soup can, turning it slowly in his hands, rubbing the label almost sensually with the pads of his thumbs. She wondered how many women had been held and caressed by those same hands. Dangerous hands, she reminded herself.

As if he could feel her eyes on him, he looked her way. Her stomach fluttered, and she started toward them. Get a grip, Elise, she told herself. You're going to have to separate the man and his needs from your childish, foolish attraction to him, and you had better do it soon before someone gets hurt.

Chapter Eight

The kitchen smelled glorious. The scents of frying chicken, Chinese vegetables, hot oil, and soy sauce rose from the stovetop and swirled in the air.

Lucas sat at the kitchen table with his legs propped up on the seat of an adjacent chair and watched with fascination as Fritz fussed over an electric wok on the counter. Upstairs, Elise was taking a bath before dinner. Although he didn't know why. The woman barely broke a sweat when she went jogging, and with the rich enticing perfume she used, she always smelled like a delicate spring flower garden. He wondered how much good old Chuck had paid for an ounce of the stuff. He'd bet his life the man blew a week's pay easily. He also knew she was on the phone with Sanders while she soaked, trying to straighten out paperwork he or Winston had bungled.

"You haven't told her, have you?"

Lucas snapped out of his daydreaming at the sound of Fritz's voice. "About what?"

"Cut out the innocent act," Fritz growled. "Elise has no idea you're so filthy rich you could buy her firm with the snap of your fingers, does she?" He took the wooden spoon he was using from the wok and rapped it sharply on the edge of the pan.

"What difference would it make?" Lucas asked. He pulled his feet from the chair and sat upright. "And don't use 'filthy.' I made my money honestly and legally. It's hard-earned, clean cash."

Fritz flashed him a look of disdain. "Don't play silly games with me either, Lucas, or with her for that matter. She honestly wants to help, but you're not showing her all your cards. I have no idea why, but I'll tell you only once, moron, hurt her and you'll answer to me."

"What makes you think I'd hurt her?" Lucas asked defensively and inched up more, ramrod straight. It was the last thing he had on his mind. "Listen, I just don't want the city of Scranton to know I'm anything but the poor abandoned kid who's now all grown up, all right? I have my reasons."

"Does it have anything to do with Mike's death?" Fritz sent him a pointed look.

"Yeah, it does. I'd like to wait before I reveal any of my personal finances. I want to let things simmer a bit. See what plays out, see what happens."

"And if she finds out?" Fritz gestured, inclining his head toward the ceiling where the bath was located above them. "Then what?" He unscrewed the cap from the soy sauce and sprinkled more on the vegetables.

"I'll tell her the truth. Hell, I'll tell her now, if that's what you want."

"Tell me what?" Elise asked and stepped into the kitchen from the hall. She was barefoot, dressed in an aqua sweat suit, and her hair fell loosely around her shoulders.

"I'm rich," Lucas admitted stonily, "but I'm trying to keep a low profile, so I can stay incognito. Sort of like a James Bond image, only in reverse."

"Yeah, right, cut me a break." She went to an

overhead cupboard beside the refrigerator and rummaged on the shelf. "And I'm going to be one of your super sleuth babes who gets to wear those slinky clothes with all that electronic paraphernalia strapped to my body." She removed a bottle of ibuprofen and shook out three tablets. "Are you guys into the booze again?"

Lucas shrugged, raising his hands in defeat as he shot Fritz an *I told you so* glance.

Elise filled a glass of water, swallowed the tablets, and chugged down the water.

Fritz turned from the stove. "You okay?" A worried expression marred his normally comic face.

She yawned. "I have a dull nagging headache. Jet lag finally caught up with me. I know Winston and Sanders have, too. Sometimes I feel like I'm working with two loose screws rather than accomplished architects. Mother used to say if you want a job done right, do it yourself." She sighed, her eyes following the steam rising from the pan. "When are we going to eat? I'm tired, but not too tired to miss this gourmet treat. It smells fabulous, Fritz."

"Take five on the couch," Fritz instructed. "I'll give a yell when we're ready to eat." The two men watched her walk wearily away.

"What's on your menu for dessert, Iron Chef?" Lucas asked.

"Chocolate cake, what else?" He grinned. "It's made from Mom's old recipe. Fit for the likes of Lady Godiva. One of Elise's favorites, too."

"There's only one slight problem," Lucas drawled. "Lady Godiva lived in the second century, and chocolate was introduced into England in the eighteenth century."

"Get out, how'd you know that?" Fritz raised a questioning eyebrow.

"I have a minor in history."

"Holy Fright! Why history, dude?"

Lucas shrugged. "I don't know, I guess I found it fascinating." He looked through the archway into the living room where Elise was stretched out, eyes closed, in a recliner.

"You know Elise has a meeting with Pedmo tomorrow morning." Lucas rubbed at the tension in the back of his neck. The dilemma with Children and Youth Services was wearing on him like a heavy coat of armor, slowly weighing him down hour by hour. He prayed Elise was up for the challenge.

Fritz snorted. "Pedmo is about to go down like a rock sinking in the Lackawanna River, pal. Lizzie has done a lot of legwork on your case. When she sets out to win, no one in his right mind should mess with her. You've never seen her go on a twenty-four hour bout of insanity when she gets passionate over an issue."

"What should I do?"

"Absolutely nothing if you value your life." Fritz smiled broadly. "Just step aside and wait for the fireworks to begin."

****

It was late when Lucas arrived home from seeing Todd at the Johnsons'. Elise was watching the news, cuddled up on the couch with a fluffy afghan. Although Todd was disappointed Elise hadn't accompanied him, she did insist Lucas take her smartphone. Todd spent most of the time punching the Johnsons' number into it and listening to the phone ring endlessly. Lucas wondered how many minutes they had used up on her account as a result of their antics. He hoped she had unlimited. But he had to admit, it had been a brilliant idea. Todd had the time of his life with one small rectangular piece of electronics.

He moved to the couch and dangled her watch before her eyes.

"You got it fixed?" Yawning, she raised up on an elbow to take it from him. A smile spread across her face. She searched through the covers, found the remote, and snapped the television off.

"Yes, it only needed a new battery. How are you feeling?" He sat down at the end of the couch, put her pillow on his thigh, and watched her strap on the watch. Her wrists were delicate, her fingers long and nimble.

She yawned. "Fine, how much do I owe you for the watch?"

He tugged her down until her cheek was on the pillow. His left hand rested naturally on her shoulder. "Nothing, it was the least I could do for a few minutes of in-car, off-the-cuff entertainment."

"Bet it's not the kind you usually have in that shiny package you tool around in."

His hand moved to her hair. It was silky soft, and he pushed it from the side of her face and stroked her temple lightly. "Are you implying I lead a less than respectable life?"

She rolled to her back and stared up at him. Her eyes were so bright blue, it almost hurt to look at them.

"Have you?" she asked.

"To be honest, Elise, I've known a few women. The last one I thought might be real, but I guess I underestimated my talents in selecting the right one." He toyed with the hair at her forehead, rubbing it between his thumb and forefinger.

"What happened?"

He shrugged. "She was a busy model who worked out of New York and L.A."

"She must have been beautiful."

Not as beautiful as you and only on the outside, he wanted to say. "Yes, she was lovely, but as soon as she got an inkling I wanted to raise Mike's kid, she flew the coop."

"Oh, Lucas, I'm so sorry."

He shrugged again. "What about you?"

She rubbed a hand over her eyes and took his hand, resting it comfortably at her waist as she investigated his Seiko, checking the time against her newly repaired watch. Only Elise Springer would want to synchronize watches, he thought. It made him smile.

"New Seiko? Solar driven. Never needs winding. Nice," she commented, running her fingers over the band.

"Yes, I just got it a few weeks ago. I thought my Rolex was a bit too much with my flannel shirts."

"I know the feeling," she said with cynical sarcasm he was beginning to enjoy. "I decided it was best not to wear my diamond necklace when I pulled on these sweats tonight."

"So what about you?" he asked again.

"Me? Oh, yes, I've had a few men in my life." Her face clouded, and she hesitated as her stiff German breeding kicked in, refusing to reveal too much information. "Most of them couldn't hack my long hours, and the others didn't like my no-nonsense personality."

He stroked her forehead. "You always play the

little tough girl role."

"Yeah, it's part of the job, but it's getting old and it's mighty tiring."

"Did you ever consider giving it all up and coming home? Set up your own firm here on the East Coast?"

"I considered it, but Winston and Sanders are renowned. I was hoping to get in on the ground floor, work my way up, and garner some of their reputation first. It helps when you want to go out on your own."

He stared at her, his thoughts in turmoil. It would be so easy to fall in love with her, he thought. He drew in a sharp breath. And get hurt all over again. She would leave, just like Monique. But it bothered him even more to think some other man might get the chance.

"Something the matter?" she asked.

"No, nothing. Your brother thinks I'm not shooting straight with you." He blew out a breath, hoping to gather his wandering thoughts. How do you tell a woman you're rich? He had never been in a position where he'd had to convince someone.

"So tell me what I'm supposed to know." She arched an eyebrow.

"When I snapped at you at the cottage, it wasn't because I didn't want you to know my finances. It was because I have more than sufficient funds to cover whatever you might plan to do." He picked up her hand and brought the back of it to his lips, kissing it softly. "Do you understand? Money isn't a problem for renovating the place. I set aside an account just for cottage expenses."

"Yes, I guess so." She yawned and pulled her hand free, then turned on her side. "So you want the whole works, including all major renovations and new, updated appliances, and all new furniture? Oh, and a new slate roof, too?"

"Whatever you think best. Don't let money get in your way."

"Okay. You got it." She closed her eyes. "If I fall asleep here, be sure I'm up by eight."

Within minutes she was out cold. He sat there stroking her hair, enjoying the solitude of the quiet, empty house, and her soft breathing. He would have stayed there all night, but he also knew there'd be hell to pay in the morning if he didn't set an alarm, and they overslept.

He stood, lowered the pillow with her sleeping head onto the couch and covered her with an afghan, then bent down and kissed her lightly on her forehead before turning off the lights and heading upstairs.

****

"I must say, Miss Springer, I was really surprised when I heard you wanted to speak with me. I thought Todd Fisher was in a very warm, loving home."

Elise smoothed the wrinkles from her pale blue suit and studied Twila Pedmo as she sorted through some paperwork on her desk. A stocky woman in her early sixties, Twila Pedmo had the quick, earnest, and sober demeanor of an army drill sergeant. Her tight, curly, but thinning red hair, verging on shades of pink, came straight from the bottle.

Before Elise had left the house with Lucas hovering over her as if she was headed for the gallows, she had phoned Thomas. Mrs. Pedmo's youngest son had graduated a grade before him. She learned he had become a prominent lawyer for some political faction in the D.C. area. If the mother and son were chipped from the same block of marble, Thomas told her, she'd better be ready for battle. With that piece of advice in mind, Elise had frantically phoned the hospital. Tough, her father had agreed, with a skin as thick as a black walnut, but fair. The woman was devoted to the kids in her care.

"I have no doubt the Johnsons are very capable foster parents," Elise said, "but the boy is young and is still grieving for his father. He needs to be united with his uncle. With family. He needs a place to run and play. The Johnsons aren't physically able to be chasing an energetic child. My dad has taken a real shine to the child. He has had him at the farm. Todd loves the outdoors, and he's especially fond of Dad's Dalmatian."

"Anton? How is he? I heard he had an unfortunate accident."

"He's doing well. He sends his regards. We're hoping he'll be out of the hospital next week."

Mrs. Pedmo crossed her hands on her desk. "You have to understand, there are other ramifications here. The Johnsons are not wealthy people. What little they get from foster care helps to supplement their Social Security."

Elise had thought about that the other night as she played out the entire scenario with Pedmo a thousand times in her mind. "I know, and since they're such a generous, loving couple, I'm sure you'll be able to find them another suitable child soon. We're prepared to continue to reimburse them until you can get another child for them. We'd be most happy to have Mrs. Johnson come over and babysit as well."

"It's certainly generous of you, but you must also know it's a huge undertaking being responsible for a child."

"I'm prepared to do whatever is necessary." Elise smiled with what she hoped looked like a genuine smile despite the worried feelings jabbing at her.

Mrs. Pedro pursed her lips and looked her squarely in the eyes. "So tell me, what part will Lucas Fisher play in all this?" she asked bluntly.

"Play?" Elise repeated, thinking the woman had missed her true calling. She should have been a police detective. Interrogation was mere child's play for Twila Pedro. However, it was as natural as breathing to Elise. She could spar with the best of them. Architects, like artists and writers, were adept at defending and exalting their creations.

"Yes, I can't believe he's hanging around Scranton for any other reason than the child," Pedmo admitted.

"I don't disagree." Elise saw something flicker in the woman's eyes. "Lucas is hoping to eventually get custody of Todd. For now he wants the child not only in a home in which he feels comfortable, but also as close to him as possible until he can have his own house ready for occupancy. He'll petition the court for custody if a will isn't found soon."

"I gather he has since obtained a home here in the area?"

"Of course. He's renovating his grandmother's cottage."

This time Mrs. Pedmo made no effort to hide her surprise. Her eyebrows, penciled red to match her hair, lifted. "I'm sure you also know there are all types of rumors flying around the area about Lucas Fisher."

Elise settled back in her chair. "Not any I'm aware of."

"You should know, my dear, according to word around town, seventy-five thousand dollars was transferred into an account in Atlanta for Lucas Fisher before his brother died. Now, I'm not making accusations, and I'm sure the police will investigate and straighten it out, but it does seem rather bizarre, don't you think? Especially when a hundred thousand dollars of undercover money was never recovered after Mike's death?"

Elise gripped her handbag and struggled to steady her hands. She felt her body go numb. Why hadn't Lucas mentioned this to her? Surely he knew about the rumors. He had told her money was not a problem. He had more than sufficient funds. She wondered whether Thomas and Fritz were aware of this little glitch in his life.

"No, I don't. To be frank, Lucas Fisher's finances are none of my business. You would be entrusting the child to my father and me, not to Lucas." Her mind whirling, she forced herself not to panic. Instinctively, she changed tactics, going on the offensive. "Would you like to talk about my finances? Or my father's? I'd be willing to supply all necessary documents you might need."

Mrs. Pedmo waved a hand. "No, no, of course not."

"Then please tell me, what other complications stand in our way?"

"The stepmother for one. I'm sure you're aware she is claiming she has a close bond with the child."

Elise scoffed. "I'm sure even the courts would

question Clarisse's relationship and her motives."

"She moved here, I'm told."

This time Elise waited a moment, then spoke carefully. "It's a free country, Mrs. Pedmo. She can do as she pleases. Just tell me what *I* need to do."

"You'll have to have an acceptable room for the child, agree to an inspection of your home, have the proper paperwork in order, and get approval before a transfer can be made. Oh, you'll need a criminal background check and a 151 Form, but I suppose in your work you have those documents. I have Anton's criminal background check and his 151 child abuse history clearance already on file."

"I do." Elise pulled out a note pad from her purse. "How long will this paperwork take?"

"Only the time to fill out the office forms." Mrs. Pedmo handed her a packet over the desk.

"Do you have a number where I can fax this back? Or can I scan it through the computer and send it to your e-mail?"

"Either way is fine." Mrs. Pedmo's pink hair bobbed as she cracked a thin smile. "I personally do the home inspections, so we can set it up for any day. However, the paperwork usually takes a few weeks after it's submitted for approval."

"Not good enough." Elise shook her head, lips pursed. "Can we get it by the end of this week if I fill out the papers today?"

"Oh, heavens, no. The system doesn't work that fast."

Elise leaned forward. "Mrs. Pedmo," she said in a sweet, low whisper, "you and I both know we don't need the Governor to approve something like this. Give me a name or names, and I'll personally get the signatures."

The hackles all but rose on Twila Pedmo's neck as she shot Elise a hostile glare. "Ms. Springer, I resent—"

"—intervention and opposition, I assume," Elise finished and reached in her purse for her phone. She held it out in front of her, punched in a ten-digit number and positioned her thumb over the send key. "Now I get a name of someone who'll push this through, or I call Senator Billings. State legislators love little dilemmas like these to solve for their constituency. It makes for good press when campaign time rolls around. Poor orphaned child, police officer father dead, unable to be relocated with the people he's most fond of—his family. A child who's crying himself to sleep at night. Local foster agency unwilling to cooperate, stalling the paperwork. You know, all the heart-wrenching stuff the public loves to hear?"

The color drained from Mrs. Pedmo's face. "Heart-wrenching stuff? You're a bold, tenacious one, aren't you, Miss Springer? You must really want this child."

"You're pretty tough yourself," Elise admitted.

"Oh, all right," Mrs. Pedmo conceded. "If you give me the papers today, I'll try to have them signed before Friday. It's the very best I can do!" She stood, obviously a signal she was ending the meeting.

Elise sprang from her chair, almost dropping her phone. She extended her hand across the desk and pumped the woman's enthusiastically. "Thank you, Mrs. Pedmo, thank you. You don't know how much I appreciate your help."

"Tell me, Ms. Springer, would you really have placed the call?"

Elise laughed. "Unfortunately, not that particular one. I would have had to call directory assistance and locate the right number first."

The woman's face held a conspiratorial smile. "You are certainly a credit to Anton Springer, my dear." She picked up a file from her desk and gestured to the waiting room. "You're welcome to stay, fill out this packet of paperwork, and leave it on my clerical assistant's desk."

Elise followed her to the outer office where she dropped Todd Fisher's private folder into a wire file basket on the corner of Linda Cook's vacant desk before returning to her office.

Elise surveyed the room. Linda Cook was nowhere in sight. She was either in the restroom or getting some coffee in the office lunchroom. As soon as she heard Pedmo's office door shut, Elise slid into a seat, snatched the folder from the basket, and began to riffle through it. Amid the report of services and contacts with the foster parents, she found an entry of Pedmo's in-home visit. In the margin, a notation read, "Child likes dogs, the color blue and French fries. Not fond of green vegetables, but loves animal crackers." Elise smiled at the flowery script. So Pedmo wasn't the hard case she appeared to be.

Continuing her search, she also discovered the initial intake evaluation by Jack Morrison. It merely recommended Todd to be returned to New Castle for the child's best interests. Beneath the evaluation, there was a single sheet of paper with Clarisse Fisher's name, address and phone number on it. Elise stared at it a moment, wondering whether Clarisse had made contact with Child Welfare or if they had located her. From her purse, she pulled out her notepad again and quickly jotted down the information including Clarisse's most recent place of employment, Two Horses, a local bar.

She was about to return the folder when a niggling thought crossed her mind. She removed Clarisse's address and compared the handwriting against Twila Pedmo's and Jack Morrison's. It was Jack's writing, there was no doubt.

Footsteps in the hall forced her to slam the folder shut. She had no sooner tucked it beneath her packet of papers when Morrison sauntered down the hall with a bottle of water in his hand.

"Lizzie, I'm glad I caught you. I was meaning to call. How about Saturday night?"

"Saturday night?" She peered up at him. This time he was wearing a brown jacket with a blinding gold tie accented in what appeared to be tiny lime green palm trees.

"Yeah, I thought we'd get something to eat and catch up on old times."

Her mind ticked. "I heard there's a place called Wild Horses."

He frowned. "You mean Two Horses? Yeah, it's a new country and western joint. Pretty rowdy. Food's bad, unless you're into burgers and noise. I thought we'd go someplace with some atmosphere and class."

She gave him her best little girl pout. "Ah, Jack, I can get enough class in San Francisco. Why don't we catch a nice dinner some place and go to Two Horses afterwards? I'd love doing something different."

Relenting, he said, "Oh, all right, but it's a real dive. I'll make sure we at least stop there so you can see it. Is seven o'clock, okay?"

"Seven o'clock is fine." She glanced down at her papers. "What do you know about Todd's stepmother?"

"Clarisse?"

She thought she heard a slight hitch in his voice. "Yes, but I don't recall her maiden name," she lied.

"Cramer, but she uses Fisher," he filled in. "Nothing. I guess she was interested in custody of Todd Fisher, from what Twila Pedmo tells me."

"Now why would she think she could have custody, Jack?"

He shrugged and fidgeted with some change in his pocket. It was plain to see he was uncomfortable discussing Clarisse, even though he made a valiant effort to conceal it. "I suppose she would have had some type of rapport with the child, having lived with him over a year."

He started to say more, but Linda Cook strolled in, a cup of coffee in her hand.

Elise clutched her papers fanned over Todd Fisher's folder. She expected to see hostility in the secretary's face, but instead Linda Cook greeted her with a smile and sat down.

"I see you got the papers you need," Linda said.

Elise nodded. "Yes, thank you. It looks like your agency invests heavily in Hammermill."

The woman laughed. "The government does, you mean."

Jack Morrison glanced briefly at Elise and smiled. "I'll let you finish up here." He headed down the hallway toward his office.

A half hour later, Elise decided she had all but signed away her life and her dad's farm. Now all she would have to do was distract Linda Cook and return

Todd's folder to the basket.

But how? She pondered her dilemma for a moment, watching Linda Cook efficiently bang out information onto a form in her computer. She toyed with her pen, removing the cap. She remembered the many times she and Fritz had been caught in childish pranks. When you can't bluff, her brother always said, confront your opponent with sheer confidence and boldness, or complete stupidity.

Mustering her courage, Elise rose, plunked the papers fearlessly on Linda's desk while she slipped the folder back into the basket. "Thanks for your help."

Linda turned from her computer. The woman was blessed with uncanny peripheral vision. Her hand flew to the basket.

"This is a confidential client folder," she said, tapping it lightly.

Elise smiled. "Excellent! It means my papers will be treated with the same efficient care and confidentiality, right?"

"Of course." Linda Cook quickly removed it from her basket, then looked up, her gaze cool but not unpleasant. "Have a nice day, Ms. Springer."

Elise left, so nervous she took the steps to the street too quickly, almost stumbling on the last one. She had obtained more information than she had planned, but she was certain of two things. There were still a lot of unanswered questions, and she had not pulled the wool over Linda Cook's eyes.

Chapter Nine

The first thought crossing Lucas's mind was that a blue tornado had swooped down without warning.

Elise Springer barreled through the office door, crossed the distance between them, and slammed her fist on the metal desk so hard two pencils did simultaneous jumping jacks before hitting the concrete at her feet.

"You liar!" she shouted. Vicious claws, still splendidly colored a brilliant red, reached out, clutching the front of his shirt and jerking him by the throat.

"Having a bad morning?" Lucas asked quietly, thankful he never made it a habit to fasten the top button. "Maybe I should make a pot of coffee?"

"You set me up, you detestable jerk!" Her hand still held fast even when his came up to cover it. "You never told me about the seventy-five thousand dollars Mike gave you."

He pried her fingers loose, and she stepped back, slicing the air with the edge of her palm. "I trusted you, you lowly worm. I went in there on your behalf!" Both hands flew to her temples, massaging her forehead. She stomped to the window and back again twice. "God, what a fool I am."

"It's not what it appears, Liz." Lucas sat down, leaned back in a chair beside the desk, and hoped Fritz had not lied and this was just one of her twenty-four hour bouts of raving insanity. "Maybe you ought to sit down, and I'll explain."

"You can start spouting an explanation right now, pal, and I don't need to sit to hear your gibberish!"

If her eyes could throw darts, he'd be dead man for sure, Lucas decided. He mustered some courage. "If I had told you Mike gave me money from his personal funds to invest for him, you would have gone into the meeting with Pedmo and tried to second guess her, just to defend me. I couldn't take the chance. You got the kid, right?"

She glared at him. "Yeah, I got Todd, or almost have him, no thanks to you, pinhead."

"Liz," he said and patted the top of the desk. "Sit down. Please."

He watched her warily back against the edge of the desk and defensively cross her arms at her chest.

"It's not what you think. The money Mike dropped into the Atlanta account was from his foster parents, who sold some property and wanted him to share in their profits. It wasn't stolen undercover money despite the rumors flying about. His divorce wasn't final yet, and he wanted to be sure Clarisse wouldn't get her hands on it. He felt it should be invested for Todd."

"Do you have proof of this?" she asked. Her tone was still irritated, but to his relief, less hostile. Anger was slowly draining from her face.

"It's a little more complicated than I'd like to admit. You see, Mike deposited the money in cash, so there'd be no paper trail for Clarisse to follow. Right now, Thomas is tracing it back to New York and the bank accounts of Mike's foster parents." She stared at him with a wary expression, and he could see she was struggling to believe him.

"What other pertinent information should I know?" She chewed on the corner of her lip. "Don't even think about handing me any bull, Fisher."

"Of the one hundred thousand dollars Mike received from his foster parents, only seventy-five thousand was actually deposited for me to invest. There's twenty-five thousand of the total missing as well."

It took a while for her to register what he had just told her. "How did that happen?"

He shrugged. "Originally, his plan was to deposit twenty-five thousand in four separate installments. My accounts in Atlanta show only three."

"And you didn't question him?"

"Elise, I was in Atlanta. He was here in Scranton. Of course, I never questioned him. I received three payments. I had no reason to believe he wouldn't pay the last one as we planned. Anyway, my accountant, who helps takes care of the business end of the garage in Atlanta, was handling the transactions. When I found out there were only three deposits, I figured Mike was having a cash flow problem and needed to buy a car or fix up his apartment. How often do you discuss your savings and finances with your brothers?"

"I don't."

"Exactly." He stood, pushing back his chair, and leaned an elbow on a new filing cabinet positioned diagonally behind him. "Remember when I told you yesterday I had adequate funds to cover the cottage repairs?"

"Sufficient," she corrected him.

"Sufficient then." He leveled a gaze her way.

"Actually, I took care of it this morning." He opened the top drawer of the cabinet and withdrew a checkbook with a card. "I dropped fifty thousand into this account for you to use. As soon as you sign the signature card and return it to the bank, you're in business to work on the cottage."

"Fifty thousand? Holy cow!" She arched a brow. "Aren't you going a little overboard for paint and carpeting?" She took the checkbook he handed her.

"The slate roof will be pricey. I don't know what you'll need. I don't know what the materials might cost." His hands flew palms up. "I don't care what you do, just get it operational. I need the place livable as quickly as possible."

"Wait, why do I have to I sign the card?" Warily, she flipped up the cover where temporary checks were concealed. "Why use my name?"

"So you can pay the bills, why else?"

"I'm not going to be here for very long," she pointed out.

He studied her a moment. She had let her hair fall loose about her shoulders. The soft blue suit she wore hugged her body and fell in perfect lines to accentuate her trim figure and baby blue eyes. It made her look youthful and fresh, and he knew she had selected it for the meeting to give the appearance of innocent trust. She also looked incredibly sexy. He thought about begging her not to return to California, but it would be an effort in futility.

"I know. We can put your dad's or Fritz's name on with a blind signature, if you'd like. I'd prefer if my name and money are not flashed about at the moment. This business about Mike is not resolved, and I need to keep a low profile. Trust me on this."

"So you think the undercover money does exist?"

"I think it not only exists, but I also think someone is waiting in the wings hoping to discover it or waiting until we do. This morning I found a back window in the showroom jimmied. Someone was in here snooping around. Perhaps hoping to find some information to lead him or her to it."

Elise pushed herself from the desk with worried eyes. "We should go to the police, Lucas. It's the sensible thing to do."

He shook his head vehemently. "I can't be sure it wasn't just kids pulling a prank. And I want the police out of it—completely uninvolved for the moment. They already suspect me, and it might be best if everyone thinks the same."

"Why?" She heaved a sigh, not understanding his logic.

"Listen, Elise, what if there's someone close to Mike who knows the money wasn't recovered? If my name is cleared, he'll have to make doubly sure he doesn't get careless searching for it. With me as a prime suspect, he just might let down his guard and hopefully make a few mistakes."

"So even if someone finds it, what difference does it make? Thomas will clear your name."

"Yeah, but I want to clear Mike's. I don't want the entire police force to think my brother was a thief." He considered telling her he didn't think Mike's death was an accident either, but instead, he pushed up the sleeve of his flannel shirt and checked his watch. "Are you hungry? We can finish this over lunch." He remembered Fritz's description the other night. He hoped she had calmed down and was over her anger. If only he could tell her the truth...the real truth...that he was rich and he didn't need anyone's money for anything—even to take care of Todd. All he wanted to do was catch Mike's killer and clear Mike's name for both Todd and himself.

She smiled. "Starved. I know a small diner where they make the best vegetable lasagna."

Half an hour later, he sat across from her in a secluded corner of the restaurant, watching her shovel the final bite of pasta between her lips as she related the incidents in Pedmo's office.

She sighed contentedly and leaned back, tapping her nails on the red checked tablecloth. "Now tell me the rest of your dark secrets. I tend to take bad news better on a full stomach." Her blue eyes danced merrily.

He smiled. He'd remember that next time. "I should have made you breakfast before I sent you into battle with Children and Youth Services."

He reached across the table and took her hand in his. She was wearing an expensive opal ring he hadn't seen before. It looked so delicate, like her, especially compared to the chunky black watch with all its beepers she wore tucked up high on her wrist under the sleeve of her suit.

He rubbed her ring finger. "Another gift from Chuck?" he asked with a grudging tone.

"As a matter of fact, it is," she said and pulled her hand away.

"So this guy is...what?"

"Generous?" she offered, as if she could read where he was going with his questions and wanted to head him off.

"Could you be more specific?"

"What's more specific than generous?" she asked dryly.

He leaned forward and said in a hiss, "Dammit, Lizzie, don't play coy. I hate head games." He could see flames leap in her eyes. Her face went from white to red to white again.

"Are you asking me if I'm sleeping with him?" she asked. "What are you? Part of the Springer brothers' protect-little-sister brigade? Did they make you an honorary big brother?"

"Yes. Answer my question."

"I will not! I don't need this, you know. You have a lot of nerve." Throwing her napkin aside, she signaled for the waitress, who was one table away. "Can we have our check, please?"

Before the receipt even hit the table, she had it in her hand and was storming toward the cash register.

Teeth clenched, Lucas rose and threw some bills on the table for a tip. He caught up with her tearing across the parking lot as she headed to the car.

"Lizzie, wait up!"

She slid into the passenger's seat and slammed the door with a sharp crack that made him wince. If he didn't get something else for her to drive, the poor car would be in pieces and the buyer in Atlanta would never get a chance to smell the leather cleaner on the seats.

He opened the driver's side, heaved his tall frame down, and shoved the key into the ignition. "You know, your brother is right, you are a raving maniac when you are on a mission...or maybe when your hormones go ballistic...or maybe when you need chocolate."

"Oh, terrific, so you're analyzing me now? I hope you weren't discussing this with those two baboons I call brothers."

"No." He threw the car into gear and peeled out of the parking lot. "But we did discuss Lady Godiva."

"What? Are you morons? What's with Lady Godiva?"

"Chocolate, I guess. Hell, I don't know." He swiped a hand across his face. Being around this woman made all logical reason fly out the door. He could barely think straight. He continued, "I once watched a television show about women who are addicted to chocolate for the good feeling it causes, and they have withdrawal symptoms when they don't get enough of it. I noticed you didn't have any of Fritz's chocolate cake last night."

"Oh, dear Lord, you three really *are* certifiable imbeciles! I didn't eat chocolate cake because I wasn't hungry for dessert!" She jammed her sunglasses on her face and muttered, "Where are we going, Freud?"

"I don't know that either." He mustered all the strength he had to keep from sniping back at her. He nudged the accelerator, pressing her backwards into the seat. "Liz, I was only curious about Sanders."

"Sure, sure you were," she countered. "Why don't you just run a criminal background and credit check on him while you're at it? Get a private investigator to dig up some dirt. Maybe have a quick interview with his elderly grandmother, too. Do you want her address?"

Refusing to rise to her bait, he turned on the radio and turned the volume down to low. From the corner of his eye, he watched her fall silent, settling herself stiffly in her seat and snapping her seat belt. Minutes later, he turned off into Nay Aug Park, glided the car into a parking place, and cut the motor.

"We need to talk," he said in a quiet voice and turned toward her.

"So talk. Just so it's not about my personal life," she muttered. She refused to look at him. She removed her sunglasses, squinting out the windshield. Through the open window, the cry of a redwing blackbird taking flight rent the air.

"No, it's about mine." He reached over and unsnapped her seat belt. "Can we get out? It's a beautiful day. Let's walk."

****

The air smelled of spring. Crisp, sweet and earthy, Elise decided, as they made their way up to the Davis Wenzel Tree House overlooking a 150-foot rock-strewn gorge below. The Tree House area was deserted. Then she remembered it was approaching late Wednesday afternoon when most people were ending their workday and heading home for a relaxing evening.

Lucas propped his forearms on the rail. For a moment they stood, forgetting their differences, peering into the gorge, drinking in the warmth of the sun and panorama below them.

"You know, Fritz, Tom, and I often came up here when we were in high school," he said.

"And brought your dates, I'll bet." She suppressed a sly smile. Nay Aug Park was a well-known haven where lovers gathered to exchange a few embraces without interruption.

"Yes, but many times we came alone. I remember my senior year in high school when Fritz and I skipped chemistry class one afternoon, just to sneak up here.

Thomas was already in college. He always knew he wanted to be a lawyer. Fritz and I stood in this exact spot, trying to figure out our future. Fritz decided he wanted to have his own business so he could set his own hours." Lucas chuckled. "Now he works ten-hour days, six days a week because he's boss and owner."

"And you?"

"Me, I wanted to race cars and be rich."

"I'll bet your grandmother loved those goals."

Lucas propped a booted foot on the lower rail. "When I was growing up, I always resented her frugality. She provided the basics, nothing more. I knew money was tight, so I never complained. There were days when I swore I'd never eat another peanut butter and jelly sandwich again once I was out on my own. If it wasn't for your parents, I swear I would have never been exposed to all the possible food groups."

A soft breeze kicked up and blew her hair into her eyes. She pushed it aside and leaned backwards against the railing. "She did the best she could, Lucas."

He nodded and looked up for moment at the blue sky dotted with a tiny wisp of clouds. "Yes, with what she had, I'll not deny that. Later, when I was in the Army I used to send her money to help supplement her Social Security checks."

It took Elise every ounce of control to keep desolation from sweeping over her. Lucas's words made her heart ache. She could imagine him sacrificing his own needs to send money home. Even wild and reckless as he was, he would have considered his grandmother another underdog he needed to help.

"Lucas, maybe it's not a good idea to rehash the past," she suggested.

He went on despite her suggestion. "I kept it up, even when I set up my own struggling business. When she died, I discovered she had been investing my grandfather's pension from the railroad instead of spending one red cent of it on me or herself. She also took the money I sent her and squirreled it away into stocks and bonds, of all things."

He glanced over at her. "I thought I was successful when the specialty body shop started booming and netted me a pretty penny, but she had already made me my first million."

Elise sucked in a breath. "First million?"

"Yeah," he said turning to her, squinting under the bright rays of afternoon sun. "She knew nothing about stocks so she randomly chose to invest in gas, oil, computers and pharmaceutical companies."

She felt her face register shock. "You really *are* rich, aren't you?"

He came toward her, grasping the rail beside her as he slowly nodded, his lips set in a tight line. His hand came up, and she felt his knuckles slide softly down the side of her face.

"Yes, very rich. Does it make a difference, Lizzie?"

Stunned, she didn't know what to say. They stared at each other. His eyes, bright silver, met hers of sky blue. "Of course not," she finally admitted. "Why should it?"

He stepped closer and faced her. "Good, because there's something I've wanted to do for the last two days."

"What?"

"This," he whispered, lowering head as his lips

descended closer and closer to hers. "It's the only thing I think about since you arrived."

Her hand went reflexively to his chest. She pressed herself against the rail and felt the cold steel bite into her back. "Lucas, this is not a good place, and the timing's all wrong."

"It's the perfect place and time, Liz. Nothing can happen, don't you see? You're safe."

"Lucas, no."

Her plea went unanswered as his lips brushed lightly over hers. His hands circled her, and he drew her tightly against him. Her heart pounded clear up to her throat. The kiss became more insistent, and she found herself responding. Her lips parted. His tongue slipped in, mating and tangling with hers. He broke away and kissed her cheek, his lips traveling down her neck to the soft spot at her shoulder, and then back to her mouth again. The heat of his body burned against her, hard and demanding, just as relentless as his lips.

"Lucas," she moaned between breaths. "Lucas, we have to stop." She nudged his chest with the heel of her hand, and he pulled away. His eyes had darkened to smoky gray.

"What? What's the matter?" His forehead creased, and he stared at her as if he could feel her fear.

"Nothing." She shuddered, even though the sun was warm and inviting. Her hands trembled, and she gripped the rail. She closed her eyes and swallowed, hoping to erase the frightening thoughts swirling in her head. Philip Cullington had made a mess of her life. She had thought she'd never feel comfortable again in another man's embrace. For the last four years she had felt safe, carefully avoiding any relationships, making her work her first love. Now Lucas Fisher had come along to awaken yearnings she was sure had died.

"Someone hurt you," he said quietly.

She hung her head. "I don't like to talk about it."

"Like or want?"

"Either."

"Okay, fair enough, it's part of the past," he said gently and pulled her into his arms again. She leaned her forehead against his chest and felt his lips skim the top of her head. "I promise, Liz, I'll never hurt you. Not on purpose. Never on purpose."

"Lucas, this could muddle so many things we're not prepared to deal with." She rested her cheek against his laundry-faded shirt. He smelled of earth and sky, sunshine and spring breezes.

"I know," he whispered into her hair.

Her gaze found his solid, masculine one and she pushed herself away. He heaved a sigh, letting her wiggle out from his embrace, and ran his hands through his hair. "Listen, Lizzie, I'll take it slow, if you want. Hell, you can pick the speed, and I'll be content just to be in the race."

Collecting her emotions, she looked out over the rail to the opposite side where fishermen below in Roaring Brook looked like miniature toy figures. Could she risk an intimate relationship again? Could she risk being hurt emotionally one more time? She had to return to San Francisco. She had a career to pursue.

"I'm not certain I know what I want," she said truthfully. "I don't even know if I want to be in the rat race I'm currently in."

She felt his breath fan her ear. "I understand. I'll give you a few days to work this all through."

"A few?" She turned and faced him and found herself smiling. "My, you certainly are a magnanimous sort, Lucas Fisher."

A grin tugged at the corner of his mouth. He kissed her lightly on the temple. "Hell, yes, considering we're down to nine, counting today."

Chapter Ten

Lucas stood inside Whitman's Paper and Paint Store, surrounded by the pungent scents of vinyl wallpaper, turpentine, and paint, and wondered how he had allowed himself to be tricked into abandoning his work at the garage. Then he remembered it all had come about with Elise's urge to redo the bedroom at the farm for Todd.

Actually, it had started with her persistent wheedling about the bare kitchen cupboards and the need to grocery shop. It had been an eye-opening experience in itself, and he finally admitted to himself he had discovered how the phrase "shop till you drop" came into existence. Woman pitted against marketable commodities. In less than forty-five minutes, she had filled a grocery cart with more food than could possibly fit into the cupboards and refrigerator and which barely fit into the trunk of the Trans Am, now parked outside.

Though he had to give her credit, despite her unflagging obsession to use every minute to its advantage, she was as competent and efficient at managing details as she had professed. Over the past few days, she arranged to have the electricity at the cottage turned on and already had a contractor on the job, replacing the cottage's slate roof. And lists. Lord, the woman could make lists. On anything. From napkins to the margins of a candy wrapper.

However, nothing had prepared him for Whitman's Paint and Paper. It was like stepping onto another planet.

"What are we looking for again?" He watched her leaf through the pages of a pattern book with a speed that defied logic. She was standing before a long rectangular table in the back of the store with two dozen books piled haphazardly around her. Shelves circling the room held hundreds more. "Blue dogs?"

"No, white wallpaper with blue paw prints and with a corresponding blue border with dogs. I know it exists, I just don't know where." Her eyes never left the book she was working with. "It has to be in stock, too."

"Run this by me again. How do I tell if it's in stock, and what shade of blue?" Lucas rubbed his bleary eyes with the palms of his hands.

"Ah, French blue, something like this." She paused only long enough to point to a flower so small the average person would need a magnifying glass. She flipped the page before he had a chance to commit it to memory. "Don't worry about the stock, the store manager will check on it."

Lucas scowled. Every pattern had begun to look like the next, melting into a haze of swirling tones. God, he needed an aspirin and a beer. If she kept this up, he'd be too dizzy to eat the hundred pounds of food jammed into the trunk.

"Can't we do this tomorrow? I really need a break here."

"No time," she mumbled. "Pedmo is coming on Monday."

"Monday?" A little bell of alarm went off in his head. "Since when?"

"Since the meeting. It must have slipped my mind." She never raised her head.

"Maybe we should get someone to help us," he suggested.

"I did." She waved her hand toward a circular table where a thin man with fuzzy gray eyebrows was rummaging through a stack of books that would put a library to shame. "I snagged the manager on the way inside while you were rearranging groceries in the trunk."

"You're absolutely sure this wallpaper exists?" He squinted at her with a skeptical look, and she nodded, her fingers nimbly turning the pages of yet another book.

"Uh-huh, I saw it once when I was selecting paper for a day care center our agency was contracted to renovate."

"Oh, terrific. There are at least five hundred books here, and we've been through what? Two dozen? I imagine you have someone lined up to hang the dang rolls?"

"Uh-huh, you and Fritz. But only if you'd stop talking and help me find it."

"Me and Fritz?" His voice came out in a hysterical wail. "Get serious, Liz, I've never wallpapered a room in my life." Hell, he couldn't wrap a Christmas present unless it was packaged in a box with four crisp corners and there were yards of paper to waste.

"Neither has Fritz, but he's watched my mother do it many times. I have to interview some nurses from Home Health in the morning, otherwise I'd help. Anyway, it's just one wall and pasting a border around the ceiling. It's a piece of cake." Her hands continued flashing through the pages.

"Piece of cake? Are you *sane*? Unless Fritz has flashbacks, we're doomed." Lucas slumped down wearily onto a nearby chair and cupped his face in his hands.

Two seconds later, he heard the store manager's cheerful voice. "Got it! Right here, Miss Springer!"

He looked up in time to see Elise take the offered book and mark the pattern with a paint chip sample. She grinned at the tiny blue paw prints and tipped the book for him to see. Across the top, Lucas could see a strip of coordinating border with all breeds of puppies tumbling on top of each other.

He was about to jump up, shout hallelujah, and sweep the manager into a bone-jarring hug when Elise paused, staring out into space.

"I wonder whether the department store down the street carries bedspreads in this color range?"

"Oh, sure, I imagine they do," the manager assured her. "Here, let me give you another paint sample to take with you."

Grimacing, Lucas plodded behind her as she sauntered to the counter to verify the measurements and pay the bill.

Outside again, he stopped in the sunshine beside the Trans Am. Earlier he had spied the sign for a bar and grill, a block up the street. Farther away, a state liquor store stood on the corner.

"You need that phone of yours?" He frowned at her and jammed a hand in his back pocket. "I figure I can make a few calls while you bolster sales in the linen department down the street."

She pulled the phone from her purse and spoke in a

disgruntled tone to match his. "You know it would be easier if I had a car and you had a phone. You wouldn't have to stand around waiting for me like a moping pain-in-the—"

"Okay, okay! I know, I know." Oh, how he knew. He touched the screen to her phone and opened the number pad. "I'm taking care of the car right now. I intended to stop by the garage and get one. A shipment came in today from Atlanta. To save time I'll have it delivered to the house instead. I also promised your dad I'd stop by the hospital, so we'll have to swing by there first."

"Dad never mentioned it to me." She stared at him with a puzzled gaze.

"It probably slipped his mind, like Pedmo did yours." He opened the door to the Trans Am and retrieved a spare set of keys from the glove compartment. "Here, take these. I have an errand to run myself."

"You know, Lucas, it's not a terrific idea to keep the spare keys locked inside."

"Don't worry, I don't make it a habit."

He didn't want to tell her there wasn't a car built he couldn't access. Hell, he had learned how to break into an automobile when he was only thirteen. He checked his watch. "Go...get moving! You have thirty minutes to come up with the Russian blue blanket."

She let out a quick unladylike snort. "*French*, Lucas. French blue bedspread."

His hand plowed through his hair impatiently. "Cripes, we're not holding an international summit here. Just buy the damned thing and get back here. Pronto."

She took the keys he thrust at her and looked in the direction of the bar and grill. "Don't even think about it," she warned. "The last thing I need is for Dad to see you with a buzz on."

Lord, the woman had mental telepathy along with her interior design skills. He punched some numbers into her phone. "Hurry up, or the food in the trunk is going to cook before we get it home."

"I hope so. I'm tired of kitchen duty. When is it going to be your turn?"

He grinned at her. She was wearing a yellow tank top with a pair of snug-fitting, faded blue jeans that made his mouth water. "Listen, Frenchie, I'm willing to negotiate. I've got the yard work, laundry, and garbage duty."

She groaned and held up a palm. "Forget it, just forget I asked." She took off down the sidewalk, her sandals slapping on the hot pavement.

He waited until she was out of sight before he spoke briefly on the phone, opened the car and laid it carefully on the passenger seat. Lizzie Springer was in for a delightful surprise. He couldn't wait to see her face when they arrived at the farm and she saw the car he had chosen for her. Whistling merrily, he locked the door and strode up the street and into the bar.

****

Elise promised herself she wouldn't let Lucas Fisher aggravate her, but fifteen minutes later, it took all of her willpower to ignore the empty Coors can he'd flung behind the seat when she slid into the Trans Am with her purchases.

"Maybe I'd better drive." She held out her hand, palm up.

Judy Ann Davis

"One beer, Liz, that's all I had." He shoved the key in the ignition and smiled as the engine roared to life.

She turned and peered behind the seat where a brown paper bag and a nicely wrapped small rectangular box were wedged between the heaps of packages they had collected all afternoon. Unless she was sorely mistaken, it looked like it held a six-pack. "What's in the bag?"

"Coke. Plain ol' cola, Miss Curiosity."

"Yeah, cut me a break."

He heaved an exhausted sigh. "Why don't you ever believe me? It's soda, I tell you. See for yourself."

She reached back and retrieved the bag. True to his word, it held six cans of carbonated drink and a package with two plastic snap-on lids.

"It's for your dad," he explained, his face registering pleasure at having bested her.

"My dad? I can't believe he can't get cola at the hospital." She eyed him skeptically. "Did he ask them for some?"

He shrugged. "What do I look like? Anton Springer's personal dietitian? I imagine the only thing he can get in the hospital is some ginger ale which, by the way, looks like cattle urine and is usually served flat to boot."

When they reached the hospital, they parted while Lucas parked the car, agreeing to meet shortly in her father's room. She was surprised to find her father looking incredibly better. He sat upright in his bed, foot propped on some pillows, reading a copy of *Stock Car Racing*. One leg of the new pajamas she had bought him had been cut open carefully on the seam to allow room for the cast covering his lower leg and ankle.

120

She kissed him on the cheek.

"Lucas coming, too?" he asked, setting the magazine aside.

"He's parking the car." She wandered to the window and gazed out. Below her, in a far corner of the distant playground, she watched a group of little girls play jump rope. In another corner, a group of boys was shooting hoops. "How much longer do you think they'll hold you hostage?" she asked.

"I can go in a few days or stay until the middle of next week. I told the doctors there's no sense in rushing this old body out the door."

Surprised again, she turned and eyed him skeptically, pondering his reluctance to leave. "Don't you want to come home, Dad?"

He repositioned himself on the bed. "That's not the point, Lizzie. While I'm here, I get physical and occupational therapy sessions each day. It makes more sense to stay here a bit and get the help, right?"

Yesterday, when she had phoned the hospital to talk with his doctor, she learned the medical staff already had her father using a walker. The doctor had chuckled and said he had vehemently refused to use a wheelchair. If he had intensive physical therapy now, his doctor thought he'd be able to rely on crutches and perhaps move into a walking cast sooner than they had expected.

Elise nodded. She knew what her father was implying. He had never been a man to rely on anyone, and a wheelchair and the thought of being less than self-sufficient scared him to death. She had to admit the hospital stay was helping him. His face was pain-free, his voice was steady, and his demeanor cheerful. He was also starting to charm the nursing staff.

Casting a warm and approving glance at him, she spoke. "It's your choice, but remember, if you change your mind and get homesick, it won't be any problem. We'll manage with or without a wheelchair."

At the sight of Lucas in the doorway, Anton Springer brightened even more. "Well, well, just the man I wanted to see. Did you bring some?"

"Coke, just like you asked." Lucas grinned and popped the tab on a can he pulled from the bag under his arm. He slid the wrapped present, done up with a bow on the nightstand beside the bed.

Anton Springer took a Styrofoam ice bucket from the nightstand and held it out to Elise. "Could you get me some ice?" he asked with a hopeful look. "I want to put a few cans in to chill for later tonight."

She studied him a moment. He wasn't fooling anyone. The ice was merely a ploy to get her to leave the room. And Coke? She didn't even know what was going on with that particular craving. For some reason, she thought, he wanted to be alone with Lucas. Reluctantly, she picked up the bucket and headed for the door.

On her way back to her father's room, she stopped at the nurses' station to get their opinion about her dad's progress. She was glad to hear he was healing faster than even the surgeon could imagine. Behind the counter, she overheard an older nurse telling a co-worker about her emergency room shift last week when she had taken care of one of Mary Jo Meyer's boys, who needed stitches in his forehead. "Those children are always falling down," she said. "Clumsy little tykes. This one was running and hit the coffee table. Now why does a mother let children play tag in the house?"

Puzzled by the very same question, Elise headed back down the hall to her father's room where she found a gray-haired nurse hovering near the foot of her father's bed and fussing with some charts. She handed Lucas the ice bucket.

"Now be a trooper, Lily," Elise heard Anton Springer tell the nurse, "your charts can wait a while longer. Can't you see I have company? I want to talk to the kids without someone tinkering with these damned machines."

The nurse's gaze flitted from Elise to Lucas to Anton and back again. "Maybe I could just get a temperature?" she asked hopefully.

"Now, now, Nurse Ryan, I haven't had a dad-burned fever since I came into this knife-wielding place," Anton replied. "Let's not get me riled and have my blood pressure soaring."

The nurse laughed lustily, clutching her clipboard to her ample breasts. "You win, Anton. How can I refuse my favorite patient? I'll give you a half hour, but I'll be back. Count on it. As soon as you finish your soft drink, I'd suggest you dispose of the can. It's a real appealing product around here, and I'd hate for our other patients to develop a taste for it since it's not on our menu."

Anton Springer winked. "That's my girl. I knew you'd accommodate an old gent."

"Oh, go on with you," she said, and still chuckling, headed for the door.

Elise circled the bed and found a seat near the window. "Now, what was that all about?"

"Routine, just routine," her father said, smiling. He

took a sip from the can and smiled appreciatively at Lucas, smacking his lips. "Now, what were you saying about restoring a red '67 Camaro, Lucas?"

It was then Elise smelled rum, or thought she smelled rum. Mystified, she stood and walked to the side of the bed.

Carefully, her father switched the can to other hand and placed it on the nightstand where Lucas was sitting by the door. Elise noticed the present on the nightstand had disappeared. Waving his hand, her father batted the air. "Jeez, don't hover, Lizzie, you're making me nervous. Have a seat. You must be tired from all the shopping Lucas was telling me about."

Elise eased herself to the foot of the bed and stood there listening to Lucas and her father discuss exhaust systems and carburetors. After a few minutes, she inched up the opposite side, but Lucas's feet shot off the ground before she could reach the nightstand beside him. He propped them on the edge of her father's mattress, crossing them at the ankles. It was a blockade, pure and simple. She watched her father remove the can and switch it back to his other hand.

Eyes hooded, Lucas peered up at her. "Something wrong, Lizzie?"

"I smell rum."

"Nah." Face poker straight, he stared at her. "It must be my aftershave. It's called...let me think...Bay Rum?"

Without warning, his feet slid off the bed and he stood, checking his watch. "Well, Anton, I guess it's time to hit the road. I'd like to get your lawn mowed before dark." He set another can with a snap-on lid in the ice bucket. "This one's ready, and you don't have to fool with those tricky tabs on the top."

"Thanks, Lucas." Anton Springer chuckled. "Now you two run along. Is Lizzie feeding you?"

"If our trunk is any indication," Lucas said, "she's planning to feed the entire neighborhood." He grabbed Elise by the elbow and propelled her toward the door before she even had a chance to plant her usual kiss on her father's cheek.

Outside the hospital, Elise stomped to a nearby bench in the shadows where the air was chilly for a spring day and sat down. She pointed to the space beside her. When he slouched down, she swiveled to face him. "Don't even think of trying to come up with some fairy tale story to lull me into mental serenity. You sneaked rum into the hospital room!"

Instead of cowering, Lucas threw back his head and let out a peal of laughter. "Guess we didn't fool you, or Nurse Ryan. Though I must say, Nurse Ryan was a tad more compassionate."

"You should be ashamed of yourself!"

"Oh, put a lid on it and lighten up." Smiling, he leaned back against the bench and looked up at the sky, gloating. "It was a mission of mercy, Liz. He asked for some."

"Mission of mercy? Lucas, have you any idea what can happen when you mix pain pills with alcohol?"

He lifted himself off the seat and fished for something in his back pocket. His tight jeans, molded to his well-muscled body, barely allowed him room for his hands. He pulled out a small plastic bag. Grinning, he tossed it in her lap. "He's been palming the pain pills for the last forty-eight hours, so he could have a couple of rum and Cokes. Come on, Liz, cut the man a break here. Fritz and I introduced your Dad to Captain Morgan when we started to play a few hands of weekly poker at the farm. It's a change from beer. What's the big deal? And thanks to our discriminating tastes, your dad has acquired a taste for the dear Captain's Private Stock."

She spoke through clenched her teeth, "I can't believe you two were in cahoots. You're like a couple of irresponsible teenagers." She watched his face fade to a dark, dangerous scowl. She crossed her arms at her chest.

"Now you listen here, Elise Springer. If your father asked for an entire bottle of top shelf Kentucky bourbon, I would have driven to Kentucky to get it—and I would've slipped it past the goddamned nurse's station. I owe him that much."

"You don't owe him a thing."

He twisted toward her. "Your father is in the hospital because of me."

"What? No way." She looked at him with a confused look.

"Yes, he is. Earlier, the morning of the accident, we got into a heated fight." He ran his hand through his hair in exasperation. "God, it was the best fight I've ever had with your old man. He sure can hold his own. No wonder Thomas is a lawyer."

"About what?" she asked.

"Thomas and I wanted to put more pressure on the local police about Mike's death. Your dad said it was best to let things ride for a while. He seemed to think putting any squeeze on the local cops to re-evaluate the accident might cause more suspicion. He said dishonest people are prone to make mistakes. He's always been the one who keeps a clear head, who heats up the least. Anyway, we fought, and he left the house, obviously to give me some time to cool off and rethink my impulsiveness."

"So you think you're responsible he was injured?"

"I think if I hadn't worked him up, he might have been more cautious." He stood.

"I wouldn't beat myself up over it," Elise said in a calmer voice. "An accident is just that—an accident." She mulled over what he had just told her. "What exactly did the local cops report?" she asked.

"The local cops said Mike lost control and hit a tree. I understand they were the first ones on the scene."

"And the state police?"

"They agree, but they also speculated he could have been forced off the road and then hit the tree."

"That's quite a difference," she said.

"Yeah, a big difference."

Chapter Eleven

They were within two miles of the farm when a police siren wailed its warning, and a black and white township cruiser with red lights flashing tore up the pavement behind them.

"Oh, terrific," Lucas muttered, annoyed. He glanced at the rear view mirror. "Just what we need, some stimulating police activity to cap off an already fun-filled day."

"How much were we over the speed limit?" Elise asked. She pulled her sunglasses off and propped them on the top of her head.

"We?" The look he gave her was deadly, but his tone was less threatening. "I can think of a lot of things *we* could be sharing at the moment besides a speeding ticket."

"Seriously, Lucas, *how fast*? We couldn't have been more than five miles over." She felt the car smoothly decelerate as he slipped through the gears above the steady click of the turn signal.

"Yeah, well, I'm sure that cop back there is dying to take the word of a woman who drives like she's in a NASCAR race."

"Don't you dare tell me you've never had a ticket."

"A few," he conceded, grinning. He guided the car onto the apron and turned off the ignition. "Just sit tight, okay? Let me handle it."

The cruiser door slammed and a burly officer stepped up to the side of the car. The Pontiac's low-slung construction obstructed Elise's view from the passenger's side. Only the officer's meaty thighs were visible through the driver's open window. His bear-paw hand moved cautiously to rest on the gun at his hip, his left thumb tucked behind a belt encircling his bulky waist.

"How about stepping out, buddy?"

Instantly, Elise recognized the voice of Ted Meyer, a local cop and husband of her high school friend.

Like his father before him, Ted had joined the local law enforcement division a few years after high school. Now retired, old Sam Meyer had been a hard-nosed local cop who reveled in terrorizing those who were defenseless or weak, especially the teen population armed with new licenses. He had stopped Elise one night coming home from a high school basketball game and ordered all four females from the car while he searched it for alcohol. Their open cans of Pepsi had been unceremoniously dumped out in the gravel with the warning there had better not have been any booze. Elise remembered her father had been furious when he learned of Sam's little strong-arm tactic.

"Well, well," she heard Ted say as Lucas vaulted from the car, "if it isn't Lucas Fisher. So the local bad boy is back to visit his hometown and old haunts, huh? If you're thinking about looking up all the bimbos you screwed, Fisher, forget it. You're too late. They finally got themselves some common sense and better taste and married respectable citizens."

"Yeah, I heard Mary Jo finally took the plunge with you," Lucas drawled.

The next instant the car rocked violently.

"Watch your filthy mouth, smart aleck, or I'll cram your tongue down your throat! Hey, what's that I smell? Beer? You been drinking, Fisher?"

"Only one, and it was hours ago. Sorry. Not enough to make you the hero-of-the-day, Meyer. Get your hands off me."

"You trying to impede an officer at work?" Meyer's voice escalated with his growing anger.

The car rocked again.

Heart thudding, Elise eased the door open and scrambled out, rounding the car by way of the front. She was not surprised to find Ted Meyer gripping Lucas by his shirt while he muscled him flat against the gleaming back fender of the Trans Am. Both men were so caught up in the moment neither of them noticed her approach.

Gathering her wits, Elise spoke with a calm control she hardly felt. "Is there a problem here, Officer Meyer? Or are you just trying to polish the finish on this beautiful Trans Am with the rivets on Fisher's Levi's?"

Ted Meyer's hands flew up and away from Lucas Fisher as if he had touched hot coals. He stepped back and stared at her as a look of surprise replaced the earlier hostility on his jowly face. "Liz? Lizzie Springer?" His surprise quickly faded to frantic silence as his eyes searched the area along the weedy berm for another vehicle.

"I see your memory serves you well, Ted." Elise cocked a hip against the fender and crossed her hands at her chest to suppress her rage. The last thing she wanted was to be in the middle of a testosterone war between two males. "Is this a private party or can anyone join in?"

"Stay out of it, Liz," Lucas warned through gritted teeth.

"You with *him*?" Ted jerked a thumb at Lucas.

"It was either Lucas or hitchhike," she admitted with a half-hearted smile. "You know what they say about bumming rides from strangers, Ted."

She was amused as he fumbled for something to say. She had never been fond of Ted Meyer. Even in high school, he had been a loud and obnoxious bully. When her best friend, Mary Jo, had announced she was dropping out of her third year of college to marry him, Elise had been dismayed until she learned he had pursued her with a vengeance, making it a point to pester her with calls and unannounced visits. Seven months after their wedding, it was no surprise when the first of their three children arrived.

Face beet red, Ted Meyer tugged at the neck of his uniform. "So when did you get into town, Liz?"

"A couple days ago. How are Mary Jo and the kids?"

"Fine, fine. How's your dad? I heard he busted up his ankle."

"And leg. However, he's doing well. In fact, Lucas was just giving me a ride back from the hospital. Dad's old truck should be pronounced unfit to drive in a demolition derby." She smiled, hoping to lighten the mood. She liked nothing about Ted Meyer, but he was an officer of the law. All she wanted was for everyone to stay calm and to keep Lucas out of an altercation.

She blew out an anxious breath of air and asked, "Seriously, we weren't going over the speed limit, were we?"

"Sixty in a forty-five."

Lucas drew himself up straight. "That's a lie—"

Elise cut him off in a chiding tone as her arm came out and lightly smacked him on the chest with the back of her hand. "Now, now, Lucas, maybe it's possible. You know how distracted we were trying to catch up on old times and recent activities around Scranton." Her hand came up to shade her eyes against the brilliant glare of the setting sun. She squinted up at Ted. "So what's been happening since I left? What's it been now, twelve years since we've graduated?"

Ted shrugged. "Nothing much. The area is still the same. Oh, we're trying to put in a local recreation area for the kids next to the Ice Cream Parlor out on Sawyer Road, complete with a new ball field. Maybe even miniature golf. Hey, would you like to be on the committee? The old gang would love to see you." He eyed her with open appreciation. "You look real good, Lizzie. Reeeeeal good."

"Thanks, but I'm not staying long. I'm just here until Dad is on the mend."

"Ah, Liz, it doesn't matter. Come anyhow. We're meeting next Thursday night. Maybe you could just lend us some fresh ideas. It's going to take a lot of fund-raising."

"I imagine so. Maybe you should think about asking—"

Out of the corner of her eye, she saw Lucas give her a baleful look.

"—Fritz," she finished. "He knows nearly everyone in a fifty-mile radius."

"Already have," Meyer admitted. "Did he send you

the flyer about a community Summer Festival in June to raise money for the high school band? It's supposed to be at the Country Club. Big splash. Mary Jo's on the planning committee and is forever having some sort of meeting at our house."

"It sounds like fun. I plan to stop over and see her before I leave."

He motioned toward his car. "Could we talk in private for a moment?"

She glanced at Lucas, who was eyeing Ted Meyer with a look hot enough to melt steel. He was all but itching to send a fist into the man's chunky nose. She shrugged, and then nodded.

"If you two are going to trade secrets, I'd keep a reasonable distance, Liz," Lucas interjected, straightening his shirt. "The man has trouble keeping his hands to himself despite his fancy badge and pledge to uphold the law."

"Why, you—" Ted Meyer lunged toward Lucas again, but Elise's hand flew up to flatten against Ted's stout chest.

"Take it easy, guys. Come on, Ted, he's baiting you on purpose and you know it. Just like old times," she said. "Let's go over by your cruiser. I can only spare a second. We have a trunk full of groceries." With teeth gritted, she threw a warning look at Lucas as they passed.

"The guy's bad news," Ted said in an irritated whisper. "Watch your step, Liz. Fisher ain't the best company to keep. Ten years hasn't dented his hard-ass attitude. He's still the same low life without a care in the world. You'd only be one of his many flings."

"I would like to believe we have all matured some,

Ted. Fritz and he have always been best friends."

"Yeah, and I never could figure out what Fritz saw in Lucas Fisher."

"Maybe something we don't." She patted him playfully on his arm. "Hey, thanks for the advice. Tell Mary Jo, when I get a few minutes, I'll be over. I can't wait to see the kids, and she can fill me in on the fundraisers."

"Sure, sure," he said, throwing a final irritated glance Lucas's way. "Tell your Dad I said hello." He hefted his thick frame into the cruiser and pulled out onto the highway, gravel spraying beneath his wheels.

Elise sauntered back to the car.

"I thought I told you to stay put!" Hands planted on his lean hips, Lucas all but shouted the words at her.

"And be a witness to your murder? I don't think so, hot shot."

"You never listen to anything anyone tells you, do you? You are hell-bent on handling everything your own way. Your bullheaded German mettle just won't back down, will it?"

"Oh, yeah, right, and don't tell me your docile Irish temperament wasn't sending Meyer's blood pressure soaring." She glared at him and straightened her shoulders. If he wanted a face-off, she was in the mood to go a few rounds.

"Why didn't you just proposition him right on the spot? Cripes, from the look on his face, he would have flung his over-stuffed body right on top of yours, right here in the weeds. *You look real good, Lizzie. Reeeeeal good.*"

"Hah! I suppose implying his wife was one of your high school bimbos was your convoluted way of getting us off the hook?"

"Your jeans are too damned tight."

"So are yours, buster!"

"Do you use always use that sultry, soft-spoken stuff on every male who stumbles across your path?"

"Not after this. I'm going to give the Lucas Fisher Mr. Know-It-All attitude a shot instead." She scowled and didn't try to disguise her annoyance. "Maybe we can get a decent meal. Behind bars. Maybe they would even serve me *chocolate* to keep me calm."

"Have you no shame?"

"Have you no brains?"

Livid, he said, "I could have handled this, Liz. I don't need to hide behind a woman. Any woman!"

Liz felt her face flood to the same matching color, but she willed herself to stay calm. "No, you don't. Meyer was itching to knock you alongside the head and leave you lying on the pavement for the next car to run you over. You know he was." She turned, staring down the road, and drew in a ragged breath, her voice softening. "I don't need more trouble. Not now, Fisher. I have my hands full already. Raising bail money wasn't in the job description when I agreed to help you."

She glanced at him sideways and their gaze met and held. She saw angry heat flicker in his gray eyes and then slowly fade.

"Get in," he said gruffly, yanking on his door handle.

She rounded the car and slid in, welcoming the comfort and security of the wrap-around leather. She sighed and stared at her hands. "I'm sorry, Lucas, I just became unnerved when I thought someone might get hurt and you might be that someone."

She waited for him to respond. When he said nothing, she glanced up. In the next instant his face loomed over her as his mouth come crashing down. What should have been an angry assault exploded into a brutal tangling of teeth and tongues. He went crazy, kissing her so deeply and thoroughly her head reeled and her heart jumped clear up to her throat. She found herself responding with the same shameless passion. It ended all too quickly. But before he pulled away, she heard him hiss against her ear. "Don't let it happen again."

He settled himself behind the wheel.

Wordlessly, she nodded, feeling dazed. She drew in a breath to calm her jangled nerves. When she opened her mouth to speak again, he held up a hand.

"Don't analyze this, Liz, like you do everything else. Good God, did you ever consider psychiatry as an alternate occupation? Just go with the flow."

She fell silent and touched her swollen lips. Whatever anger had been driving him had now dissipated. "I was just going to say the ice cream in the trunk is undoubtedly now a milkshake."

He snickered. "Well, we've got beer, we've got milkshakes. Guess that just about wraps up dinner for tonight."

****

There was nothing more beautiful in Lucas Fisher's eyes than a shiny new car, washed and gleaming in mirror-like colors, ready for an owner to take control. When he pulled into the Springer farm, both the new silver Corvette convertible and a shiny burgundy Tahoe were parked in the driveway. They shimmered under the fading light of the afternoon sun. He pulled up behind them and cut the engine.

"Oh, Lucas, have you lost your mind?" Elise vaulted from the passenger's side. "These must be right off the line."

"Almost," he said grinning and steered her toward the Corvette. He opened the door and lifted the floor mat where he retrieved two sets of keys. The fresh scent of new carpet, plastic and leather spilled out. "Get in," he coaxed.

"I can't drive this," she said, breathlessly, slipping into the black leather bucket seat. "What if I wreck it?" Her fingers trembled as she caressed the buttons on the front panel. It was loaded—CD player, OnStar, satellite radio, and its own GPS system. "No, I can't. I just want something...less audacious."

"Audacious?"

"Okay, ostentatious then."

He rubbed his forehead. "Good grief, Corvettes are supposed to be flashy."

"Lucas, this is a mobile magnet for speeding tickets. Don't you have something I can lease? Something older, less expensive?"

"No, the lease cars aren't ready yet."

She took one more longing look and slid out, stepping toward the Trans Am, waiting for him to open the trunk. "Even a sports utility vehicle would be more practical."

"I don't want you to drive just anything." He sighed and unlocked the trunk, reaching for a grocery bag.

"Why not?"

Because you're exquisite and you deserve only the

best, he wanted to say. She was going to be difficult. No, stubborn. Downright predictably stubborn. "Listen, Liz, I'm trying to start up a leasing business and restoration and specialty garage here. Corvettes are the caviar of my banquet table, so to speak."

"Then get me an old one." She started toward the house with an armload of bags.

With two bags in each arm, he stalked up the walk behind her. "For the love of God, don't say old. There's no such thing as *old* Corvettes. Antique or vintage, maybe, but cripes, never old. Listen, look at it as advertising."

"Advertising?" She whirled to stare at him and walked backwards.

"Marketing. Advertising. Call it what you want. I have to get the word out I'm in the leasing business. Hell, the two mechanics I hired are driving something off the floor, too. How do you suppose you get started? People see your cars on the road, parked at a curb or in a lot, and take notice of the dealer's name on the license plate holder or a sticker." He watched the wheels begin to grind in her head.

"There's no dealer's name on it."

"Jeez, Liz, what are you? An undercover cop for Chevy? I'm not pasting any stickers on such a fine piece of machinery. It only needs a license plate holder with my business name. They aren't in yet."

"I guess I can give it a try." She pulled the door open and held it with her elbow, allowing him to catch it behind her. "If I don't like it, will you promise me I can have something else? When Todd comes, I really need an SUV with a backseat so I can haul him, his car seat, and his toys and things."

He grinned at the back of her head. "What do you think the Tahoe is for? And, yeah, I can get you something else, but I'll guarantee you'll fall in love with the Vette."

Inside the kitchen, they set about unpacking the bags. The answering machine blinked with only one message, a plea from Chuck Sanders to call him day or night. Lucas reset the machine and found himself begrudging Winston and Sanders for intruding on her time at home and their precious time together.

"Does the guy ever function on his own?" he asked, pulling canned goods from a bag.

"The only reason I'm here is because Chuck is doing my work there. I'll give him a call later." She began to unload a bag of cereal boxes.

He moved beside her and pulled out a box of Frosted Flakes. "Care to give me a rundown on the nutritional value of this?"

She swiped it from his grip and pressed it to her chest. "It's very nutritious."

"Yeah, I'll bet."

"It's for Todd when he visits," she said.

He didn't believe her for a minute. Ever since he could remember, Tony the Tiger had been a regular around the Springer household. He didn't need to guess who was Tony's biggest fan.

He grabbed another bag and attacked the refrigerator. "The new computer is wired and we now have Internet," he told her, jamming vegetables into the refrigerator bin. "I gave Bryan the spare key and had him set it up when he dropped off the vehicles. You can take a look at it while I mow. We can have a late dinner. I'll throw some steaks on the grill and then we'll take your car for a whirl." He straightened and moved to where she stood on tiptoe struggling to reach the upper shelf, took the boxes from her outstretched hands and slid them easily onto it.

The smile she gave him was heart-stopping. "You really mean it?"

"Of course I mean it." It was the truth. He had seen her sketchpads all over the house. Some had rough drawings on them, others were more refined. Sometimes he recognized a window, doorway or roof. Sometimes a whole facade or layout of a building. It seemed no matter how she tried, she couldn't resist the urge to create. "You haven't touched your computer since you arrived. I figure by now you're having withdrawal symptoms. I should have known it would be from electronics and not chocolate." He grinned.

"Oh, Lucas, thank you. I'll load my software on yours and see how it performs. I was hoping to do some computer-generated drawings." She gave him a quick hug. Her face glowed with excitement. Slowly she lifted her hand and traced the sharp outline of his jaw. "What am I going to do with you?" she whispered and touched a feather light kiss to his lips.

It was more than he could bear. Before she could even try to step away, he swept her up in his arms and felt himself losing control. His body burned with a tight, hot sensation. Urging her closer, his lips tasted hers more hungrily.

Behind them, the phone rang. Once, twice.

Lucas felt her stiffen. "Don't," he said through a whispered groan, his arms still wrapped around her. "Please, pleeeease, let the answering machine get it."

Through three more rings he nipped at her lower

lip and planted kisses over her face. They heard the machine click on and blurt out its quick message, then the caller respond in a soft feminine voice:

"Lucas, darling, it's Monique. I know you must be there, so just pick up the damn phone."

Elise's eyes flew open. Her hands fell away from his chest and she stepped away.

The message droned on. "I've left seventeen messages on your machine in Atlanta and finally had to shake your phone number and whereabouts out of one of your pathetic little mechanics down at the dealership. Honey, I miss you so-ooo much. You're not still mad at me, are you? Listen, I have a few weeks off between shoots. How about we get together just like old times? Give me a call and I'll catch the next flight out to Atlanta or Scranton. You know my number, lover boy."

The answering machine shut off with a soft click.

Elise stared at him. "Monique? Lover boy?"

"Listen, Liz, this is *really* a long story. It's over but I guess she just doesn't get my message." He saw disgust or maybe pain cross her face for a brief second. He cursed silently and reached for her, but she backed away, putting distance between them.

"Lizzie," he pleaded. "I can explain."

She drew herself upright. "Yes, I imagine you can," she agreed and headed for the stairs, not waiting for the explanation.

Chapter Twelve

Elise sat at the kitchen table and jotted notes in the margins of the list of care nurses from Home Health. It was a miserable Saturday morning, even though the sun climbed over the rooftops of the barns in sparkling rays and the robins called merrily to each other as they searched the yard for a tasty breakfast.

Upstairs Fritz and Lucas were making a gallant effort to wallpaper Thomas's old room without killing each other. At various intervals, Elise could hear a series of curses filter down the staircase. Things had become so hot, she had sent Todd outside to play with Bess. Through the open window, she could see him throwing the Dalmatian a tennis ball. The boy and dog had become inseparable pals.

Yesterday evening, she had tried several times to call Chuck Sanders, only to get his answering machine. She finally convinced herself the impending crisis had passed. She had a fleeting touch of remorse she had not been available to help handle it.

Now, as she sat in the kitchen waiting for the third person recommended by Home Health to arrive, she was discouraged. In the last hour, she had interviewed two licensed practical nurses on the list. The first had been an elderly lady with the temperament and disposition of Rambo, and she had made no effort to hide it. The other, a blonde reeking of White Diamonds, had arrived looking like she was interviewing for a modeling position with *Vogue Magazine.* Both of them were clearly not a match for someone as down to earth as her father.

She glanced at her list again. Cindy Peters. Registered nurse. *Has a difficult time relating to people*, it merely said. Elise sighed. Just the endearing words to make the morning a total wash.

To make matters worse, she had avoided Lucas since they parted after the telephone message from Monique. He had mowed for over two hours until darkness fell. During that time, she had toyed with the computer, worked at her old drawing board in her room, and sketched out a possible renovation for the showroom in the restoration facility before she crawled into bed, forgoing dinner. She had been too exhausted to even care about eating and too weary to think about a confrontation with him. She had no desire to compete with a flashy, jet-set model. Lucas Fisher, good-looking and wealthy, could have his choice of beautiful, desirable women. She needed to keep her life in perspective, she told herself. At the end of next week she would be returning to San Francisco, where a career with Winston and Sanders was waiting.

She wondered whether he had come to the same conclusion. He had left early, skipping breakfast and leaving a note that said he was stopping at the garage and the hospital and picking up Todd afterwards. With some free time on her hands, she decided to drive to the cottage and look around. She needed to get a feel for the place, although she was sure she would take every step possible to ensure its complete restoration, right down to repainting the kitchen cupboards. She had also brought three boxes of Mike's personal books and papers to the farm and stored them in her room. Even though Lucas was adamant there had been no clues as to the whereabouts of a will or the money, she couldn't quite bring herself to believe a smart cop would not have made preparations, especially with a young son to care for.

The low growl of a motorcycle sent her curiously moving toward the front door. Up the drive, a bike and rider made their way to the entrance and stopped. A small figure jumped off, struggling to muscle the Harley upright and set the kickstand.

The rider was a girl, Elise realized, as soon as she saw the tiny heart-shaped face emerge from under the bright red helmet with a blaze of gold across its side. Dressed in jeans and leather boots, the girl had blonde hair scraped back from her face and tied in a ponytail. She flung her leather jacket over the seat of the bike and eagerly took the steps two at time.

"Can I help you?" Elise moved to the screen door.

"I'm Cindy Peters," she said, shyly.

Elise's jaw dropped.

"I'm here to interview for the job as a nurse." When the young woman saw her look of astonishment, she whirled and batted her hand at the bike. "It's my brother's. I lent my car to him to take my mother to the hospital for some blood tests."

Recovering, Elise stepped out onto the wide front porch and gestured to a set of dark green lawn chairs. "Let's just sit outside. The sun is so gloriously warm."

With a nod, the girl took a seat across from her. "I know I'm not dressed for an interview," she admitted frankly, her face blushing, "but I had no choice, and

Home Health said the position would be on a farm."

It didn't take more than a quick glance to realize the young woman was definitely not what Elise had pictured in her mind as a nurse for her father. She had wanted someone older and more robust, someone who could easily help muscle her father around if need be. Cindy Peters looked barely over twenty-one and a hundred pounds soaking wet.

"You seem so young," Elise said at a loss for words.

"I'm twenty-five," she admitted, then added, "I have my RN, and I'm willing to do anything extra you might need around the house. I can dust and vacuum."

Elise felt her forehead crease in a frown. "Are you aware your recommendations are far from stellar?"

Cindy Peters hung her head staring at her hands a moment before she looked up. "Yes, I'm not a great conversationalist, Miss Springer, and I'd hope I wouldn't be hired just to amuse people."

"Good listeners beat talkers any day," Elise agreed, wondering why she was even trying to prolong the interview or put the young woman at ease. Yet there was something earthy and intriguing about Cindy Peters underneath her plain facade. "Do you have any hobbies?"

"I like old movies," she said. "You know, with Fred Astaire, Cary Grant, or Vivian Leigh. I love to fish, and I'm a gourmet cook."

Old movies? Fishing? Gourmet cook? Now they were finally getting somewhere. Elise smiled as Todd scrambled up the steps and skidded to a halt in front of them. Although he had been outside for only a few minutes, his jeans were already smudged with mud and grass stains, and one sneaker had a lace untied.

Cindy motioned to the boy to draw near.

"Is that your bike?" he asked.

"It's my brother's." She bent and tied his sneaker. "There, buddy," she said, ruffling his hair. "Makes it easier when you have to run and play with your imaginary friends."

"You have imaginary friends?" he asked.

She winked at him. "Doesn't everyone?"

He peered up at her. "Can I sit on your bike?"

"Sure. How about before I leave?"

Grinning, he faced Elise. "Can I go see Uncle Lucas?"

"If you wipe your shoes," she instructed, smiling back. He made a half-hearted effort to scrub his sneakers on the doormat before he tugged the door open, letting a mud-covered Bess slip in ahead of him. His sneakers pounded on the oak stairs.

"Let's go inside," Elise said. Together they headed for the kitchen where she offered Cindy a seat by the table. "Would you like something to drink?"

"Anything is fine. A soft drink if you have it."

Elise handed her a glass and can. "Now tell me the truth, what happened with your last case?"

The girl paused and stared at her a moment. "The patient, a male, wanted more than just my nursing skills," she admitted in a low voice. "I couldn't afford to file a complaint. I need the work. I have a lot of loans to pay from school."

Elise felt her stomach do a backflip as she pushed the sickening image of Philip Cullington groping at her into a far corner of her mind. "It looks like you have some experience with children."

"They're the easiest to talk to," Cindy admitted, smiling. "I like kids. I'm from a family of eight."

"Eight?"

Their conversation was interrupted again when Todd tore back down the steps and skidded to a halt before the refrigerator. He tugged at the door handle. "Uncle Lucas and Fritz want another iced tea." He pulled out two cans of Coors Light and was half way across the room when Elise stopped him. "No, not those," she said, gently. "I'll have to get it from the pitcher."

He shook his head and dug in, clutching the cans to his little chest and staring at her wide-eyed. "No, Uncle Lucas said they were in shiny cans, like the handles on my bike. Like a silver bullet."

"Oh, did he now?" Elise pried the cans from the boy's grip and set them on the counter. She smiled, amused at the thought of foiling Lucas's plans. "Why don't you go play outside with Bess for a bit more? I'll take the iced tea up to them in a minute."

"Good, 'cause Uncle Lucas is reeeeal grouchy." The little boy wrinkled his nose and raced off again with Bess trotting beside him. The screen door banged shut behind them.

"Now, where were we?" Elise asked, smiling and glancing at Cindy Peters.

****

Upstairs Lucas batted at a soggy piece of paw print wallpaper starting to peel from the wall and creep slowly onto his sweaty head.

"Jeez, Fritz," he growled, whirling and hammering it back in place with his fist. "You have to be a freakin' human octopus to hang this stuff. I thought it was pre-

147

pasted." They were both covered from head to foot in paste, water, and scraps of wallpaper.

"Maybe we soaked it too much," Fritz said, frowning. "Did you read the instructions?"

"Hell, no. Did you?"

"Why should I? I'm not in charge here."

Lucas sighed. "If any one of us were in charge, dude, we wouldn't *be* here."

"Good point. Hey, I got an idea. We'll just try some of this paste we used for the border and smear it on the wall instead." Fritz handed him a large paintbrush, its handle sticky and crusted with paste. He squinted at the seams curling away from each other. "Mother made it look so easy."

"Everything your mother did looked easy. This is a damned catastrophe, thanks to you. You were supposed to have taken mental notes in that fuzzy pea brain of yours."

"Me? Wait a second, don't blame me. This wasn't my idea! How did you ever let my crazy sister talk you into this?"

Too weary for a rebuttal, Lucas leaned his head against the soggy wall. "Your sister could talk Lucifer out of hell," he whispered. "I need a beer. Just one lousy beer. I wonder what happened to our little sidekick?"

Fritz glanced at the sawhorses they had set up on layers of plastic drop cloths. Two glasses of iced tea, untouched, sat on the end of the planks. Elise had absolutely forbidden them to have any alcoholic beverages until they finished.

Lucas followed his gaze and shot him a sour look, then gestured with a paste-crusted finger at the iced tea.

"Don't even offer me that swamp water Elise calls iced tea. Where is Todd?"

"If I know Lizzie, she intercepted his beer run. Honestly, Lucas, don't you think the silver bullet description was pushing it a bit?"

"Then why don't you make yourself useful and get us a can? Don't tell me you want to drink that crap?"

Fritz measured another piece of paper. "What's got into you?"

"Everything. You name it. Your sister, for starters."

"Don't tell me she didn't like the car? No one— absolutely no one—would pass that up. It's everyone's dream machine." With a retractable box-cutter in hand, Fritz deftly sliced off a piece of wallpaper from the roll.

Lucas grunted. "She didn't even take it out. We had a little tiff last night. Monique left a message on the answering machine."

"I thought it was over."

Lucas pushed his hand through his hair, only to realize he had now covered his head with paste. Cursing under his breath, he growled, "It is over, moron."

Fritz regarded him with a curious look. "Wait a second. So what does my sister have to do with Monique? What's going on here?" His eyes were wary now.

Lucas scowled. "Nothing, that's the problem."

"Did you tell her you're rich?"

"I told her." Lucas stooped to dunk the last piece of paper in the water tray. He didn't want to add it only seemed to make things worse.

"Does Dad know you're...ah, interested?" Fritz helped him take the last piece to the wall and set the seams.

"You want him to have a relapse?" Using a brush, Lucas smoothed the paper up the wall. "What do you know about Sanders?"

"Chuck? Nice guy. He stopped in here once when they were flying to a convention in Pittsburgh."

"Is there something between them?"

Fritz considered it for a minute. "Naw, I think it's just a creative partnership. She was engaged once, but not to Sanders."

"She was?" Lucas felt a jolt of shock and wondered why she had not mentioned it the other night in the living room. Then he wondered why it bothered him.

"To a Philip Cullington. His daddy was a big wheel in the construction industry some place in California. They went together for three years and then it just seemed to suddenly fall apart...evaporate. Next thing I knew, it was over. Hey, that seam looks crooked, doesn't it?"

Lucas threw him a threatening look. "Shut up and get the beer before I beat the crap out of you."

"Ah, come on, Lucas, you know Elise." Fritz surveyed the papered wall a moment more, scowling. "She'll break my wrists and ankles."

"I wish. Get a move on. I'll start cleaning up." A glint of humor flashed briefly in Lucas's eyes. "If you don't come back with a can, I swear I'll cancel all my insurance policies with your company. Right down to the last penny."

Fritz's hands went up defensively as he slowly backed out of the room. "Okay, okay! Hey, I understand a thinly veiled threat when it's delivered with tact and subtlety."

****

Fritz entered the kitchen in his usual electrifying way, Elise thought, as she watched him bound off the bottom step and swagger into the kitchen. Oblivious to Cindy Peters sitting at the table, he went straight to the refrigerator and searched the shelves.

"Who owns the sweet ride in the front yard?" He pulled out two cans of Coors Light.

"Cindy's brother."

Brows wrinkled, he turned to look at her before his gaze swung to the young woman. He smiled, flashing even white teeth. "Whoa, you're a little thing to be on a big sucker like that."

"My older brother, Fritz. The family clown," Elise said by way of introduction. "You'll get immune to him, everybody usually does. I just hired Cindy to help when Dad comes home. She's a registered nurse and a gourmet cook."

"Gourmet, eh?" He tried unsuccessfully to wipe the paste from his sticky hands onto his already soiled tee-shirt. "I'd shake your hand, but then we'd be stuck to each other and you'd be forced to take me home with you."

Cindy laughed as Elise grunted out a sound of disgust and rolled her eyes heavenward. She said, "How about turning off the charm for a moment and washing up so you can give Cindy a quick tour of the house and grounds? I want to see how far Lucas and you have progressed on Todd's bedroom. And could you please check on Todd? He's outside with Bess."

"Lucas is finishing up." Fritz snickered and tossed her a can of Coors. "Here, take him his Prozac before he goes bonkers. He definitely isn't cut out for playing with sharp objects, but he's got the paste under control."

Minutes later, Elise found Lucas bent over a bucket of water, scrubbing his hands. The sawhorses were stacked and the room partially cleaned. She surveyed their handiwork. For amateurs, it didn't look too bad. The seams would need to be rolled one more time. She held up the can of beer. "Delivering your paycheck."

He looked up, hurriedly dried his hand on an old towel, then strode toward her and snatched the cold can, popping the tab and taking a long swig. "There is a God," he said, sighing deeply. "What happened to my sidekick?"

"Which one? Fritz? He defected." Elise walked to the opposite side of the room and leaned against the wall, arms crossed. They studied each other silently.

"I hired a nurse."

He took another sip of beer. His eyes glittered like a panther's. "You went to bed last night without eating dinner."

"I think she'll get along well with Dad."

"You never let me explain, Liz." He set the beer aside and walked toward her. He stopped and stared at her. The seconds ticked by, slowly and uncomfortably.

"She says she's a gourmet cook. At least we'll have some decent meals." She felt him closing in, just like a predatory animal.

"It's all over with Monique," he said quietly. "Over, you hear me?"

"Fritz is giving her a tour of the house." Her voice was now a bare whisper. The tension crackled between them. A hand came up, palm flat against the wall beside her head.

"Are you listening to me?" His face was inches from her.

She nodded.

"Good. Wonders never cease."

She pressed her hands against his chest to ward him off. The stillness of the room only heightened their sensual awareness of each other. "Lucas, you're covered with paste," she stammered.

"I know. Just one kiss, Lizzie, only one. You're looking at a broken, desperate paperhanger who's craving a morsel of compassion."

Their lips touched in a fury of emotion. She felt his frenzied need as he urged her to respond, dragging his lips over hers again and again. It was a highly charged mating of mouths that finally clashed and tangled, and when she felt her lungs burn she realized she needed to breathe. He broke away, allowing her to gulp a mouthful of air.

"I needed that." He drew in a deep breath and stepped back, giving her room, but there was no mistaking the lust lingering in his gray eyes.

In the hall, the clatter of feet brought them both to attention. Todd burst into the room. His eyes were bright and animated as his gaze swept over the new decor. "This is all mine?" he asked breathlessly. His little arms swung up and outward from his body as he embraced the room.

"Yes, as soon as we finish up and put the furniture back." Elise watched him pick up a wooden roller and curiously inspect it. "What's this, Eee-lise?"

"It's a roller, and it's used to smooth out the seams." She loved the way he drew out the vowel at the front of her name. "Here, I'll show you." She demonstrated how to roll the seams, gently sliding the roller up and down the walls.

"Come here, you can do it," she invited and pulled him in front of her, kneeling and cupping his little hands around the roller. "We have to go easy so we don't rip the damp paper."

The little boy giggled as they worked the roller up and down the wall. She felt Lucas sneak up and kneel behind her.

"You help Todd," he whispered in her ear, leaning over her. "I'll just lend encouragement."

His hands slipped under her shirt and caressed the bare skin at her waist. She laughed and tried to bat them away with one hand and still hold on to the roller and Todd's tiny hands.

"Shhh," Lucas whispered, nuzzling her on the side of the neck. "This is one job I know how to do."

"Isn't this fun?" Todd squealed excitedly, working the roller up and down the wall.

"Absolutely," Lucas murmured in agreement. "Keep it up, sport. We have the entire wall to do."

"Lucas!" Elise felt a series of shocks course through her as his hands worked their way upward. "Lucas, stop it," she said with a hiss.

From the open doorway, she heard Fritz clear his throat. "Looks good, guys, maybe you ought to take a break."

"Go away," Lucas said and planted another kiss at the back of Elise's neck. "We're not finished yet."

"Oh, buddy, I think you are," Fritz said and followed it with a nervous chuckle. "Mrs. Pedmo is here."

"Here?" The words came out simultaneously as

they turned together and flew apart. The roller in Todd's hands clattered to the floor. Lucas fell to a sitting position with Todd on top of him. Elise popped upright like a jack-in-the-box.

"Yep, *right* here," Fritz assured them, leaning casually on the doorjamb. Beside him, a stern-looking Mrs. Pedmo stepped into the room.

It would have been totally embarrassing, Elise thought, as she tried to straighten her tee-shirt, if it hadn't been for Todd who jumped up and raced toward the door waving the roller in the air at Mrs. Pedmo.

"They're teaching me to flatten the wallpaper," he said proudly, grinning up at her smiling face. He pulled Mrs. Pedmo into the room. "Look! Dogs! My favorite animal. All around the ceiling, and here's where they walked on the wall." He pointed to the paw-printed paper.

Elise cringed and felt her face flame. She had no idea how she was going to explain to Mrs. Pedmo the scenario she had just witnessed. She glanced at Fritz who merely flashed her a wily grin, waved, and slipped away down the hall.

"How fortunate you could stop by, Mrs. Pedmo," she heard Lucas say, moving toward her, completely at ease. He extended his hand. "I thought you were stopping here on Monday?"

The pink-haired woman was more gracious than Elise had hoped. She smiled and acted as if she had never seen a blessed thing. "I saw your cars and thought I'd just stop by and get this home visit over with." She glanced appreciatively about the room, her eyes pausing on the can of beer for barely a second. "My, it certainly will look appropriate for someone like this young man."

She ruffled Todd's hair affectionately.

Elise slid a sideways glance at Lucas. Instead of looking sheepish or distraught, he was now grinning outright at Mrs. Pedmo. "Maybe you'd like a drink of iced tea, Mrs. Pedmo?" he asked.

"Yes, oh, yes," Elise stammered, "and I can show you the rest of the house."

"Oh, no need." Mrs. Pedmo waved her hand, dismissing the idea. "I've seen it many times when I used to play bridge with your mother, but I'll take a glass of tea. We do need to talk."

"I'll wash up, change clothes, and be down in second," Lucas reassured her. He swiped at the paste on his shirt.

"That might be a good idea." Mrs. Pedmo surveyed him with a quick, motherly perusal, a twinkle in her eye. "Looks like you have as much paste on yourself as on the walls."

Lucas turned to Todd. "Why don't you go find Fritz? Or take Bess out on the lawn for a few minutes? I'll be out in a minute to play ball with you."

Downstairs, Elise's stomach quivered uncontrollably and her hands shook as she poured the tea. Outside on the porch, Fritz and Cindy were discussing Cajun cooking. Out on the lawn she could hear Todd squealing as he tossed a tennis ball to Bess. Elise handed Pedmo a glass. "We can sit in the living room where it's comfortable if you like."

"Oh, heavens no. This is fine." The elderly woman's gaze circled the airy, light-filled room. "I always admired your mother's kitchen. It's so spacious, warm, and inviting." She pulled out a chair and sat at the kitchen table.

Lucas returned shortly. He had washed his hands and arms and pulled on a clean tee-shirt and jeans. Traces of paste still clung to his dark, glossy hair. He took a seat across from Twila Pedmo.

"You realize, my first concern is Todd," Mrs. Pedmo said, shifting into her foster care mode. "He goes to pre-school in the morning and will need proper supervision in the afternoon."

"I've already hired a registered nurse to help with Dad and in the afternoons with Todd when necessary," Elise said. "Cindy is from a large family and gets along well with children. She's outside with Fritz, who's acclimating her to the premises."

Mrs. Pedmo looked over at Lucas. "I understand what's happening here, Lucas, and I can't say I blame you. If it wasn't that I respect Anton Springer as much as I do, I doubt all this would be possible. However, it takes more than just setting up a house or business to raise a child. Children need more than material goods and a roof over their heads. Much more. They need love, attention, discipline."

Elise sensed Lucas's anger as a chilly black silence surrounded them. She knew Lucas was aware he would have to prove to Pedmo and Child Services he would be there for Todd. He already had made it clear to everyone he was willing to rebuild his life. He leaned forward, his eyes inky black. There was a hard edge to his voice. "Are you saying I'm not capable of providing any of those?"

"No, I'm telling you it takes a lot of time, energy, and work."

"I'm quite aware of this, Mrs. Pedmo. I, more than anyone, understand the term 'abandonment' and its implications."

"Yes...yes, of course, you do." the elderly woman stammered and offered him a weak smile. "You also should know there are people who'd rather see you *not* get custody."

"I'm also aware of that. But what about you, Mrs. Pedmo?" He lifted a brow, and Elise cringed at his rash behavior. "Just where do you stand?"

She interrupted. "Lucas, Mrs. Pedmo has been more than accommodating."

Mrs. Pedmo dismissed her comment. "It's all right, Elise. I don't take sides, Lucas. I just take care of my charges. The law is responsible for determining a custody suit if we can't resolve it."

Mouth set in annoyance, Lucas leaned forward again. "Just so you know, I'll fight anyone who steps in my way to get the child."

"And money?"

"I'll use every damn penny I have."

Todd appeared in the doorway, barreled into the kitchen, and made a flying leap into Lucas's lap. "Bess lost the ball, but Cindy let me sit on her motorcycle. We have more tennis balls, don't we?" He touched Lucas's hair with a grubby hand and giggled. "You have paste in your hair, Uncle Lucas. Ooo-oh, it's sticky, too."

Lucas resettled him in his lap and enveloped him protectively in his arms, the child's silky head resting underneath his angular chin. "You have mud in yours, sport." He blew in his hair and the little boy giggled again.

Removing a package of cookies from the cupboard, Elise prodded Todd. "How about taking some cookies out to Cindy and Fritz?" She sensed their conversation with Mrs. Pedmo was far from finished. She handed him the bag. "Now only one, we're having dinner in an hour. And please don't feed them to Bess. I have dog biscuits for her."

When the boy scampered away, Mrs. Pedmo spoke. "You realize, Lucas, I know more about you than most people around here. It helps to have a son who can make the right contacts."

"You have my admiration, Mrs. Pedmo. You do your homework." Lucas leaned back in his chair. "I'd appreciate your discretion in not divulging anything more about me than may be necessary."

She frowned. "I'll do the best I can, but I think you should be aware there's now a third party involved."

"Impossible!" His easy charm faded. A fist thumped the table. "Who? Can you tell me, who?"

"You know I can't tell you. I'm probably pushing the limits of confidentially by even divulging this much information."

He leaned back again and eyed her with open frankness. "What's going on? Why are you doing this? Why are you telling me?"

She rose. "To put both Elise and you on alert. After working this job for over thirty-five years, you get a gut feeling about certain things, about people you meet, about what's best for a child." She glanced at Elise. "I'll have everything in order by Tuesday. You may move Todd any time afterwards."

Elise walked her out onto the sprawling front porch encircled by white spindled rails and watched until her car pulled out of sight. Lucas came out and stood beside her.

"I guess we messed this one up badly." Elise felt

the cool surface of the pillar against her cheek as she rested her head and stared at the dust rising from the long drive leading onto the main road.

"I don't think so, Lizzie." He slipped his hand onto the back of her neck in a gesture of reassurance. "But I suspect someone else is about to."

Chapter Thirteen

Elise leaned forward, peered into the mirror, and scrutinized the eye shadow and blush she had just applied. She had almost forgotten about her date with Jack Morrison. If it hadn't been for Twila Pedmo's cryptic disclosure earlier that morning, she might have called it off. She found nothing fascinating about the man, yet she had the feeling if there were anyone who might know what was happening with the custody case of Todd Fisher, Jack Morrison was sitting in the pole position.

Elise remembered her high school years when her brothers had played sports. As an only doted-on child, Jack Morrison always had the best sports equipment, the best golf clubs, and a new sports car to take him to and from practices. After his high school graduation and five years of dabbling in liberal arts, he had obtained a degree in sociology only after his father decided he had no immediate goals toward self-sufficiency and put his foot down. Jack's father owned a very successful family printing business and Jack inherited a great deal of capital when his parents passed away. It was also rumored he had a fondness for gambling and losing. Fritz had described him as a willful slacker.

Downstairs Elise heard the rattle of pots and pans as Fritz moved about in the kitchen. The tantalizing smell of garlic, basil, and tomato sauce drifted up the stairs and her stomach complained with a soft rumble. Her brother had invited Cindy to join them for a pasta dinner. The young nurse had enthusiastically agreed, returning home only long enough to relinquish the bike to a younger brother and find an older one needed the use of her car. Not surprisingly, Fritz offered to provide transportation to and from her house.

Musical cars. Elise had played the game several times during her high school years when Fritz was home from college. She dreaded the confusion his visits made to their social lives with their friends. Oh, how she hated driving her father's beat-up old pick-up because Fritz had a date and needed the family car. Her thoughts turned to Lucas. He had been anything but overjoyed when he discovered her intentions for the evening. She was thankful for Fritz's presence. It had helped to defuse any outbursts.

Twila Pedmo's disclosure had caught them both by surprise. Elise knew of no other close relatives of Lucas Fisher unless there was a distant cousin waiting in the wings. She promised herself she'd talk to her father the first thing tomorrow and see if he could offer any suggestions.

With quick efficient motions, Elise straightened her red and white checked jacket, under which a slinky red tank top boldly set off her white, designer jeans. She hoped the outfit was dressy enough for a low-keyed restaurant and casual enough for a late night excursion to Two Horses. No matter what, she would not be deterred. Somehow, she would convince Jack to take her there. She wanted to see the illustrious Clarisse Fisher, if only from a distance.

From behind her, a pair of small, bright eyes appeared in the bathroom mirror. There was no mistaking the soft gray color, a gene handed down to all the Fisher men. Todd Fisher held a fistful of uncooked spaghetti in his hand and his *Fox and the Hound* book in the other as he regarded her with mild curiosity.

"You smell good." He leaned closer to peer at the jars and tubes of make-up spread out on the marbled vanity. "Can I try some?"

Elise grimaced. "I don't know whether Uncle Lucas would like you to wear my make-up."

The little boy's lower lip ballooned out. "Do we have to tell him?"

"Doing something Uncle Lucas might not like and not telling him could get you in trouble, squirt," she said, ruffling his soft hair. "I've got a better idea. We can still use the make-up. How about I make you look like a clown or maybe an Indian?"

"A clown." His decision needed little thought as his face lit up with eagerness. "I like those silly clowns, and I love the circus," he told her, "and I really, really like to eat those animal crackers in a circus box."

Elise pulled out a bench from beneath the vanity. "Well then, hop up here and let's see what we can do."

With quick, creative strokes she shaded an area around his eyes and mouth in white eyeliner and then lined the perimeters with a dark blue liner. His nose became a colorful blob of red, and two more rosy spots accented each cheek. From her bedroom drawer, she dug out an old green sock hat she had worn in high school and had sentimentally refused to throw out. Rolling up the brim, she tugged it over his pale hair and turned him toward the mirror. Her efforts were rewarded with a high-pitched giggle.

"I *do* look like a clown," he said, excitedly, sliding off the bench to stare at himself in the mirror. He twisted his little cherub face from side to side. His antics were endearing, and she felt a hollow spot in her heart tear open wider. Would she ever have a child of her own, she wondered, to share pure, uninhibited antics with?

"Yes, you do. Cindy will have to help you take the make-up off before you go to bed," she instructed, smiling.

He nodded and looked at her with a sober expression, "Eee-lise, can you help me find Ranger?"

"Ranger, your beanbag dog?"

He nodded again dejectedly. "It has to be somewhere...maybe in all those boxes at the cottage."

"I'll tell you what, we'll go out there together sometime this week and see if we can find it."

The little boy brightened immediately. "Ee-lise," his small fingers rested on her sleeve. "Are you a possum's ability?"

She wrinkled her forehead. *Possum's ability?* The child had used the same phrase the night she had met him. "I don't understand."

"Uncle Lucas said if we become a family, I won't have a mother because there's no one who's a possum's ability."

"Ah-ha, I see." Possibility? As a mother? Terrific, now the kid was going to rip out her heart straight through her rib cage. "I can't be a possibility, Todd, because I don't live here."

"Are you going away?" His little voice cracked with disappointment.

164

"Not for a while, kiddo. Let's not worry about it." She stooped and bussed him lightly on the top of his head.

"Will you be home before I go to sleep?" A hopeful spark flickered in his eyes.

"I'm afraid not." She squatted next to him and handed him the spaghetti he had abandoned on the counter in his excitement. "But I'll check on you when I get in, and tomorrow morning you can tell me all about your first night in your new room. We'll have breakfast together. Now go show Cindy, Fritz, and Uncle Lucas what you look like."

He scampered away, and Elise gathered up her make-up and checked her watch. She wanted to be sure there was no delay in meeting Jack Morrison. The last thing she needed was any type of confrontation between Lucas and him.

With her purse slung over her shoulder, she headed for the hall stairs only to find Lucas propped against the doorframe of his room.

"Well, well, ready for the big date," he drawled and sniffed the air. "And wearing another of good ol' Chuck's famous, sexy-scented waters. Cripes, the man must have bought out Bloomingdale's."

She halted, eyeing him as her stomach did a quick somersault. Even in his faded Levi's and a worn blue tee-shirt, he was gloriously handsome. A six-foot-two specimen of lean muscle. "I thought you'd be returning Monique's calls. What's it been, five messages on the machine since yesterday?"

She tried to step around him, but he straightened his rock-hard body and blocked her path. She felt his smoky eyes take in every detail of her appearance.

"I thought you were just going to dinner," he said.

She shrugged. "Afterwards, maybe dancing, maybe the Mohegan Sun Casino, maybe we'll even try some country and western line dancing, who knows? I've never tried the two-step either."

"Not in that get-up you won't."

She looked down at her jeans. "What's wrong with what I'm wearing? Not an Oleg Cassini, but it's got potential."

"Too much potential. Even with the jacket on, that tank top is pushing respectability."

"Come on, Lucas, it's not. Would you tell me to change if you were taking me out?"

He grinned the kind of grin that made her heart slip clear into her matching red sandals. "Not on your life."

"I rest my case."

"But you're not going out with me. You're going out with sleazy Morrison."

She shook her head wearily. "This Morrison thing is getting tiresome. I'm a grown woman, Lucas, and I'm going to be late." She tried to push past him.

"Put a blouse on," he instructed. His hands shot out and spun her around in the opposite direction. "This is not negotiable."

She stared at him over her shoulder. She was beginning to feel herself losing control. Why did they always have the need to square off in opposite corners over every issue? "And if I don't?"

"You'll keep the scum bag waiting until you do."

Biting back a burning desire to plow a fist into his hard gut, she whirled and stomped to her room. Tearing off the jacket, she removed a red silk blouse from her closet and jammed her arms into it, right over the tank top. Her hands shook with such fury she almost ripped off the buttons. Back in the hall, she faced him again.

"You are a total jerk. You need professional help! No, I take it back. You're beyond even serious therapy."

His hand came up to straighten her collar beneath the jacket. "Okay, so shoot me."

"I'd consider it, but the time I'd spend explaining it to the police would hardly be worth the effort." She paused, a slight smile on her lips. "Unless it was Ted Meyer, and then it would be pure heaven."

That brought a quick response. His hand shot out, and he pulled her against his chest. "Admit, Ms. Springer, there's chemistry between us. It's tugging at me as much as it is at you."

His head lowered to hers, but her fingers covered his lips to halt the kiss. "Listen, even if I were to admit there's an attraction, this 007 agent isn't letting you put me in any lip lock."

"Why not?"

"Because it took me three tries to get this face and lipstick perfect, and you're not ruining it." She smiled and stepped around him, heading for the top of the stairs.

"Lizzie." He halted her again.

"What now?"

"You did a great job on Todd's room. The kid is ecstatic. I haven't seen him giggle and laugh this much in weeks."

She paused to search his face and saw unselfish warmth and affection in his eyes. The kid was getting to both of them. Big time. "It was fun, wasn't it?" she asked and remembered how she had been caught with

Lucas's groping hands. She started for the steps, only to be halted a third time.

"Lizzie, be careful. Morrison might ask you a lot of questions. Don't give him any more ammunition than necessary. I don't know who we can trust."

She sighed and clutched the handrail. "Lucas, I'm trying to *get* information, not give it out." She hesitated a minute. "Do you really think Morrison might be involved?"

"I don't know. I suspect he knows more than he lets on. He lied to you about not knowing Clarisse. I'd downplay any involvement with me."

This time she laughed. "Lucas, I'm driving your thirty-five-thousand-dollar car. The man's not particularly bright, but he's not a complete dimwit either."

"You're driving a forty-five-thousand-dollar car. It's loaded." A smile made his ruggedly masculine face appear more angular and alluring. His gaze locked with hers. "He's probably clueless. If he asks, tell him you're still trying to decide if you want to buy it. Tell him anything. Tell him you're test-driving it before you decide to lay down cash."

He tossed his head toward her bedroom. "By the way, I saw the drawings on your desk for the center's new showroom. The idea of a semi-circular display never crossed my mind. It's brilliant."

"Lucas, I can't afford that car."

"I didn't expect you to buy it. I'm giving it to you."

"Whoa, no way will I accept it as a gift." Her emotions warred between being elated by his praise for her work and irritated he thought he could manipulate her with an expensive gift. She glanced at her watch.

"I'm going to be late. Don't forget to read Todd the new book I left on the bed. Please see if you can get him hooked on something new. If we read *The Fox and the Hound* one more time, we're going to start barking. And you and I need to talk. First thing, tomorrow."

"If you say so." He slipped back into his old familiar self. "Make sure you're home at a respectable hour, Ms. Springer. We don't want the neighbors to gossip. Your reputation is at stake."

Her reputation? Oh, how she longed to smack him alongside the head. Oh, how she ached to remind him he was the one who had gained notoriety countywide for his reckless behavior.

"Be a good boy, Lucas," she replied instead. "And don't wait up. It may be a long night." She hurried down the stairs.

His response filtered down just as she reached the bottom step.

"It better not be."

****

Elise hated to make assumptions about anyone, but with Jack Morrison, she decided to dismiss her long-standing rule. He had, by far, the most hideous wardrobe of any man who walked the face of the earth. With black slacks and a lagoon blue sweater over a plaid peach shirt, he looked like a walking box of Crayolas.

She jerked open the door to his white Mercedes and slid in as soon as he pulled into the drive, not wanting to be under the scrutiny of Lucas Fisher any longer than necessary.

"Am I late?" he asked with a worried frown.

"No, I'm starved." She buckled her belt. "I thought

we'd tackle some Italian food if you don't mind."

"Sure, why not?" His shoulders heaved in indifference.

She waited until he drove to the end of the lane, out of sight from the house, before she unbuckled her seat belt and shimmied out of her jacket. When she began to unbutton her blouse, she saw Jack Morrison watching her warily out of the corner of his eye.

"Now wait a second, Elise," he choked out. The car swerved as he pulled onto the highway. "Don't you think we should wait until *after* we eat?"

"Just drive, Jack! Be quiet and don't say anything to tick me off tonight. I've run out of places to hide the bodies." She yanked the blouse from her jeans and shrugged free, shoving the tank top back behind her belt. Then she grabbed her jacket and slipped it on. "I'll be damned if I'm wearing what everyone thinks is appropriate for little Lizzie Springer."

"Big brothers giving you a hard time, huh?"

"Something like that." She repositioned herself in the bucket seat and ignored his chuckles.

"It looks like a party at your house."

"Fritz is into the sauce again. Spaghetti, I mean."

"That boy could always cook up a storm."

"Yes, he could," she agreed. Although the real storm, she thought, was inside the Springer residence and had no connection to spaghetti sauce.

"Whose new silver Vette?"

She started to say hers, then changed her mind. "I'm leasing it." It wasn't the truth, but it wasn't a lie either. It was a trade off in the world of reality, she rationalized. Her showroom designs for the use of the car.

****

After they finished their meal at G's Wood Grill and after Jack Morrison had given a blow-by-blow account of the last ten years of his life, the only valuable piece of information Elise had gleaned from the dinner date was the pasta and shrimp alfredo was the best in the area. When Jack suggested they hit the casino, she countered with Two Horses. He seemed reluctant at first, telling her it was a four-star dive, but she persisted until he finally relented.

She understood his uneasiness as soon as they entered the smoky, crowded interior. Decked out in a Death Valley theme, the hangout held everything from cactuses to cattle skulls, obviously all plastic renditions. The bar's motley group of patrons consisted of bikers in black leathers with chain wallets and colorful tattoos, second-shift factory workers with no homing instincts, and young couples either fond of the kaleidoscopic atmosphere or in love with the western two-step.

A lengthy search led them to a table for four in the far back of the bar room, away from the vibrating dance floor and the band wearing Stetson hats and snakeskin boots and blaring out heartbreak music on steel guitars.

Elise looked around curiously in hopes of locating Clarisse.

"I told you this was a fiasco," Jack grumbled and signaled to a cocktail server to no avail.

Across the room, two men ambled toward them. The taller one, wearing a brown leather bomber jacket, had a pleasant smile. His friend beside him, in a blue plaid shirt and engineer boots, grinned openly.

The leather-jacketed man spoke. "Mind if we share these seats? The place seems to have filled up fast

---

tonight."

Jack straightened in his seat and glowered. "Yes, I mind. Find your own damn table."

Both men's eyes narrowed and they glanced at each other, frowns on their faces.

"No, no, of course not." Elise felt her pulse skitter and motioned to the vacant chairs. This was the wrong place to aggravate anyone, she thought. "Come on, Jack, the place is standing room only. We have two vacant chairs."

The two men, obviously regulars, slumped down. They were barely seated when a server moved instantly toward them.

"I'm Nick and this is J.B.," the man in the jacket said. He looked up and winked at the waitress at his elbow. "Two Michelobs for us and put whatever the lady and her gent want on our tab."

"Whisky and water," Jack said.

"Just ginger ale for the moment." Elise glanced at Nick. "Thanks."

He smiled. "Come on, you don't have to be polite. I'm buying."

"No, actually I just had a glass of wine with my meal, and I need to let the system change gears." She smiled.

"Like switching from high test to regular or vice versa," J.B. commented. "Know what you mean."

As soon as the drinks arrived, the men took a few sips and left to scout the place for willing dance partners. Afraid she'd never have a free moment alone with Jack Morrison, Elise turned to face him. She had hoped to worm the information she needed out of him, but decided on the direct approach instead.

"Tell me, Jack, does it look like Dad and I will be able to provide a foster home for Todd?"

He frowned into his glass. "I don't think a custody case will surface any too soon, if that's what you want to hear."

"Why not?" she asked.

"With the number of people jumping in and claiming their undying love and devotion for the kid, it will take a while to sort things out unless someone comes up with some concrete evidence about Mike Fisher's intentions."

"Like a will?" She slid her gaze to him and offered him a worried look she didn't have to invent. "Be a sport, Jack, I have nothing in this. Just tell me who the key players are."

"I could lose my job."

"Dad and I are going to lose the kid, Jack, and eventually, the whole pathetic cast will have to step on stage and make an appearance."

Jack Morrison heaved a sigh in agreement. "You already know two. The third one is the kid's grandfather."

Grandfather! Lucas's father? Jack's revelation made her stomach do a war dance. She felt the color drain from her face. The man had deserted his own sons, so why on earth would he want to be saddled with a grandson? She shifted in her seat and took a sip of ginger ale, willing her hands to be steady. The money. Of course, it had to be for the insurance money.

Her head was still spinning from the news when Nick and J.B. sauntered back to the table.

"Hey, they're playing a Texas two-step," Nick said. "Want to dance?"

Elise forced a smile and shook her head. "Sorry, I don't know how."

"There's nothing to it. Right, J.B?" He held out a strong, tanned hand.

One quick glance at Jack and Elise knew his temper, aggravated by the alcohol, was on short fuse status. The men had not only invaded his space, but now they were hitting on his date.

"Jack can show me," she said. "Thanks anyhow."

"Where are you from?" Nick asked. He buckled down into his seat.

"Scranton, but now San Francisco."

"Ah, you're kidding, right? A West Coast gal now? Then you really have to let us cowboy clones show you how to take a spin around the floor. Tell you what, I'll buy you and your date another round if you give it a whirl." He smiled and signaled the waitress.

There was something oddly disturbing about the man. Maybe it was the coaxing grin, the glint in his eye, or maybe it was just her gut instinct, but Elise knew there was more than what visibly showed. Somehow, he looked familiar, all too familiar. She glanced over at Jack. His eyes were getting hazy from the bottle of wine he had consumed at supper and now the whiskey. She was afraid she'd be driving him home. "Sounds like a plan. You game, Jack? Another drink?"

Jack shoved his empty glass away and took a sip from the second one the waitress set in front of him. "You want to dance? Go dance. I'd be a fool to pass up good whiskey," he said with a slur and waved his hand toward the dance floor. "Go ahead, give it a shot."

Minutes later, she was fumbling her way across the floor and enjoying the gentle, coaxing advice from Nick who appeared to be an excellent dancer.

"I assume you're a regular," she said. "Do you know a waitress called Clarisse?"

He twirled her effortlessly in the opposite direction and tossed his head to the right. "See the blonde waitress in the corner who's talking to the table of bikers? That's Clarisse."

Elise watched the hard-edged dishwater blonde throw back her head and laugh. Even from where they danced, Elise could tell Clarisse Cramer Fisher was in her element. She wore a fringed leather mini skirt with a low-cut blouse. A horde of turquoise bracelets wound up her slim wrists. She laughed lustfully with a solidly built man with meaty wrists and leaned forward to offer him a better view of her cleavage, probably in hopes of attaining a generous tip.

Could this woman, Elise asked herself, really become the legal guardian of Todd? How had all this come about? Why would Clarisse, who knew nothing about children, want custody of a four year old? Her thoughts were a blend of red-hot fury and ice-cold bewilderment as she allowed herself to be shuffled about the floor.

The commotion started somewhere in the opposite corner of the room. First, loud shouting erupted, followed by a boisterous exchange, sprinkled with some colorful oaths, and the scraping of chairs. Suddenly the crash of tables being upended drowned out the lead singer's impersonation of Clint Black. As if on cue, the band quit playing.

Heart in her throat, Elise scanned the room long enough to see the entire place rapidly convert itself into an indoor battleground. A chair sailed through the air, along with a volley of beer cans and bottles.

"Let's get out of here!" Nick shouted, ducking as a metal napkin holder skimmed his head, landing with a thud and sending paper flying into the air like a flock of startled doves. He pulled her toward a door in the back and out into the darkness of the back parking lot, illuminated by a single halogen light. Behind her, other people rushed from the front exit heading straight for their vehicles. Engines roared and tires squealed as cars and motorcycles peeled from the lot.

From a crowd of people rushing out the back door, J.B., breathing heavily, pushed his way toward them. "Hell of a night. I heard it started with some bikers in an argument over who had the best machine to ride from here to the coast. What sane person would want to ride their backside for days on only two wheels?"

Elise's worried gaze flitted to the door. "I have to find Jack."

"No, no way, you can't go back in there!" Nick gripped her elbow with firm pressure and ushered her toward a corner of the lot. Behind them, the wail of police cars split the air. A local cruiser pulled up to where they stood and Ted Meyer's hefty body crawled out from behind the wheel.

"Elise Springer, you're the last person I'd expect to find in a dump like this." He lumbered toward her. "You'd better let me take you home. Go sit in my cruiser. The state police are stopping every car as it leaves the lot and passing out DUI's."

"I haven't been drinking," Elise said defensively. "I didn't even drive here, for Pete's sake. I came with Jack Morrison and I need to find him."

"Does he have the white Mercedes?"

She nodded.

"I passed it leaving as I came up the road. You'd better get in and let me get you out of here. Pronto."

"Never mind, I'll take her," Nick spoke up.

"Listen, buddy," Ted Meyer's double chin grew rigid, "butt out, before I find a reason not to like you."

With cool calmness, Nick flipped open his wallet and flashed a state police badge. "I said she's with me, and I'll drop her off. I have to go out that way anyhow."

Red-faced, Ted Meyer stared at Nick, before he gave them both a scathing look and plodded away to the front of the building.

"But you don't know where I live." Elise rubbed her forehead, willing her brain to kick into gear. The light went on. "Whoa, wait a second, you're one of Cindy Peters's brothers, aren't you?"

"Yes, we're all dead ringers for each other in some very odd way."

Dead ringers, Elise thought. He and Cindy could have been twins. She stiffened. "This was a setup, right?"

Nick laughed. "Now why would you assume that? Hey, I'm off duty today, but my car needed some work so I borrowed Cindy's. When she found out I was about to hit the town, she suggested I try some country and western. The band was supposed to be good, but we'll never know."

"Do you know Lucas Fisher?" She sensed he was artfully avoiding the issue. He couldn't possibly know she'd be at Two Horses unless he, or someone else, followed her from the time she left the house.

"I knew his brother better."

Elise turned to J.B. "I suppose you're in law

enforcement, too?"

He held up his hands. "Oh, pul-eeze, I value my life. I don't make it a habit to touch anything loaded with brass, steel, or lead. I'm just a friend who gets a kick out of computers, cars, and country and western music."

Chapter Fourteen

Lucas sat in a tiny, smoke-filled bar on the east side of Scranton and glanced around the dingy room where vacant, scarred tables with captain's chairs were more plentiful than the customers, most of whom were huddled around the bar at the front of the room.

He had not expected the phone call that arrived shortly after Elise left with Jack Morrison, but he was relieved she had not been there. She would have insisted she should be with him, and he figured the fewer people who knew about the meeting soon to take place, the better, although one o'clock in the morning was a hell of a time to meet with someone he loathed since the day he was able to speak his name.

He was angry with himself. How could he have been so careless? He had always considered himself a grounded, calculating businessman who never missed tying up any loose ends or forgetting any details. That he had not taken the time to verify his father's whereabouts had been a miserable mistake. Until seven hours ago, when he received a call from the garage and learned someone from Alaska had stopped in and was looking for him, he truly believed John Fisher was six feet under. He had not had any contact with him since his stint in the Army when he learned the old man was perilously close to death.

A tired-looking waitress in a wrinkled black and

white uniform approached. "Hey, handsome, what'll you have?"

The urge to order a beer was tempting. "Got any iced tea?" he asked.

"Tea?" She looked at him oddly, raising a harshly plucked eyebrow. "Well, yes sir. Sure. I guess I could round up a glass. Would you like anything to eat?"

He shook his head. When she turned to leave, he added, "Oh, miss, could you brew it fresh? I'd prefer it strong, laced with lots of sugar, and in a high ball glass over ice, too." He handed her a fifty-dollar bill.

"Sure, sure, anything you want, mister." She smiled wanly and jerked a thumb toward the empty tables. "It's so slow around here I could hop a boat to China and bring the tea leaves back if you'd like."

Lucas pulled out another fifty-dollar bill, sliding it across the table. "When my friend joins me, don't mention the tea, just ask if I want another round. Keep the change."

"You serious, mister?" she asked, brightening. She laughed. "For tips like this my lips are sealed and I can brew you a glass you'll never forget."

Lucas frowned. Never forget? He hoped not. He hated iced tea. He had tried to acquire a taste for it while living in the South. Even the sweet tea served below the Mason-Dixon Line held little appeal, although it was better than the colored water they served up North. However, he needed a clear head since he was driving. After he had opened his dealership and car restoration facility ten years ago in Atlanta, he had seen more than his share of twisted metal, the result of drivers who had downed too many drinks in too few hours.

The glass of tea arrived barely minutes before John Fisher swaggered through the door. He had aged miserably, Lucas decided, watching him with a guarded hatred he hoped didn't show. It was evident the man had been drinking. At one time John Fisher had been a fit, muscular man, used to the harsh outdoors and accustomed to scaling monstrous oil rigs. Time and whiskey had rounded his waistline and once-lean face. He swayed unsteadily on his feet as he approached the table.

"So, my boy, you came." John Fisher slumped into a seat opposite him and peered at Lucas through bloodshot eyes. "I knew you would. Couldn't sleep wrestling with the thought your old man might best you?" He signaled to the waitress who hurried over. "Bourbon, straight up. Make it a double. Jim Beam Black, if you got it." He motioned to the glass Lucas held. "I see you started without me. You must have inherited my Irish drinking gene."

"Don't flatter yourself. There isn't anything we have in common." Lucas gripped the iced tea glass so tight he prayed it wouldn't splinter in his palm.

John Fisher chuckled. "An Irish temper as well." He took the glass the waitress deposited on the table and took a swallow, smacking his lips. "There's nothing like smooth, well-aged booze to top off the evening or a good business deal."

Lucas leaned back in his seat and took a sip from his glass, feeling the disgusting, sweet liquid slide down his throat. "I had hoped you were dead."

"Almost was. I fell from a rig, busted my pelvis and punctured my lungs. I ended up with a plate in the skull and enough damage to buy me out from under that damn monkey business with a settlement and a little disability cash on the side. So, I bought me a little fix-it shop near Fairbanks, but the timing must have been wrong. It didn't fly."

Lucas snorted. It was as clever a way to say he drank the profits as he'd ever heard. "So tell me, what brings you all the way to Scranton?" The bastard had not attended Mike's funeral nor even sent a lousy bouquet of flowers. Was it possible he hadn't known until someone notified him about Mike's estate?

"I figured it was about time we established some family relationships. I'm not getting any younger."

It took all of Lucas's willpower not to reach across the table, grab his father by his sweaty neck, and squeeze it until his red eyeballs rolled onto the table. "Not with me, you don't. You gave up your right to family bonding thirty-some years ago, old man."

"I figure we have something worthwhile now. Or someone."

"If you're talking about Mike's son, his name is Todd."

"Yeah, Todd. That's it." John Fisher leaned forward, speaking in a slurred voice. "If we play our cards right, you and me as the only surviving heirs can split the insurance money and maybe find the bundle of cash everyone is talking about. You know, the undercover stuff?" He paused. "I heard talk you're trying to start up a garage. It looks nice. I stopped in there today and looked around. Some extra money would sure go a long way to help you."

"And your grandson?"

"There's always some well-meaning couple out there willing to give a kid a decent home. Hell, what would I do with a kid in Alaska?"

Lucas felt his blood began to boil. He would walk on shards of glass before he'd every consider giving Todd to anyone, especially to the worthless piece of scum before him.

The waitress returned with another round of drinks. She offered Lucas a faint, reassuring smile. "Gentleman at the bar said this round is on him."

Through the escalating fury almost blinding him, Lucas saw Bryan, his right-hand man and computer tech, standing at the bar. Tipping a can of Coors to his lips, he acknowledged Lucas in a mock salute.

"Friend of yours?" John Fisher asked.

"Yeah." Lucas leaned forward. "Listen, you old bastard, I don't know what your game is, but 'the kid' isn't going anywhere. I lived the horrors of not being wanted. Todd will never know what I had to endure. I want to raise the boy. By myself, if necessary."

"It wasn't my fault. Your mother was a nag, the kind of woman who wouldn't give a person any space. She'd suck the very air out from around you, if you let her."

"Space to carouse and whore, you mean, while she carried your second child."

"I tried, I really tried." John Fisher voice took on a whiny edge to it.

"Tell me about it. You tried so hard we never knew you even existed!" From his breast pocket, Lucas pulled out a checkbook. "What will it take you to give you your 'space' again?"

John Fisher's eyes registered shock a moment, then narrowed to cagey slits. "Hey, are you trying to buy me off?"

"I'm trying to make you disappear for good this time," Lucas said through a hiss. "How much?"

"You don't have enough."

The remark pleased Lucas. So the old man had no idea he was wealthy. It meant his secret was still safe for a while. He was certain he could count on Mrs. Pedmo to keep a tight lip.

"I'd take a loan if I had to, just to get you off my goddamn back," Lucas admitted. "As luck would have it, the stock market has been pretty good to me."

"Rumor has it there's as much as a hundred thousand dollars the cops never recovered."

"Even if you found it, do you think you'd be able to walk away with it? You'd end up in a cell so small you'd never have room to breathe." Lucas removed a pen from his coat and scribbled in the checkbook. "What's it going to be?"

"I could use one of those fancy cars of yours," John Fisher said. "It's a long drive back to Alaska, and my '98 Plymouth is on its last legs."

Lucas ripped the check from the book and motioned to Bryan. "My friend here will make sure you're put up in the best hotel in town." He handed him the check and turned his attention to young man who came to stand at his elbow.

"Give him the best Suburban on the lot."

"A hundred thousand dollars," John Fisher said under his breath staring at the check. "Sure looks like the stock market was really good. Hey, how do I know this check is good? It's made out to cash."

Lucas snatched it from his grip and handed it to Bryan. "After Mr. Fisher here signs some papers from my lawyer tomorrow morning relinquishing any attachment to Todd, accompany him to the bank and make sure he has his spending money to return to Alaska, okay?"

Bryan nodded curtly.

"And have one of our mechanics personally escort him to the Ohio border."

Bryan nodded again.

Lucas stood, his chair grating on the floor. "From now on, old man, I never want to see your face, and I never want you in the kid's space, either. Got it? As far as Todd is concerned, you really *are* dead."

With visible effort John Fisher rose, grabbing the table for support. He nodded and turned to walk away, then turned back. "Since you're so generous with your money and advice, I think there's something you should know."

"What?"

"I'm not Mike's old man."

Eyes narrow, Lucas stared at him. "What did you say?"

"You heard me." John Fisher smiled an evil smile.

The implication of the words sank to the pit of Lucas's stomach like a stone. If John Fisher was hoping for a visible reaction, he was determined to use every ounce of effort not to give him one. "Well, what a relief," he said with a faked laugh. "But how can I be sure you're not just blowing hot air?"

"I'm not."

"You gave him your name."

"No, your mother gave him my name," John Fisher said harshly.

Lucas pursed his lips. "Who was it? Who was Mike's dad?"

John Fisher lifted his shoulders. "You figure it out," he said with a sneer and walked away.

****

Elise paused at the foot of the step leading up to the front door, glowing yellow under the rays from the porch light. For as long as she could remember, the light had been left on until the last person was safely inside each night. Outside the night was chilly and the rains had heightened the smell of the damp earth and mingled it with the sweet odors of new mown grass, lilacs and spring flowers. It was a refreshing change from the smog and exhaust fumes to which she had been accustomed in the city. If it weren't for the far-off rumble of thunder heralding another downpour, she could have stood there all night watching the stars play peek-a-boo with the clouds.

Inside she found Fritz fast asleep on the couch. Beside him lay a note pad with messages to call Jack Morrison and Chuck Sanders. She checked her watch. Already it was past one a.m. Jack Morrison could wait forever, she decided. Undoubtedly, he had been checking in to see if she got home safely. She'd let him wonder. He had abandoned her like the coward he was. Chuck, on the other hand, she would call first thing in the morning.

She climbed the steps and slipped past Lucas's room. The door was open and a lamp burned beside the bed, but he was nowhere in sight. A small green light from the computer in the spare room gleamed at her like a tiny cat's eye.

Still wide awake from the incident at the Two Horses, Elise went to her room and retrieved a flash drive she had found among Mike Fisher's belongings.

Powering up the computer, she clicked on a word processing program and slipped the flash drive into the port. When it refused to read the data, she shifted to a database program and clicked on a file marked personal. The screen filled with what looked like an address book. She decided not to take any chances and printed a hard copy before going on to the other directories, marked finances, cases and contacts, and miscellaneous. The last of four database files refused to be read by the processor's database so she closed all the files and made a copy of the lone file, then another copy of the entire flash drive before she perused the address book.

Outside the rains began again, starting with the soft rumble of thunder and quick bold flashes of distant lightning. She cursed softly as she moved quickly down through the list of names, knowing soon she would have to shut down to avoid any interference from an electrical surge or outage. Halfway through the list, she stopped the cursor on Ted and Mary Jo Meyer's names. She stared at the lines listing both an address and home phone number.

"Elise? Whatcha doing?"

She jumped at the sound of her name. Framed in the doorway, Todd stood sleepy-eyed, clad in his wrinkled pajamas, holding *The Fox and the Hound* at his chest. Beside him, Bess stood vigilant guard and let out a soft whimper.

"Hi, sport, can't you sleep?" she asked as she shut down the computer.

He came to stand beside her, resting his tousled hair against her shoulder.

"Don't you like your new room?"

"I don't like the noise outside."

Elise removed the flash drive and out of habit hit the button on the processor checking to see the CD drive was also vacant. The slot opened and the CD tray popped out.

"Hey, you have a cup holder, just like Uncle Lucas has on his computer. But J.B. told him he can't use it."

"No, I guess not, Todd," she said and chuckled. "It's another way for the computer to read information or play music." She stared at the drawer as it closed silently. J.B.? It couldn't be a coincidence, could it?

"Who's J.B.?"

"He works for Uncle Lucas." He yawned. "Uncle Lucas calls him the computer genius. What's a genius?"

"A very, very smart person. Tell me, what does J.B. look like?"

He shrugged. "He has dark hair. His name is Jerome Bryan something, but he hates to be called Jerome, so we call him J.B. He wears boots with little straps over them."

Engineer boots, she mused. Nick's sidekick at Two Horses. Lucas had someone following her.

Behind them a crack of thunder exploded, and Todd all but jumped into her lap.

"Don't be afraid," she said soothingly and stroked his silky hair.

Quickly she retrieved her flash drives, gathered up the papers, and swiveled in the chair. "I'm not fond of storms either. How about you go to the bathroom while I change into a pair of sweats, and I'll tuck you in? By morning this will be over."

"Will you stay a while?" he asked. "Uncle Lucas stays when I'm afraid. Sometimes he lies down with me

188

until I fall asleep."

She nodded, trying to imagine Lucas Fisher, lean-faced and tough, giving comfort to a small child late at night, and found it wasn't as odd an image as she thought. Behind his hard exterior there was a gentleness she had never seen in most men, and she found herself attracted to it. "Sure, of course. Do you know where Uncle Lucas went?"

"He got a phone call. He promised he'd be back. He will, won't he?"

"Yes, I'm certain he will."

Minutes later, illuminated only by a small night light, she lay on the pillow opposite Todd with his small hand wrapped around her thumb.

"I'm not going anywhere," she whispered softly.

"I know," he murmured with a sleepy yawn. "I won't let you."

She smiled into the darkness, warmed by the thought.

Outside the rumble of thunder grew louder.

"Eee-lise, do you really think God's bowling?"

"Uh-huh," she said and rolled on her side. He snuggled up next to her, poking the back of his soft head of hair under her chin. "And the lightning is when he snaps heaven's lights on and off."

"Uncle Lucas says it's when he bowls, knocks down all the pins, and gets a strike."

"He does, does he? Well, that sounds like a winner to me. My dad once told me when God plays with his snow globe, he shakes out some flakes and we get our winter snow. What do you think?"

Todd giggled, despite his tiredness. "Wow, he must have a giant one." He fell silent a moment. "Elise?"

"What?"

"I love you. Do you think you could be my mom? I know Uncle Lucas likes you. A lot."

Softly, Elise raised a hand and smoothed the baby fine hairs beside his ear. They were as soft as the richest silk, and she felt an overwhelming sadness, a heartsickness so wrenching tears welled up in her eyes. The only thing the small boy wanted in the whole world was to be loved.

"I love you, too, Todd, but I don't know about the mom part," she whispered honestly and was glad it was too dark for him to see her watery eyes. "We'll have to see. Let's get some sleep."

****

It was nearly five o'clock in the morning when Lucas finally pulled into the drive. He crept up the steps carefully to avoid making any noise and then silently moved to Elise's room where the door was ajar. The bed was still made. He stared it a moment, not quite believing his eyes. Anger and disappointment welled up inside him. So she was spending the night elsewhere, he concluded with a dull ache that wrapped itself around his heart. With Morrison, perhaps. Yet J.B. had told him she had caught a ride back to the farm with Nick Peters. Unless Jack Morrison returned and picked her up again.

Well, what did you expect, Fisher? You have no strings to tie her to you. She's an adult who's allowed to make choices and decisions on her own.

Sickened, he moved to Todd's room and quietly pushed the door open. From the side of the bed, Bess came alert and raised her head. As soon the dog recognized him, she dropped her head back down on the carpet.

He found both Elise and Todd snuggled beneath the bedcovers. French blue bedcovers, he reminded himself. Her hair was mussed and spread out on the pillow, like strands of cornsilk baked golden brown from the sun. One arm was tucked beneath her pillow, the other wound around the small boy who slept as deeply and soundly as she.

He stood there a long while just watching them sleep, burning the impression into his memory, and wishing with all his might the scene would be repeated over and over for the rest of his life.

Chapter Fifteen

Elise stood beside the breakfast table with a box of Frosted Flakes poised above her bowl.

"You what?"

"I paid him off to get him out of the picture, out of my life."

"Oh, Lucas, no. Even if John Fisher isn't Mike's real father, unless you can prove otherwise, he still figures into the picture."

"Not legally he doesn't. I had papers drawn up which he signed and which now give all custody rights to me."

"You don't think it can be reversed?"

"Certainly not if we find out who Mike's real dad was." He gestured to her upraised hand. "Pour your cereal, for God's sake."

"And if we don't?" Slumping down into a seat, she dumped cereal and milk into the bowl.

"If we don't, then we can always prove John Fisher isn't Mike's dad with DNA tests."

Elise scrubbed a hand over her face. "Back up a second. How will you do that? We'd need blood samples or something from Mike."

"We already have them. The police took samples right after the accident for drug testing. All I'd need is John Fisher's, too."

"Oh, this is scary, Lucas. You could be opening

Pandora's box. This could cost a pretty penny. Your father will hit you up for even more money. Once he finds you've got money to burn, there will never be an end to the blackmail."

Coffee cup in hand, Lucas shoved himself away from the table, went to the sink, and leaned against it. "Maybe, but it's a chance I have to take. Anyway, he came right out and said he didn't want Todd. Like Clarisse, he was hoping to find the money. Everyone, it seems, wants the damn money. I want the child. What did you find out from the sleaze?"

"Morrison? Not much. The place went berserk and I didn't have enough time to worm my way far enough into his good graces. I think you may be right. He knows more than he's letting on. I need more time." She sighed, rose, and carried her empty bowl and spoon to the sink.

"Forget Morrison. I don't want you seeing that jackass again." Lucas swallowed the last drop of coffee and set his empty cup on the counter.

Elise smiled and rinsed her bowl. "Jealous?"

He arched a brow. "What if I am?"

"I'd say you're being unreasonable, stubborn...and sweet." She lifted her face to look at him.

Gently he pulled her into his arms and her heart beat a quick staccato as his mouth, warm and hard, came down to meet hers. His arms encircled her back and he nudged her against him. Her breath quickened as the heat of the kiss became more intense. Her hands fell to his waist and she pulled him even closer, heedless of her damp hands.

"Okay, you two, knock it off, the kids are here and we want our breakfast," Fritz said, coming through the doorway. Seconds later, Todd came barreling down the steps in his pajamas.

Lucas released her gently, but brushed a light kiss over the top of her hair before she stepped away. He threw a disgruntled look at Elise's brother. "Fritz, I swear I can't decide whether you're my best friend or worst enemy. Do you ever live at your own place?"

"Hey, bonehead, don't blame me because your timing's wrong." Fritz crossed the room, opened the cupboard, and scanned the shelves. Turning to Todd, he said, "Well, buddy, around here it looks like breakfast is cereal or more cereal. Fortunately for us, someone must have stock in General Mills and Kellogg's. What'll it be? Wheat, rice, or corn?" Fritz lifted the boy in his arms and made a special effort to help him choose a box.

"I could make you both eggs," Elise offered.

"Don't put yourself out, Paula Deen. Just pour me a cup of that hemlock you brewed."

While they gathered bowls and spoons and sat down to eat, Elise related as cryptically as she could with Todd present what had happened the previous evening.

"This puts a whole new spin on everything," Fritz said between bites of cereal. He waited until Todd finished and scampered upstairs to change his clothes. "Even if you determine John Fisher wasn't Mike's father, what do you prove? If there's someone else out there hoping to cash in on Mike's estate, wouldn't he have had to step forward by now?"

"Maybe he isn't aware of Mike's death," Elise pointed out.

"Or maybe he can't reveal himself without ruining

himself or his family," Lucas offered.

"Yeah, and maybe he's dead or just maybe this person doesn't exist. Maybe Lucas's dad is lying," Fritz said. "All of this speculation doesn't get you any closer to finding the money, clearing Mike's name, determining the real cause of his death, or his true intent for the custody of Todd."

His brutal honesty brought a flash of pain to Lucas's eyes. Even if Fritz's intent was to point out the truth and keep them from chasing flimsy leads, Elise wished he would be more tactful. She touched Lucas's arm gently. "He has a point, Lucas, but we're not giving up. I'm going to visit Dad at the hospital. Perhaps he can help us piece some of this together. It's worth a shot. Dad knows half the people in the county, so maybe he knows something about your family connections." What she didn't tell him was she planned to stop at the state police barracks and see Nick Peters. She had a hunch the last database on the disk was somehow connected to Mike's work.

"You'd better call Chuck before you leave," Fritz warned Elise. "When I spoke to the guy last night his parting shot was if you didn't get back to him pronto, he was a dead man. I asked him if he'd wanted to take out a life insurance policy, but he declined."

Elise laughed. "I'll do it before I leave."

****

"You have to come back to San Francisco right now," Chuck Sanders pleaded. "I'm serious, Elise, the biggest contract of our lifetime is about to go down the drain."

"I can't, Chuck," she said, changing hands and ears with the cordless phone. She stood next to her drawing table in her bedroom and flipped through the blueprints for Lucas's showroom, already under construction. Beside a pile of notes, more paperwork was stacked high and screaming for her attention. The cottage was almost completed, except for a few cosmetic changes to the kitchen and bath. "Paul and you promised me this next week."

"Elise, listen to me. Levinson agreed to all five contracts. All five. The only stipulation is you manage them. All five. Is the signal getting through? He wants to meet with us as soon as possible."

"Hold him off. Give him some kind of excuse. Tell him I'm still in Scranton."

"I told him, I told him. The man is not civil to any of us. You know how he hates Paul. It's a no go unless he's able to deal directly with you. He's adamant about this." He lowered his voice, and Elise knew he was struggling to disguise the strained and frantic tone he had earlier used. "Here's how it works, kid. It's not every day an architect lands designs for five major hotels. You do it and you're on your way to national recognition as an architect. We have to think of your future here."

My future? Elise felt her stomach do a quick summersault. "Wait, you never said they were my designs."

"What do you think we've been talking about? I showed him the plans you created for Simson and Associates. You know, the ones they discarded and we tucked away in the dead files? The one with the lounge placed directly in the center of the recreation area, so parents can relax, read, and still watch their kids play video games, use the equipment room, swim, play ping pong, whatever."

"I don't get it," Elise said.

"I didn't either until I realized Levinson's plan is not just to build a chain of hotels. Anyone can do that. He wants to build family-oriented ones. He wants to create an atmosphere in each hotel geared to enticing businessmen who want to travel with their families. That's when I showed him your designs. It was like the merging of two intellectual wave lengths."

"What am I going to do, Chuck?" Elise asked. She pinched the bridge of her nose and drew in an exhausted breath. She had made a promise to her father and she was committed to helping Lucas. How could she just pack up and leave? And what about Todd? How would she ever explain it to him?

"Get back here. Now."

"If I don't?"

"We lose the contracts."

"And I lose my job," she said exhaustedly. "It hardly seems fair, Chuck."

She heard a long silence over the phone. "Elise, try to remember Paul is my partner."

"Well, at least you're honest," she said, juggling the phone to her other ear again as she searched for a pen. "Give me Levinson's number." She quickly jotted it down and said, "Maybe I can stall him. Can you deal with Paul?"

"I'll try. You have forty-eight hours starting tomorrow. That's all I can promise you, kid. Would it help to say I'm sorry?"

"No," she said as much to herself as to him and hung up.

****

Anton Springer looked happy and robust for a man who had just spent his last week in a hospital. Elise found him sitting in the lounge with his crutches, reading the latest copy of *USA Today* and chatting with Mrs. Pedmo.

He looked up and smiled. "I was just telling Twila about your job in San Francisco."

As if Mrs. Pedmo sensed Elise's need to be alone with her father, she rose.

"You needn't rush off," Anton said apologetically.

"We could stay here all day and trade stories about our kids and the good ol' days, Anton, and we'd never finish. I've paperwork to do." She smiled at Elise. "Your father and I were reminiscing about all those childhood pranks our kids used to play. I especially like the one where Fritz and Lucas let the air out of the tires of old Sam Meyer's police car."

Elise groaned. "Oh, great, I'm sure you now have a terrific impression of Lucas Fisher."

"Lucas Fisher was no easy kid to raise. But behind his bad attitude, there was a kid with brains and the willingness to work hard." She patted Anton on his hand and picked up her purse and briefcase. "I'll stop by again and see how you're doing."

"I'll walk you to the elevators," Elise offered, rising and following her through the lounge door. She punched the down button. "It's really nice of you to stop and see Dad. He really enjoys your company."

"And I enjoy his," Mrs. Pedmo replied. "When I lost my husband, I thought there was nothing else left besides work until people like your father convinced me I could have a life again, once the healing process began. Even Todd will eventually readjust after the initial shock of his father's death has passed and he has stability back in his life. It's funny, kids seem to go through the process so much quicker than older folks."

"Can you tell me why Jack Morrison recommended Todd Fisher be sent back to New Castle?" Elise asked.

Mrs. Pedmo paused for moment, pursing her lips. "Jack Morrison is a decent caseworker, Elise. Maybe not a rocket scientist, but as good as he can be, realizing his shortcomings. One, he's never had any children, and two, he has never known the poverty or loneliness so many of our economically disadvantaged kids have experienced. When Jack recommended Todd be sent back to New Castle, his intent, I believe, was to place the boy back in familiar surroundings near friends and neighbors so he could better adjust to his father's death. You realize Mike had only moved to Scranton a little less than a year before the accident."

"But why couldn't he have waited until Lucas arrived?"

"Until your dad spoke up and suggested it, Jack was going with what seemed the most logical and appropriate approach for the immediate needs of a grieving child." She looked across the room where Anton was seated. "I must say, your father is a very imposing, stubborn man when the need arises."

"You'll get no argument from me."

****

Anton Springer set his newspaper aside on the coffee table in front of him. The lounge was deserted except for the two of them.

"You might as well tell me, Elise. You have that God Almighty, horrified look about you like the world is coming to an end."

Elise slumped into a chair opposite him. "Chuck Sanders called this morning. I have a shot at cinching the designs for a five-hotel deal, but I have to go back to San Francisco."

"How soon?"

"Looks like Wednesday unless I can stall them."

"And you don't want to?"

"No, not exactly." Elise blew out a breath. "If I go back, Paul Winston will never let me return." She related her phone call with Chuck Sanders in capsule form. *And I don't want to leave, not yet. Not right now.*

"But you have vacation due you."

"I also have a job," she reminded him. "I'm also knee-deep in helping Lucas Fisher. Then there's Todd to think about."

"Ah ha," Anton Springer said.

"And just what does 'ah ha' mean?"

He smiled. "I guess I should say it means nothing, but from what your brother tells me, there might be something."

"Fritz talks too much."

"He always was the household jabberwocky, wasn't he?" Anton Springer laughed heartily.

"Dad!" She watched him settle back in his chair and raise his injured foot to rest on the coffee table.

"Have you spoken to this Levinson fellow?"

Elise shook her head. She had been dreading making the call and was actually thankful it was Sunday. "I guess I wasn't sure what to say. I was looking for an excuse so believable the man would cave and agree to a postponement."

"Lizzie, Lizzie." Anton Springer held up a silencing hand. "For crying out loud, you're telling me the woman who is known as the greatest manipulator of the human race, your brothers and me included, can't come up with a way to deal with a man who wants, no craves, your expertise?"

Stunned, Elise stared at him. "Dad, you don't understand. He's our major client. I can't go ordering him around. The man's a multi-millionaire." She sighed.

"So's Lucas Fisher, and from what I hear you've got him standing on his head and wallpapering. And not just wallpapering—wallpapering with Fritz! I'm enormously disappointed I missed that."

She smiled. "It was rather amusing. They used so much paste we'll have to blast the wallpaper off when we need to redo the room."

"You were lucky they didn't eat it."

She laughed, but her mood grew serious as she walked to the window and looked out at the trees already dressed in full spring green. "Dad, John Fisher showed up the other night and told Lucas he wasn't Mike's father. Do you think he was telling the truth? Or was it just a way to try to hurt Lucas?"

Anton Springer drew in a deep breath and blew it out. "Whew, I honestly don't know, Elise. If your mother was living, she would have probably been able to tell you. If Lucas's grandmother confided in anyone, it would have been her. Does it really matter?"

"I don't know. Fritz says it doesn't." Elise stared at the sky, a clear bright blue. She hated the thought of going off on a wild goose chase. "I do believe it matters to Lucas."

"Let me think on it," Anton said. "Right now you've got enough to muddle through."

Chapter Sixteen

Surrounded by shrubs in need of pruning, the Meyers' small ranch house sat back from the road with a gravel driveway ending at a double-car garage where Mary Jo's beat-up blue Mazda was parked inside. A weed-filled lawn extended from front to back, the rear portion encircled with a battered wire fence. A rusty swing set occupied a corner of the enclosed lot along with a huge tire filled with muddy sand. Three-wheeled plastic Big Wheels lay abandoned, their colors fading in the bright sunshine.

A tired-looking Mary Jo greeted Elise and Todd at the front door, and shortly thereafter three noisy children, ranging in age from ten to five, barreled up behind her.

"Take Todd around back to play," Mary Jo instructed the children. She hugged Elise warmly, ushering her into the small foyer. "Let's go to the kitchen," she suggested, "and have some coffee."

She stopped on the way to pick up a stuffed animal and rubber ball and throw them into a laundry basket doubling as a toy chest. At one time, she was a tall, slim woman with vibrant hair the color of lemons, but three pregnancies had added twenty additional pounds and faded her hair to the color of a dull penny.

"How's your dad?" she asked.

"Much better. In fact, I was at the hospital earlier

this morning," Elise said.

"Good to hear he's getting better." Mary Jo removed two mugs from the cupboard, poured them each a cup of coffee, took them to the table, and slid into a seat. "Whenever you want to visit him, I can watch Todd for you. He's familiar with my kids. Sometimes when Mike Fisher's sitter had other obligations, he would drop Todd off here."

So that explained why Mary Jo's name was in Mike Fisher's address book, Elise thought with a welcome sense of relief.

"Actually, we hired Cindy Peters to help with Todd and also Dad when he comes home," Elise told her. She sat forward and crossed her hands on the table. "So tell me, Mary Jo, what's been happening in your life?"

Mary Jo shrugged. "Kids keep me busy. I'm working with a committee to purchase new equipment for the playground at our elementary school. Pretty soon your poor father will be bombarded by kids selling candy, cookies, and candles to help raise money."

Elise sipped her coffee and studied Mary Jo's face. "Why don't you get a few local businesses to donate some money? They like to help with community and educational projects."

Mary Jo bit her lip and looked away. Her face clouded with uneasiness. "No, Ted doesn't want me bothering the local businesses. He feels they'd be obligated to give because I'm a police officer's wife."

"So get someone on your committee to ask." Elise watched an anxious look appear on Mary Jo's face and she could see Mary Jo was not comfortable with any suggestions, so she changed the subject. "Did you know Mike Fisher?"

"Yes. Why do you ask?"

Elise shrugged. "Just curious. Just wondering what he was like."

Now Mary Jo's face looked almost pained. "I didn't know him real well, but he seemed like a kind man. A good father. He adored Todd. I've heard he was a good cop. He didn't appear to have the hard edge that seems to be part of Lucas's nature, if you know what I mean."

"Do you think he was capable of stealing a hundred thousand dollars of undercover money?"

"Oh, no." With eyes cast downward, Mary Jo nervously fidgeted with the handle on her cup. "Well, at least he..." she paused and stammered, "he, he didn't seem to be."

Elise pursed her lips and watched her friend with a keen eye, saying nothing more. She seemed tense, almost fearful. Was she telling the truth about Mike Fisher? Did she know him better than she cared to admit? Or was there something she was hiding?

Outside, a car pulled up, tires crunching on the gravel driveway. Mary Jo stood, moved to the kitchen window, and parted the sun-faded curtains. "Oh...oh, it's Ted. He must have noticed your car and is dropping by to say hello."

Word travels fast, Elise thought. Only Jack Morrison knew she was driving a new Corvette convertible. The community gossip network was alive and functioning.

Ted Meyer came into the kitchen through the side door.

"Hello, Ted," Elise said, smiling. "Sorry about last night, but Nick Peters was going my way. He had to pick up his sister."

Grunting noncommittally, he went to the cupboard, took out a cup, and poured himself some coffee. "So tell me, how fast does the silver streak out there go?" he asked, eyeing her above the rim of the cup.

Elise considered the question a moment and laughed. "I don't know. I haven't pushed the pedal to the floor yet. Tell you what, I'm willing to take it out sometime and find out, but only if you're game to ride shotgun. No way am I going to risk getting a ticket from the local police department."

"Smart girl," he said, cracking the barest of smiles. "You and Mary Jo fall into the reminiscing trap yet?"

"Almost. I was about to ask her whether she knew anyone who knew Mike and Lucas's grandmother."

A furrow creased his brow. "Why do you need to know?"

"So I could get a better insight into who Mike Fisher was," Elise said. It wasn't a lie. If it would help her to understand Todd better, she would do whatever was necessary. Any information might help her while the little boy was still recovering from the loss of his father. She made a mental note to pick up a book on children and the grief process at the bookstore.

"A cop. What's there to know about cops?" Ted Meyer asked, then snorted.

He seemed piqued, and Elise was glad when Mary Jo's oldest child, a girl with big brown eyes, came racing into the kitchen.

"Cookies," she said breathlessly. "Everyone wants cookies and we're thirsty, Mom."

"Not now, Rachael," Ted Meyer said to her. "Can't you see we have company and we're talking?"

"Please?" the little girl asked.

"I told you, get back out there and play!" Ted barked and pointed to the door.

Fear was all Elise could think as she watched the girl's eyes widen as her face and posture froze. She shrank back toward the door, her eyes skidding to her mother.

"Go on, do as your father says," Mary Jo said softly. "I'll bring a tray out in a second." She shooed her daughter out the door with a wave of her hand.

The door banged shut.

"Damn, Mary Jo, when are you ever going to teach those kids to shut a door properly?"

Before she could answer, Elise interrupted, hoping to defuse what might be an ensuing argument. "So fill me in, Ted. What's new in the old neighborhood?"

"I guess right now, Lucas Fisher. I didn't know he was staying at the farm."

"Until the cottage is restored."

"How long will it take?"

"A couple of weeks."

He frowned. "People are starting to talk."

"About what?" Elise smiled, amused. She knew exactly what they were talking about.

"What do you think?" He grunted. "You and him."

Elise shook her head in disbelief. A decade later, and the old neighborhood hadn't changed. Everyone had a voracious curiosity to know everyone else's business.

"If you get a chance to offer some news to the local grapevine, Ted, you might remind everyone Fritz is there most of the time and so is Todd." She had promised herself she would ignore comments like this, but the need to defend Lucas was almost overwhelming. She found herself more annoyed than angry. "You might want to add we're both over twenty-one and self-sufficient. We make our own way in the world. Oh, and my father is well aware of who is staying at his house."

"Listen, Liz, I'm trying to be your friend here," Ted Meyer said gruffly. "I'm just passing on what I heard. He's always been a wild sort of guy, known for his reckless side, fast cars, and one-night flings."

She refused to take his bait. "Listen, Ted, if you don't see it with your eyes, don't invent it with your mouth. I dislike vicious rumors."

"I'm just telling it like it is, Liz. You asked." His face reddened. "Hey, I gotta go." He hitched up his pants and left abruptly, the side door creaking as he went outside.

"Don't mind Ted," Mary Jo said in a low voice. "He's a little cranky from working overtime. One of his buddies is off sick with the flu and everyone is covering his shifts."

"Are you happy?" Elise asked suddenly, the words spilling out of her mouth before she had a chance to analyze her thoughts. It was heartbreaking to see a woman as bright as Mary Jo give up everything to live such a squalid existence.

"I adore my kids," Mary Jo said. "I don't know what I'd do without them."

Elise grimaced. She hadn't said she adored or loved Ted. "Did you ever think of going back to school and getting your degree? You were thinking about elementary education, and you'd be a natural, Mary Jo."

The woman's eyes grew distant. "Ted and I talked about it, but right now the money just isn't there. Did I tell you we're saving to buy a small cabin and some land outside Scranton? Ted wants a hunting camp, and it would be perfect for the kids."

"You could always take out loans, ask your parents for one, or check into scholarships," Elise persisted.

"Ted's pride would never allow it." Mary Jo shook her head and paused a moment. Then, as if coming back to reality, she rose and slapped her hand lightly on the table. "Anyway, enough about me. Tell me what little Lizzie Springer has been doing while I get these kids something to eat and drink."

****

Dressed in street clothes, Nick Peters sat at his work station, which looked more like a garbage heap than a state trooper's work area. Cardboard cups, candy wrappers and a day-old bologna sandwich fought for room with pencils, books, and a group picture of his eight brothers and sisters in a simple wooden frame. The man was clearly overworked.

"Is this creative clutter?" Elise asked when he hopped up to clear a pile of papers from the chair beside his desk.

"No, this is actually tidy and rather organized for me," he admitted. "Cindy and I only share our dad's features. Our work habits are at both ends of the spectrum. This office drives her crazy every time she stops in. She wants to dive in and clean it up. So what can I do for you?"

From her purse, Elise withdrew the flash drive with a copy of the database. "There's a database of Mike Fisher's on here I can't read. I was thinking perhaps it had to do with work."

Nick Peters turned to his computer beside him and inserted the flash drive. After a series of faulty tries, the screen filled up with information. "Looks like a copy of Mike's logs and reports for work. You couldn't get it to work because it's software specific."

"What kind of logs?"

"His work schedule, cases, notations. He must have checked out a laptop to do some work at home. This is routine stuff we usually try to get done in the office, but it's not always possible. This is the original flash drive, right?"

She stared at him, trying to decide whether to tell the truth. He turned to her and waited for her response. There was a long silence as each waited for the other.

When it was evident she was not about to lie, he laughed and said, "Okay, that was a dumb question, even for a cop. Don't answer it, and I won't have to get a search warrant. It's not going to do you any good without the program-specific software. I guess I should remind you, it's confidential information."

He turned back to the computer, and she stood and moved behind him, peering over his shoulder.

"You know, this makes me a little uneasy letting you see this," he said and swiveled his head to look at her. He paged down the screen, stopping occasionally to scan the contents. "But I'm a sucker for a woman who smells heavenly."

"So keep inhaling and keep your finger on the down arrow. Wouldn't it make for an interesting legal case if confidential information *was* on a flash drive not owned by the police?" She smiled, squinting at the screen. "How well did you know Mike Fisher?"

"Enough to know he was a damn good cop."

"Would he be the type to run off with undercover money?"

"Absolutely not. Hmmm..." He scrolled farther down through the material. "There's nothing really important here, Elise. It looks like a lot of traffic reports and violations. Probably old stuff from his job back in New Castle."

"Did you see him the day he died?" Somehow she had to try to get an insight into what had happened prior to the accident. Lucas had admitted he knew nothing about what had occurred in the days leading up to it. The lack of details had been needling her for days now.

"Yes, come to think of it. Mike stopped by before his afternoon shift. We had our usual talk complaining about dumb things at work." He turned back to his desk and pulled out a notebook, flipping through the pages until he came to a page and stopped, running a neatly trimmed nail down the list of what looked like a telephone logbook. "The entries for the day were routine. He made a few calls."

He looked up at her. She had moved and was now leaning over his other shoulder again. "You really should consider undercover investigation. We need more nosy people out there working for us." He smiled. "Here, the last call, placed at about eleven p.m., was to Mary Jo Meyer's house. He must have needed a sitter for the next day. He died at one the next morning."

Puzzled, she sat back down. "Let's be candid, Nick. Was he the kind of man to lose control of a car?"

"Are you kidding? Those Fisher boys shared a car gene even if they weren't raised together. I've never seen anyone handle a vehicle as well as Mike, except maybe for Lucas. But then, accidents do happen even to the best drivers. He was coming off a shift and he might have been tired."

"The police report said the driver's side was dented as well as the passenger's side."

"Yeah, it was, which means someone could have hit him, and then he hit the tree. There could be endless possibilities when you think about it."

"Give me a few," she said, wanting to visualize the accident herself.

Nick shrugged and turned his eyes toward the ceiling, contemplating an answer. "Well, he could have swerved to avoid something like an animal crossing the road, lost control, traveled farther and gone over the bank. We're still working on that particular theory, Elise, if it makes you feel better. Maybe he swerved to avoid another car coming toward him and crossing the center line."

"Who filed the accident report?"

"Initially the township, but then because it was one of our own involved, the state police also investigated."

"And you've seen the report?" she asked.

"Yeah, what are you getting at?" Confused, he squinted at her.

"Something someone missed?"

"On the car?"

She nodded. "On the car or on the report. What make and color of car was Mike driving?"

"A white Honda." He heaved a sigh. "Tell you what, I'll take a look at it one more time. I'll have to do it on my own time, though."

She smiled. "Thanks. Take Fritz with you, will you? His insurance-minded brain is pretty good at picking out unique details. One last question."

"Shoot."

"If a cop wanted to hide something...anything, like money, perhaps. What would he be thinking? What would be going on inside his head?"

Nick chewed the inside of his lip. "He'd stay away from traditional places. Safes, cupboards, mattresses, mirrors, closets, the logical ones every average Joe falls for. He'd choose a spot so obvious no one would ever think about it, a place you or the public might pass by without giving it a second thought. You know the theory of overlooking something right under your nose?"

"Thanks, you've been a big help." Elise rose and extended her hand.

He shook it with a hard, firm grip. "I'll try to keep you updated."

"I appreciate it, really I do." She smiled warmly and collected her purse.

"I have a question," he said and returned her smile with an equally warm one. "Are you and Fisher a solid thing yet?"

"It's beginning to look that way," she admitted.

"I was afraid of that," he said and shook his head. "Just my luck."

Chapter Seventeen

With the top down on the Corvette, the sun shining bright, and a soft warm breeze sifting through her hair, Elise drove into Scranton enjoying the mild spring day. Fritz and Cindy were taking Todd over to Cindy's house for dinner with plans to raid the attic for old baseball cards stashed there by her brothers when they finally outgrew their mania for collecting cardboard.

It was Elise's turn to make dinner, which she decided to have at the cottage with Lucas while they reviewed the latest renovations. Her first and only thought was take-out. Mentally, she clicked off a list of possible choices they hadn't already tried. She could handle these domestic glitches, she told herself with a smug air of satisfaction, as long as there were enough restaurants and fast food joints to establish a rotation that didn't repeat itself so often anyone noticed. Even Martha Stewart would have been proud of her ingenuity.

Chicken. Fried chicken would be perfect. She grabbed her cell, dialed the number of a small mom-and-pop restaurant just down the street from Pedmo's office, and swung the car onto the highway leading to Scranton.

A half hour later, Mom and Pop were easily on her list of lifelong friends when she picked up the tantalizing, neatly packaged, white Styrofoam containers, complete with plastic plates and silverware and dinner napkins. Grinning, she headed for the car, resisting the urge to belt out *O Sole Mio*, a tribute to the sun, as she stashed the food away on the floor of the passenger seat. While she was in the area, she had hoped to make a quick stop at Pedmo's office. It was no secret Twila Pedmo was a workaholic, often working long after the finish of an eight-hour workday and many times on weekends. Sundays were no exception.

Since Elise had talked with the elderly woman on Saturday, a nagging thought kept haunting her. If there were anyone who knew the true identity of Mike Fisher's father, Twila Pedmo would be the most logical choice. Even if she didn't know, she'd be the most knowledgeable person who might suggest some leads. Elise would also ask Twila Pedmo what she knew about Mary Jo and Ted Meyer. Twila and Mary Jo's mother still played in the same bridge club. From what she had witnessed, Mary Jo's marriage was hardly a loving, warm one. She had the feeling Ted Meyer, like his father, was a pompous, verbally abusive cop, father, and husband.

With a million thoughts circling relentlessly in her mind, Elise put the car in gear and drove up the street. However, it was Jack Morrison's shiny white Mercedes parked in the lot instead of Twila Pedmo's. Frowning, Elise hesitated, torn by indecision, and circled the block. When she arrived back at the lot, she pulled her car into a parking space in the farthest corner, away from any window view. It would be best, she finally convinced herself, to confront Jack Morrison and find out the pathetic excuse he had for abandoning her the other night.

Angry raised voices assaulted her the minute she stepped into the main lobby, even before she rounded the corner to the reception area leading to a maze of back offices. She stopped just outside the hallway and peered down the corridor. Ted Meyer was inside Jack Morrison's office, the door partially ajar, and from the sound of his disgruntled voice, a very unhappy Ted Meyer.

"I'm warning you, Jack," Ted Meyer grumbled. "One more stunt like last night and you'll be finished. Driving under the influence is a serious offense, especially with your track record. You were lucky you hauled your backside out when you did. You were barely one step ahead of the state police."

"One step is all I needed."

"Get your head screwed on, Jack. You sound like a goddamn kid. Grow up, you're an adult now."

"What's the matter, Ted? You afraid I'll take a vacation behind bars, and you won't get your money?" Jack Morrison's voice was becoming as heated as Meyer's.

"Yeah, maybe I am. Mary Jo has been badgering me about the land we planned to buy for a camp. I can't stall her much longer."

"I'll get the money. Just give me a few more days."

"I'm giving you until next Friday."

Jack Morrison's voice rose an octave. "You threatening me? You're in this as deep as I am, Ted. Just remember that!"

The door to Morrison's office squeaked on its hinges as if someone had laid a hand on the knob to leave. The sound jolted Elise upright from the wall she had been leaning against. Icy fingers crawled up her spine at the thought of being caught eavesdropping. Slowly she backed out into the entrance hall, turned quickly, and dashed down the steps to her car. Hands shaking, she slid into the driver's seat, fumbling with the keys before she jammed them in the ignition and started the engine. Her eyes darted nervously toward the building while she backed around the corner, maneuvering the car out into the right lane to head for the cottage. There was no way on earth she could drive through the building's parking lot and take the chance either Jack or Ted might get a glimpse of her from Jack's office window above.

Her mind scrambled to make sense of what she had just heard. She wondered what sort of deal Morrison and Meyer had gotten themselves involved with. She wondered why Jack Morrison owed money to Ted Meyer. Was it the same money Mary Jo had referred to when she told her they were saving to buy a cabin and some land?

With more questions than before swirling around in her head, she drove to the cottage. She pulled her car into the gravel drive leading to the back of the cottage and parked. She was an hour early. Lucas had agreed to meet her at five that afternoon.

J.B. was coming out of the side door carrying a load of empty boxes nestled inside each other and met her with a warm grin and a twinkle in his eye.

"You're moving in Lucas's things already?" she asked. She hefted the food from the car as a wave of loneliness and disappointment washed over her. Lucas would be moving out of the farmhouse soon, and although she hated to admit it, she discovered she was growing fond of having him around. She enjoyed their daily banter sessions, even when their opinions were diametrically opposed.

"I'm putting the finishing touches on a few things I unpacked from storage and a few personal things he wanted shipped up from Atlanta," J.B. replied. He set the boxes on the ground beside the doghouse. "Pretty soon this place will be hopping, and once he moves in with the kid, it will be rocking. Did you know Lucas is planning to buy a puppy for Todd? He's looking at Golden Retrievers. Oh, to be the flea on that puppy's back when Lucas has to house train it."

Elise laughed. "Get serious, J.B. He gets along just fine with Bess."

J.B. chuckled. "Only because Bess has a generous canine personality, and you and Fritz are the ones responsible for feeding her. Lucas is an impatient sort. If he owned a garbage dump, I doubt he could keep fruit flies."

She laughed. "How long have you known Lucas?"

"Six years now, and I hope fifty more."

"You're very loyal."

"He's easy to be loyal to. I ran out of money in my last year of college and desperately needed a job. Lucas hired me on. At first, I helped in the restoration garage until he realized I was a computer geek. He dislikes computers with a passion, so he asked me if I'd manage his business ventures and communications. We realized we were compatible opposites. He does the head work, and as his right hand man, I handle the technical end and other things that sometimes frustrate him."

"And who made the decision to follow me to Two Horses?"

J.B. blushed furiously and stared at the ground a

moment before raising his eyes level to hers. "Well, to be honest, Nick, Lucas, and I knew the reputation of Two Horses. I'll admit they do get some good bands banging out some lively country and western tunes."

"What do you know about Monique?"

J.B. shrugged dismissively. "Monique was a handy diversion before Lucas became grounded. Maybe wiser, too?" He paused a moment, to collect his thoughts. "The woman is an intellectual lightweight. If she had another brain, it would be lonely." He looked at her with a serious gaze. "Elise, Lucas has no interest in Monique. He adores you, surely you know? He has for years and always will, whether you return the devotion or not."

Surprised, she stared at him.

J.B. shuffled his feet, rubbed the back of his neck, and glanced away. "Look, I'm out of line here. I shouldn't be getting involved in Lucas's private affairs. Forget what I said." He frowned, then gestured toward the shed. "I put the boxes I thought might contain Todd's things on top of the others so you can reach them more easily. Eventually, Lucas wants to clear the shed out. A lot of the boxes are filled with junk."

He moved toward the open trunk of his car. "If I bring in the last box of books Lucas wants stashed in his office, will you stack the contents on the bottom shelf for me? The notebook on top of everything goes in his right hand desk drawer. I really gotta run, Elise. There's a client who's coming in to the garage and wants to lease a fleet of SUVs."

She nodded and watched him remove the last box from his trunk. "Lead on. Take the box into the kitchen, leave it on the counter, and I'll take it from there."

As soon as J.B. left, Elise set the take-out dinners on the small kitchen table, hefted the box of books from the counter, and made her way to the small room at the back of the house. It had once been a sewing room and was now converted into an office for Lucas. She paused for a second at the door, feeling uneasy about entering a room that was now his private working area and filled with his personal belongings.

Finally, when the weight of the box became unbearable, she pushed the door open. The rich cherry desk she had selected occupied the center of the room, decorated in shades of navy and gray, and behind it, matching floor-to-ceiling bookcases nestled against the wall. It was perfect, just as she had envisioned it. The contractor and decorator had followed her instructions flawlessly. Soft white valances hung from the long mullioned windows and sunlight poured into the room through the blinds and danced on the polished dark hardwood floor, refinished and squeaky clean. A chair rail with soft tan grass cloth above it encircled half the room.

Elise set the box on the corner of the desk and moved to the bookcases, surprised by the collection of pictures in a potpourri of expensive silver- and gold-plated frames and occupying the two middle shelves. Except for small pictures of his grandmother and his brother with Todd, the remainder of the collection consisted of snapshots of herself, her mother and father, and her brothers. In the center of the collection was an enlarged, high-school era picture of Fritz, Thomas, Lucas and herself eating watermelon under a gnarled old apple tree outside the farmhouse kitchen door. Fritz and Lucas were having a seed-spitting contest.

Turning back to the desk, she felt her breath catch in her throat in surprise. Beneath a banker's lamp with a milk glass shade, a small college graduation picture of herself stared back at her. Wondering how he had ever managed to get his hands on it, she slumped down in the chair and picked it up. Only her brothers and her father had the picture. He had to have gone through the trouble of having a copy made from one of theirs.

Replacing it, she removed the notebook from the box and pulled the desk drawer open. Just as she was about to slide it inside, she noticed a small, maroon-colored scrapbook. Curiosity, she muttered to herself, had always been her worst enemy. Her hand hovered above it. She hesitated a second, then picked it up, flipped open the cover open, and gasped. Everything from the first newspaper clippings covering her high school track records to the announcement of her acceptance to Ohio State had been carefully and chronologically preserved beneath the plastic sleeves. There was even a local article about her appointment to Winston and Sanders.

A folded, yellowed and worn sheet of lined tablet paper tumbled out from among the pages. She carefully unfolded it, surprised to find a long-forgotten note she had scribbled to Lucas when she was in her first year of high school. It was asking him—no, telling him—to save her spot on their neighborhood sandlot baseball team. "Dear Lucas," she had written. "I'm coming late to the game after school today because I have track practice until five. Save second base for me or face torture or death. Love, Lizzie."

"You always had a blunt, knock-'em-over-the-head approach when you wanted to get your point across.

You're busted, you know."

Elise's head jerked up at the sound of Lucas's voice. He stood in the doorway, his hand shoved into his back pocket of his Levi's. She could tell he had recently showered. His hair, still damp, curled over the back of a light blue chambray shirt, sleeves rolled up to show strong arms, lightly sprinkled with hair. He was all muscle and male from head to toe, and just looking at him made her heart skip wildly.

"Lucas, I..." She paused, embarrassed, unable to speak. Quickly she shoved the note back into the scrapbook and slipped it back into the drawer. She rose.

"I know what this must look like."

His face held no trace of anger as she moved toward him.

"It's all right, Liz. I knew I could never keep it a secret once I decided to move here," he said softly.

"You've been keeping tabs on me for all these years?"

"Not exactly keeping tabs per se, just following your career. Come on, Lizzie, it's been no secret even with Fritz I've always admired you from afar. You've been my first choice of all the women I've known." He reached up and tenderly tucked a wisp of hair behind her ear as he stared into her eyes. When she smiled, he bent and kissed her lightly on the lips for barely a second and then again for two until they both found themselves pushed to that electrifying moment of intensity where no one else exists. Elise broke the embrace, burying her face in his shirt as he kissed her neck and pulled her frantically closer to him.

"Lucas," she whispered into his shirt, "this may not be such a good..."

"Shh," he whispered. "I've wanted you so badly for so long now."

He swept her up in his arms and headed for the bedroom where he set her down and like a raging fire taking hold, they stared at each other for barely a second before their arms and hands tangled with each other. Buttons and snaps popped, zippers scraped, and clothes went flying to all corners of the room. When they finally sank naked into the soft fluffy comforter on the king-sized bed, Elise heard him tenderly whisper into her ear, "There really is heaven on earth, Lizzie, my love. Let me show you."

Chapter Eighteen

Lucas sat on the front porch of the Springer residence watching the sun climb over the horizon and turn the fields and treetops to a hazy rose, pink, and violet. Its rays reflected off the tin roof on the milk house by the barn and sent flashes of light like white firecrackers soaring into the air.

He was in love with Lizzie Springer, truly in love with her, and the thought made him gloriously happy for the first time in his life. Last night was more than he had ever hoped for. She was everything he had dreamed about and wanted since he was sixteen years old. But doubts had a way of creeping up on him now with the dawn of a new morning.

Elise was a stubborn and proud woman. Proud of her creative accomplishments. Proud she had achieved such a level of success. But would she want him as much as he wanted her? Would she ever consider giving up everything she had on the West Coast to stay on the East Coast? He doubted it, and he frowned at the troubling thought. She'd have to be convinced and he'd have to find a way to convince her, even if he had to resort to bribery. Late last night, after they had left the cottage to return to the farm, he had set the wheels in motion. This time Elise Springer was not getting away from him so easily.

His thoughts were interrupted by the sound of a car

coming up the drive. J.B. stopped and hopped out. With a gray portfolio slapping against his right thigh, he scaled the steps two at a time.

"I made the deal. It went as slick as soft butter on warm bread. Levinson was thrilled to take on a serious interested investor willing to put up twenty-five percent on one hotel alone. And guess where he's building the first one?"

"Wilkes-Barre or Scranton?"

"Wilkes-Barre. How'd you know?"

"Come on, J.B. The man is getting old, thinking of retiring. This five-hotel deal is his final hurrah. His wife was raised near Wilkes-Barre. It doesn't take a Mensa mind to figure out one of them will be located here. I'm assuming you chose to invest in his Pennsylvania venture for us?"

"No, Iowa, you goofball, in the middle of cornfields." He eased back and balanced himself against the porch rail. He grinned. "Of course, Pennsylvania."

Lucas took the portfolio and leafed through it thoughtfully.

"Does Elise know?" J.B. asked.

"That's the one piece of the jigsaw puzzle I haven't been able to put into place." Lucas made a sour face.

"Oh, man, oh, man," J.B. said, shaking his head. "You like to live dangerously."

Lucas stiffened and gave him an irritated look. "What choice do I have? If I tell her, she'll think I'm intervening to keep her here. Or worse yet, she'll think it's the reason she got the contract for the hotel design. Either way, when she finds out, she's going to be madder than a snake caught in a hay baler, as her dad would so eloquently put it."

"But Levinson doesn't know there's a connection. I made sure of it. He's agreeable to transacting business directly through me."

"Then let's hope Lizzie doesn't find out until I can find the right time to explain everything. It's a good investment, right? You said so yourself."

J.B. pushed himself off the railing. "Yes, it's an extraordinary investment, but there's a big difference between a great deal and convincing a furious woman it's a great one. You two need to find a way to get on the same page, boss."

"Same page? Hell, we're not even in the same book," Lucas said woodenly.

****

Elise paced in front of her drawing board in her bedroom, reaching for her cell phone and withdrawing her hand just as she was about to touch it. The pit of her stomach ached as if she had swallowed a packet of straight pins and they were regrouping to make an upward march for freedom.

Long before sunrise, she had been awake trying to work up enough courage to call Morton Levinson. Ever since she was old enough to speak three coherent words, she had been a brave, assertive individual, yet every time she thought about telling him she couldn't return to California, every ounce of stamina she owned deserted her quicker than she could spit out the word hello.

She reached for the phone for what had to be the tenth time when it rang. Caught off guard, she jumped high enough to clear Bess lying on the floor beside her. Fumbling with the on button, she jammed the phone to her ear, willing her jangled nerves to be calm.

"Hello, Elise Springer."

"Where have you been?" Nick Peters asked curtly.

"Well, a very good morning to you, too," she shot back, relieved to hear anyone's voice but Levinson's. "Sounds like someone missed his morning coffee or perhaps lost it in the landfill on his desk."

"Funny, real funny. I tried to get you last night," he said.

"Didn't Cindy tell you I was at the cottage checking on the renovations?" She had no desire to tell Nick Peters where she'd spent half the night.

"Are you in a location to speak privately?"

"Yes. What did you find?" Elise moved to bed where she sat down.

"I took your advice and re-examined the car."

Elise waited.

"And we messed up big time, or rather the township police did." He paused, and the sound of papers rustled on his desk. "I found paint flecks on the bumper of Mike Fisher's car."

"What color?"

"White, like his, but from the lab reports, the remnants of another white vehicle."

"So someone did run him off the road," Elise said with a bitter edge to her voice.

"Someone hit him, that's for sure."

"Where do we go from here, Nick?"

"I don't know. We need to think it through. We just can't mosey around the Scranton area scratching off paint samples from every white vehicle we come across. People get a mite touchy about their cars."

Morrison's white Mercedes flashed through Elise's

mind. "Maybe we can start by checking out some body shops around town and seeing whether any were busy after Mike's death."

"No way, Elise. Someone who caused an accident where another person was killed, or even injured, wouldn't waltz into a body shop in a hundred mile radius of here unless he has a few loose screws."

As much as she hated to admit it, he was right. "Okay, you work your end and I'll work mine," she suggested. "One more thing, when Mike died that night, where was Todd?"

There was a pause. "He was at the Meyer house," Nick said. "Mike was working three to eleven, and when he was on a late shift he usually let Todd sleep over until the next morning. In fact, Mike's last phone call was to check on the kid."

"Who else knows about the paint flecks?"

"Just you and me, and let's keep it that way."

"Okay. Keep in touch, will you?" She hung up the phone and collapsed into the chair in front of the computer. *What was happening here?* She parted the curtains and looked out the bedroom window onto the lawn where a noisy pair of jenny wrens was busy building a nest in a weathered birdhouse hanging from a huge oak tree that once held her old rope swing. How could she leave Scranton now? Certainly not now, when they might be close to solving Mike's murder.

****

Fifteen minutes later, Lucas found her staring at the monitor.

"You'd do better with the television downstairs," he said, stepping into the room. "It has a better selection of channels and a remote. The picture you're watching is a monotonous rerun." He moved up behind her and kissed her softly on the side of the neck. She smelled delicious, the light fresh scent of something floral. Her nearness brought back memories of the night before.

Elise glanced up at him and smiled, despite her dreary mood. "I guess you're right, but at least the screen saver doesn't have any surprises. I know how everything is going to end."

"I take it you haven't made the call to Levinson?"

"What if he says no?" She sighed.

"What if he says yes?" He rested his hands gently on her shoulders and began to knead the knots out. "Lizzie, it's not like you to be a coward."

She drew in a deep breath and exhaled, angling her head so her eyes could reach his. "It's not that simple. The man is a multi-millionaire whose family made tons of money on railroads and coal in this state. He's used to getting his own way. He's...he's fickle and quirky."

Confused, he stared at her. "Would you care to explain further?"

She laughed. "Jeez, Lucas," she mumbled, "I didn't mean it the way it sounded. I meant this dear old man is a little more eccentric than most."

"He's just like everyone else, Lizzie. His wants and needs are the same. He eats, he sleeps, he works, he loves, and he wants to have a family who loves him back."

Kneeling beside her, he took her hands in his. "It's not Levinson that's bothering you, is it? It's me and my money."

"It's not the money," she admitted. How could she tell him their relationship was doomed? She could think of no way it could it ever work. Eventually, he'd be in

Scranton, she'd be in San Francisco. And there was Todd. The kid wanted and needed a mother. "I'm just trying to understand where we're headed, Lucas. I'm so confused."

"Because I don't fit into your plans?"

"Maybe," she agreed sadly. *Maybe because I don't fit into yours.* She knew eventually she'd have to go back to California, whether she wanted to or not. It was where her life was, where she started her career, where her apartment and belongings were.

He rose and paced the room. "Good God, Elise, it's fine to be driven, to have goals, to plan your future, but life and love don't always fit into tidy little mental squares."

"I know. I know." She felt the screams of frustration at the back of her throat. Since she had arrived, her life was unfolding like one loose-as-a-goose screenplay where all the actors were ad-libbing. "I've always been a planner, Lucas. Organized, time driven, and in control."

"And in love?"

"No," she whispered honestly and shook her head. "Not until now."

His anger faded, and he felt his heart swell to twice its size. He crossed the room and hauled her to her feet, his mouth finding hers. The kiss was so long, so hard, and so deep that he hated for the moment to end. Finally, he stepped back and clamped his hands on her shoulders. "Make the call, Elise, you're driving me crazy—and everyone else for that matter. We can sort out the rest of this later."

The doorbell rang.

He looked in the direction of the sound with a

disgruntled frown. "Now what?"

"It's probably Fritz," she said. "He must have forgotten his keys."

"Good God, we should just adopt him and make our lives less complicated." He headed for the door. "Are you certain he really owns a house in town?"

She laughed above the sound of the doorbell's incessant ringing.

"Rosie's Posies delivering for a Miss Elise Springer." The young delivery boy pushed the huge, tissue-covered vase of flowers into Lucas's hands and clambered down the steps to his van.

Bewildered and equally curious, Lucas carried the arrangement to the kitchen and planted it on the counter beside the coffee pot.

It was much too soon for any type of celebrating, he decided, as he paused to eye the delicate wrapping where a card was stapled to the top.

A secret admirer? Her brothers? Someone from work? Chuck Sanders, for instance?

The last supposition was as aggravating as it was plausible. The man was one royal pain in the ass. He'd bet dollars for dipsticks, he was trying to lure her back to San Francisco. At least this time the man had the common sense to send the whole bouquet instead of squeezing the life out of each petal for a pathetic ounce of perfume. Exotic, rich perfume, Lucas reminded himself with a pang of jealousy. The kind she adored. The kind that sent his head swimming every time he was near her.

Frowning, he went to the cupboard and pulled out a fry pan. Minutes later, as the bacon began to sizzle, he heard her squeals of excitement from the bedroom above.

"Yes, it's a go with Levinson!" she shouted and flew down the stairs with Bess at her heels. "We're going to meet at the end of the week. And guess where? Of all places—Wilkes-Barre!"

She burst into the kitchen. A radiant look of pleasure made her even more beautiful. "Oh, Lucas, he wants me, only me," she said breathlessly.

And so do I. A fierce possessiveness made him want to explode. He watched with fascination as she twirled about the kitchen, stopping to plant a kiss on his cheek.

"This calls for a celebration," he said. "Let's have a spectacular lunch."

She groaned. "Lucas, I can't. I have so much to do. I need to buy a new suit. I need to tell Fritz. I need to call Dad or go out to see him."

"I was thinking we'd celebrate by having lunch at the hospital with your Dad. He'll be ecstatic."

"You mean it? Oh, Lucas, what a terrific idea. How thoughtful."

"Not really," he said. "I figure I'll have you all to myself tonight." He caught her face in his hands and bussed her lips briefly. "Unless you want to start right now with what I had in mind for a celebration later. There's no one around, if you haven't noticed. Todd is in pre-school this morning."

She laughed. "You're going to become addicting."

"I'm hoping to." He grinned, then remembered the flowers. "Looks like Chuck Sanders knew you'd cinch the deal." He gestured to the bouquet on the counter.

Her excitement faded and her face grew sober. "No, I don't think so. Levinson said he'd call Paul and

Chuck later today." She turned to the flowers and removed the card.

"This is from Jack Morrison. He's sorry for deserting me on Saturday night." She jiggled the card in her hand. "Isn't it sweet?"

The mention of Jack Morrison's name was like an unexpected punch to the gut. Using every ounce of energy to hide his disgust, he eyed the mixed flower bouquet she was unwrapping. *Oh, yeah, real sweet.*

****

Elise watched her father smile, eyes closed, as he relished the first bite of General Tso's chicken. They were in the lounge, Anton's casted foot propped up on a footstool, crutches lying beside his chair, Styrofoam container on his lap.

"Let's hope Lizzie gets many, many more offers while I'm stuck here if you plan to bring real food each time we celebrate," Anton said.

"If this is real food, we've been having a hell of a lot of it lately." Lucas shot a sideways look at Elise.

Elise felt her face grow red, remembering the fried chicken dinner at the cottage finally consumed many hours later and in bed. "My creative energy stops just short of the kitchen, Lucas. I warned you the first day." She hoped her father hadn't noticed the secretive exchange.

He did.

"Neither of you look like you're starving," Anton said, "at least not for food." He wrapped a string of lo mein noodles around his fork. "I talked to Twila the other day." He hesitated, his gaze fastening on Lucas. "She says your father is lying. There's no doubt in her mind he's Mike's father."

Fork in midair, Elise stared at him. "Why would he lie?"

Anton shook his head. "I don't know."

"She's absolutely sure?" Elise saw no point in disclosing J.B. had confiscated the glass Lucas's father used at the bar and requested a DNA comparison with Mike Fisher. Unfortunately, it would take a few weeks before the results would be back from a lab in Atlanta and they would know for sure.

"She's certain enough to bet on it."

Anton glanced at Lucas. "She suspects your father may be struggling with guilt after all these years, Lucas, and was trying to hurt you in any way possible. Or it may be his idea of escaping it. Your mother never started drinking until your father packed up and left. Twila said she would have never turned to another man. She loved him beyond everything else."

"Even Mike and me," Lucas muttered bitterly.

Anton Springer nodded painfully. "I'm afraid so, but don't blame yourself, Lucas. There was nothing either of you could have done to make it right. Sometimes there is only one real love in your life. Any other relationships are strictly sexual or for companionship."

Elise took a steadying breath. She could see the wounded look in Lucas's eyes, the pain on her father's face. One had lost a mother he loved but never knew and the other had lost the wife he knew and loved.

Her father continued in a serious, subdued voice. "When you find a relationship so pure and genuine, you'd be a fool to let it go, no matter what the obstacles. Life's like a good poker hand. When those aces come along you hold onto them."

He stared at both of them and finally went back to his meal as silence descended like a soothing balm on the aches they were all feeling. It wasn't until the meal was almost finished when Elise spoke. "Did Mrs. Pedmo say anything about Mary Jo Meyer?"

"Besides she's married to a pompous piece of garbage?"

"Dad!"

"It's the truth, honey. The man is a control freak."

"So why doesn't she leave?"

"Come on, Lizzie, you know the answer." He eased himself back into his chair. "Three kids, no degree, and a husband who's a cop. Just where could she run to where she couldn't be found? Her mother offered to help her finish her early childhood education degree, but she had the distinct feeling it was vetoed by Ted, not Mary Jo."

"She's afraid of him," Elise whispered. She rose and walked to the window.

"The entire Meyer family always had a mean streak in them." Lucas stood and moved closer to her. She could smell the scent of his lime aftershave. His nearness made her heart beat faster. "And what do they become? Police officers. Just what we need—angry people to uphold our laws." Lucas shook his head wearily.

Anton Springer squinted over at his daughter. "You know, Lizzie, if you want to know a man, find out what makes him mad. Maybe Ted Meyer would be a good specimen to start with since he always seems aggravated."

****

The rest of the afternoon went by in a whirlwind

for Elise. With her emotions vacillating so abruptly, she felt like a human yo-yo. She was delighted when she found the perfect navy blue suit in a little shop in downtown Scranton, but disappointed when she thought about leaving Lucas to go back to San Francisco and handle Levinson's designs. She was elated when she stopped by Fritz's office to tell him of her latest success and then frightened when she revealed to him Mike Fisher might truly have been murdered. She grew mellow and depressed each time she thought of leaving Todd.

Her emotions warring, her stomach churning, she finally arrived at the farm, only to find her answering machine held an even greater surprise.

Paul Winston had called and fired her.

Chapter Nineteen

Thursdays were slow days in town, but obviously not at the Springer farm, Elise decided when she pulled her Corvette in the driveway leading to the farmhouse. She stared curiously at the sight before her. The place looked like a parking lot for an outdoor rock concert. Along with Lucas's Suburban and restored Trans Am, her dad's pick-up, Fritz's jeep, and Cindy's beat-up Ford, three cars she didn't recognize and a black stretch limo were jammed into the driveway and spilling onto the lawn.

Bewildered, she grabbed the dry-cleaned clothes on the passenger's seat and hurried up the steps. Fritz greeted her on the porch, his hands jammed in his pockets, change jingling against his nervous fingers. Bess, lying behind a porch chair, jumped up to greet her, tail wagging with glee.

"What's going on?" She draped the plastic-encased garments over the top rail and bent to give Bess an affectionate pat on her head. "I leave for fifteen minutes to get aspirin and stop at the drycleaners and the place turns into a car lot."

"The invasion of the lunatics," Fritz said and followed it with a sour scowl. "I'd kill for a double scotch on ice. All I wanted to do was take Cindy out to Nay Aug Park for a quiet walk."

"That bad?" Elise smiled. "Who's watching

Todd?"

"Right now he's upstairs trying to find his Atlanta Braves baseball cap. He's begging me to take him for some ice cream." Still scowling, he jerked a thumb over his shoulder. "Before you go in there, I guess I'd better fill you in on all the whack jobs."

"Whack jobs?" Her eyes traveled past his shoulders to the screen door where a chorus of voices was raised in angry pandemonium.

"Chuck Sanders is in the kitchen and is hoping he can beg you to come back to work. Monique is in the living room and is trying to beg Lucas to come back to her. Paul Winston is camped out on the steps in the hallway, looking like he just stepped out of an episode of the television show Mom always liked. You know, the one where you enter another dimension?"

"*The Twilight Zone*?"

"That's it. Oh, and Mort Levinson is upstairs using your bathroom."

She blinked, unsure she comprehended the monologue. "Mort Levinson? *The* Mort Levinson from San Francisco is upstairs in *my* bathroom?"

He nodded. "Yep, I figured it was better he used your bathroom upstairs than parade him past the display of tempers in the living room."

She looked down in horror at her cut-off jeans and tank top. Why, oh why, didn't she take time to properly dress this morning? She looked like Daisy Duke in running shoes. She frantically tried to smooth down tendrils of hair escaping from a sloppy ponytail she had tied up into a knot at the back of her head.

"Fritz, my bathroom is not fit for human use. I was in a hurry this morning and left it a total disaster." She envisioned a rotund Levinson stepping over her lingerie, dodging wet towels, and fighting a counter full of cosmetics to wash his hands at the sink.

"What does it have to do with the old boy using the can?"

"Nothing, nothing at all." She sighed. "If it's too late to fix it, it's too late to worry about it. How do I look?" She pulled at the hem of her shorts to no avail and straightened the spaghetti straps on the tank top.

"Like you're ready to compete in a mud wrestling contest?"

Positioned between them, Bess gave out a mournful whine as her sad brown eyes rolled toward the excitement inside the house. Fritz bent and scratched her behind her ears. "Too crowded in there for you, too, old girl?" He glanced hopefully toward the front door, but no one appeared. "Oh, by the way, Levinson wants to go for ice cream with Todd, Cindy, and me, but he wants to talk to you first."

"He wants to go for *ice cream*? What idiot invited him?"

"I did," Fritz said. "Well, actually, my little 42-inch sidekick invited him. It did get a little confusing, Liz, with all three circus rings in motion at one time."

"Fritz, have you lost your mind?"

"No, no, my dear, he certainly has not." Mort Levinson stepped out onto the porch. His paunchy figure was stuffed into a pair of casual tan slacks and a dark green golf shirt. Expensive brown Docksiders finished off his attire. He smiled. "Although I can't vouch for the others in there. Charming house you have here, Elise. It's wonderfully cozy and efficiently planned. I like your spacious farmhouse kitchen. You designed it?"

"Th-thank you. Yes, I did, when I was still in college." Elise was unsure what to say next. "Mr. Levinson, I'm—"

"Shocked, I imagine?" He grinned widely. "I really didn't mean to intrude, my dear, but my wife insisted we go shopping at the mall and then take a ride in the country so I thought I'd just stop by while she shopped and double check to be sure everything is still on for the meeting."

"I'm not sure." She hesitated. "You haven't heard? I've been fired."

"Not as far as I'm concerned, you haven't. I spoke briefly with Chuck Sanders, and he assures me Paul Winston is just suffering from a bout of insanity. The meeting is still on, but we've moved it to Scranton. I'm looking forward to your ideas and thoughts."

A bout of insanity? Elise had to restrain herself from rolling her eyes. Winston had suffered several bouts since she'd signed on with the firm seven years ago.

The screen door slammed behind them, and Todd came racing out onto the porch, interrupting with a shout, "Eee-lise, Eee-lise, Mr. Levinson is going to take me for a ride in his car! Look, have you seen it? It's as big as two cars glued together. We're going for ice cream!" Barreling into her legs and throwing his arms around her, he almost knocked her back down the steps in his excitement. "Can I go? Pleeeeease? I can't ask Uncle Lucas because Fritz says he's busy getting yelled at."

From behind them, the sound of a heated female voice drifted out the open living room window.

Elise looked up nervously, her arms still encircling Todd as she refocused her gaze on Mort Levinson. "You sure want to do this, Mr. Levinson? You don't have to feel obligated."

"Elise, I love kids. This is such a glorious change of pace from being in a stuffy city, surrounded by dolts who are convinced they know more about investments than a dozen Wall Street bankers." He ruffled Todd on the head. "And from the looks of things inside, an ice cream parlor is by far the more civilized place to be at the moment."

Cindy stepped through the door, a small gold purse slung over her shoulder. "Are we ready? I've never ridden in a stretch limo. This is so cool!"

"If it's all right with you," Mort Levinson said to Elise, "your brother is going to take his car so he and Cindy can go up to Nay Aug Park afterwards. I'll drop Todd off at the house before I pick up my wife, with your permission, of course."

Her head still spinning, Elise released her grip on Todd and nodded. "Sure, that's fine."

Levinson started down the steps, then turned. It was obvious he had not missed her shorts and top. His eyes wandered over her, then drifted to her legs. An impish smile turned the corner of his lips upward. "You really should convince Winston and Sanders to have office dress-down days, my dear. I'd be inclined to make all my appointments on only those days."

Elise laughed and felt her cheeks grow hot. "I can assure you it won't be high on our punch list at the moment."

"No, I suppose not." He grinned.

Another series of harsh words poured out in a hot

stream onto the porch.

"What a perfect beginning to a beautiful morning," Elise muttered more to herself than to those around her and looked through the screen.

"Ah, kiddo, this is where survival instincts kick in and sane men depart," Fritz said. "We're out of here."

"You'd better hurry in there before the lid flies off," Levinson urged, and with a quick wave of his hand, proceeded down the sidewalk. "They are sorely in need of your charm. Come, Todd." He gestured to the sparkling limo. "Let me give you your first lesson in drinking orange juice from a mobile bar." He turned to Fritz, still lingering on the porch. "Cindy, Todd, and I will meet you at the ice cream parlor."

Fritz nodded, but waited beside Elise for a moment.

"Nice guy," Fritz watched them pile into the limo. "Sure wish Dad could meet him. They'd like each other." He started for the steps as more shouting floated out.

"Wait!" Elise grabbed him by the sleeve, spinning him around to face her before he could slip from her grip. "What am I supposed to do?" She held fast.

He laughed. "I have no idea. Dysfunctional people are out of my league. Besides therapy, I'd suggest duct tape."

"This is a nightmare." She peered at her brother with a pleading look.

Grinning, he held up his hands, palms out. "If it looks like there might be any bloodshed, hide the sharp objects and see if they have life insurance. The last part is the important part." Elise watched him as he fled to his car, whistling a tune sounding like "Another One

Bites the Dust."

With her stomach flopping like a fish out of water, Elise turned toward the door. Paul Winston, obviously distraught, jumped up from where he was seated on the bottom step of the staircase as soon as the screen door slammed shut behind her. His face was as pale as the light tan Armani suit he wore. His usually impeccably styled hair was plastered to the side of his head as if he had been holding it in his hands.

"Elise."

"Paul." She fell silent and studied him.

"Elise." He paused, clearing his throat. "Elise, this is a huge mess. An unfortunate misunderstanding." His voice rose in a pleading tone. "You've got to help me. Levinson hates me. Chuck hates me—"

"And quite frankly, Paul, at the moment, I'm not too terribly fond of you myself."

He winced. "Elise, please."

She drew in a breath, torn by indecision. Never had she seen him so upset. On the other hand, she decided, his miserable condition triggered a small sense of satisfaction. She remembered how often over the years she had patched the broken spirits of clients he purposely and verbally injured, either to drive home a key point or to get his own way. She decided to let him squirm.

"Why don't you have a seat out on the porch where it's more comfortable and quiet?" Unless she missed her guess, he was wearing dog hair and mud on the seat of his five-hundred-dollar silk suit. The steps had not been vacuumed for a few days. "I'd really like to talk with Chuck first."

"Sure, sure," he agreed.

"Would you like something to drink?"

"Water. Water would be fine when you get a chance." He cleared his throat. "Elise, you're upset, aren't you?"

For the first time she heard genuine concern and maybe even a tinge of remorse. "Paul, I can be anything I want to be. I'm not your employee any longer. You fired me, remember?" She turned before he could respond and entered the kitchen.

Chuck Sanders rose from his seat by the kitchen table where a briefcase and a stack of papers fought for room with a half-filled glass of apple juice and an opened bag of Oreo cookies.

"I helped myself to your refrigerator, Elise. Your brother had his hands full sorting out the arriving guests." He paused as if he wanted to say more, but he seemed unsure of the type of welcome he'd receive.

"You've never been a guest, Chuck. My mentor, my instructor, my best friend, but never a guest. Certainly not here in my home." She moved toward him, and he enveloped her in a giant hug.

"Gawd, Elise, I've missed you."

From the living room, a string of expletives filtered in to them.

He released her and looked warily toward the noise. "Did Levinson leave yet? This place is a pit of insanity."

"So Fritz informed me. Luckily Levinson is on a quest to get some Chunky Monkey ice cream."

"Elise, you have to help us."

"I've been fired, remember?"

Chuck Sanders sighed. "It was a mistake. A huge misunderstanding. It was never my idea, never *my* intent."

She went to the refrigerator and removed a bottle of water. "I told Paul I'd get him a drink. He's out on the porch and looks like he's about to pass out. Once he discovers the dog hair on his britches he'll need CPR."

"Here, I'll take it." Chuck smiled and held the bottle up, examining it with a wicked sparkle in his eye. "Maybe a little additive, like a sedative, wouldn't hurt?"

"Arsenic is hardly a sedative." She pushed him toward the door. Seconds later, he was back with Paul Winston trailing behind him, his head lowered like a scolded pup. He took a seat at the table, uncapped the bottle of water, and chugged it.

"I told him he could join us if he promised not to utter a word until you and I have hashed this out."

Elise shrugged. "I guess you have the ball in your court, Chuck."

"I wish! Levinson has made it clear Winston and Sanders are out of the picture if you're not there to manage the project. Our ace in the hole is that the firm owns the designs." While he talked, Elise went to the refrigerator and pulled out a Coke. She popped the top and turned back to him. "So we have a stalemate, unless, of course, I go in-house with Levinson."

"You wouldn't! And can't." Paul Winston sputtered, jumping up and sloshing water over the front of his silk shirt.

"Oh, just shut up, Paul, and sit down," Chuck warned sharply. He glanced at Elise. "A legal battle? No way would Levinson wait."

"Oh, he'll wait. In fact, I suspect he'll be more than agreeable to wait." She was amazed how calm and collected she sounded, even though she had no idea whether Levinson really would. "And my contractual obligations notwithstanding, the firm loses the deal regardless."

Chuck shook his head and looked at Paul. "It would seem she is holding us hostage, but it's Levinson, not Elise, whose name is at the bottom of the ransom note."

"It's a bluff," Paul interjected.

"What are you, deaf?" Chuck gave him a look of disgust. "I told you to be quiet. You forget I own half of the firm as well. You haven't exactly endeared the man to us. He likes—no, he adores Elise. Now tell me, who do you think is in the driver's seat on this potential contract?" He focused his attention back to her and said softly, "Please, Elise, come back to work for us."

Setting her drink on the counter, she crossed her arms and leaned her frame against the countertop. "What's in it for me?"

"Money, lots of money, kiddo."

She shook her head.

"A healthy raise. No, a huge raise."

"Uh-uh, not good enough."

"Elise," he pleaded. "We need you. No one can handle clients like you can. Neither one of us have your touch. Half of them are already disgruntled and it's only been a little more than a week. The files look like an ad for a recycling project. Contractors and suppliers don't want to talk to anyone but you."

She pursed her lips and stared at him with an unreadable expression before she spoke. "I'll pass." She never imagined it would feel so good to say it.

"Okay, okay. I get it. A partnership?"

"Associate or full?"

He sighed like he knew he was defeated. "Full."

"Now just a second here!" Paul Winston's jaw dropped and his face blanched white.

"Oh, shut up, Paul," they said in unison, looking up at each other, exchanging a smile.

Chuck Sanders shook his head sadly. "Sometimes, Paul, just when I think I'm cracking through your thick skull and rewiring your sense of logic, a stray brain cell misfires and poof! You short-circuit. We can't do this alone. Do you get it?"

Elise watched the play of angry emotions on Paul Winston's face.

"I'll tell you what," she offered and raised both hands in a signal of truce. "Give me a day to think on it, all right? It will give you time to discuss your offer with Paul, since it's obvious he has some reservations. I have some other irons in the fire I need to sort through." *The first one is in the room next door.*

"Okay, that's a step." Chuck Sanders punched the air, grabbed her in another bone-crunching embrace, and thumped her on the back. "That's my girl! Just what I wanted to hear. How about I phone you and we can discuss the particulars later? No, take a few days, and I'll call you from the West Coast."

Elise pulled away, nodded, and smiled at his beaming face.

She met Paul Winston's somber gaze. "Make sure, Paul, whatever you and Chuck decide to offer, you're both in complete agreement."

"I understand," he said stiffly. He held out his hand. When she took it, a look of surprise and relief spread over his usually unreadable, somber face. "I know this sounds shallow and trite, but I've missed you, too, Elise."

****

Pacing the living room, Lucas Fisher shoved his hands through his hair. Where in hell was Elise? Her car had been sitting in the drive for over a half hour now. How long could it possibly take to toss the three stooges from San Francisco out the front door?

In a nearby chair, a furious Monique sat with her legs crossed, her blinding blue skirt hiked up to her silky thighs. He had never realized how beautiful Elise's legs were until he was able to compare them with someone else's. The thought was unexpected and jolting.

"Lucas," he heard Monique say, "I love you. Can't you understand?" She waved her hands in a frantic gesture and the diamond bracelet on her left wrist flashed in brilliant colors in the sunlight pouring into the front window.

He scrubbed his hands over his face. "What I can't understand is why you would think there's any future left for us. It's over, Monique. How many times do I have to say it?"

He stared at her. A million, he thought to himself. I can tell her a million times, and still she wouldn't believe me. He searched the thoughts swirling through his head. He had been blind and shallow. How could he ever have thought he could have a lasting relationship with someone who was like a small spoiled child, intent upon getting her own way? Someone who only wanted to run with the powerful, the famous, the rich?

"Lucas, darling, you can't be serious."

Her ice cold eyes flashed hot with envy as Elise

sauntered into the room. Lucas's heart hammered in his chest. Even in a pair of cut-off jeans she was exquisite. She wore little make-up, and her hair was pulled into some sort of funny knot at the back of her head and was now coming undone, tendrils fanning out around her face. She was more vibrant and exquisite than he had ever imagined, even when compared to Monique, a beautiful woman in her own right.

With a self-assured politeness and grace, she went directly to Monique. "Elise Springer. Welcome, I've heard so much about you." She held out her hand.

Monique eyed her warily, her mouth twisting into a sneer. She refused the offered greeting as well as the outstretched hand. "So you are what? Lucas's latest little diversion?" she asked.

"Oh, heavens no, I should hope not." Undaunted, Elise took a seat opposite her. "Lucas and I are old friends. We go way back, in fact, clear back to childhood when we played on the same neighborhood baseball team. Lucas was the only one I know who loved barbecued potato chips and cherry cream soda. I used to down half the can when he was up to bat and wasn't looking. Lucky for me, I never got caught."

Her eyes met Lucas's, and he felt his groin tighten. Oh, yes, he had always known whose lips had been on his can of soda. Spring and fall, he had lain in bed, freshly showered, listening to the frogs and crickets, and dreamed of those very same lips kissing him instead.

"And your point?" Monique had a haughty look.

"No point. I'm just wondering how well *you* know Lucas."

"Enough to know I'm in love with him. I know

everything about him. Much more than a silly hillbilly could ever know."

Lucas shook his head. "No, Monique, you know nothing about me. If you did, you'd realize our relationship was over a long, long time ago."

"That's not true," Monique wailed, jumping up. "You love me. You know you do. You even sent me flowers. Tell her, Lucas!"

"Flowers? What flowers?" He stared at her, frowning. Ever since he'd known her, she always had a bag of manipulative tricks. "You must be mistaken. I never sent you any flowers."

Monique sniffed and dug into her beaded purse "Yes, you did." She rooted for a moment and then pulled out a small white envelope with a card. "See, he really did." She shoved it under Elise's nose.

Elise pulled out the card. It read, "Miss you so much. All my love, Lucas." She handed it to Lucas and flipped the envelope over, taking great care to memorize the name of the florist.

"This is some mistake, a sad joke, I'm afraid." Lucas handed the card back. "I never had any flowers sent, I swear."

"Oh, Lucas, it doesn't matter." Monique rose and clutched his forearm. "Come back to Atlanta. You weren't made to vegetate in a woeful farm field. We'll fly down to the islands and catch some rays."

"I'm afraid I'm not vegetating, Monique, and the only rays I need to catch are those of hope. I'm starting up a leasing business and a spin-off restoration garage. And there's Todd to consider." It took all of his willpower to remain calm.

"I love you, Lucas. We can take the kid back with

us and get a nanny," she pleaded, "or put him in boarding school."

Elise shot from the chair so fast Lucas was sure her teeth rattled in her mouth.

With those pearly whites bared, she stormed across the living room to the front door and tore it open. "Let me tell you something, Monique, darling," she drawled, "before I tell you where to go. 'The kid,' as you refer to him, will *never* see a nanny or boarding school as long as I can breathe." She took a cleansing breath. "Now get out!"

Monique brushed past her, her sweet cloying perfume clinging to the air. "You'll change your mind," she said to Elise, "once you discover how tiresome the little brat can be."

"The child has a name," Elise said through a hiss. "It's Todd, Todd Fisher."

Monique sneered. "The kid will be a noose around your neck, believe me. You'll grow weary of tying shoelaces and wiping mud off his hands and smudges off everything he touches. You're a career woman, just like I am, Elise. Eventually, you'll go mad reading those silly, boring little storybooks night after night. You'll itch for the freedom to come and go as you please. You just wait."

She turned to Lucas and gave him a frosty glare. "She's taking advantage of you and your affections to get to your money. She can never love you like I can. *Never!* You're going to be sorry, too." She jammed her sunglasses onto her face and stormed out, slamming the screen door.

"Don't bet on it," Lucas said under his breath as he watched her leave.

****

Elise woke up the next day before the sunlight even brightened the curtains in her room. Gathering her hair and securing it into a ponytail, she dragged on a pair of capris and a tee-shirt and tiptoed down the stairs. She needed time to think, and of late, the house was more like a noisy hotel, its door constantly revolving with Fritz, Cindy, and J.B. bustling back and forth.

Her first instinct was to put on a pot of coffee, but when she checked the refrigerator she realized they were out of milk. Again. She sighed. Between Fritz and Todd, they needed to rent a cow or buy a few dairy ones again.

The keys to the old Trans Am lay on the kitchen table. She scooped them up, checking the bread drawer before quietly slipping out the back door.

Yesterday, she had called the florist in Atlanta only to find the flowers sent to Monique were purchased from Rosie's Posies in Scranton and were paid for in cash instead of a credit card. It would only mean only one thing. Someone in the area had access to information about Lucas Fisher.

How and why, she wondered, as she slid into the slippery leather bucket seat of the car and headed for the supermarket.

Only three possibilities popped into her head. Someone had extracted the information from Mike's database address book or from police records, or it was one of Lucas's own employees. It was no secret the state police had been forced to track Lucas down to tell him of Mike's death.

It was also no secret both J.B. and the men at the garage usually knew his whereabouts. Monique, herself, had coaxed Lucas's Pennsylvania phone number out of them. However, it didn't make sense why anyone would want him to patch up his relationship with Monique.

The twenty-four-hour market wasn't making an early morning killing when Elise guided her car into a parking spot near the entrance. Only a half dozen cars peppered the lot, and she easily recognized the beat-up blue Mazda of Mary Jo Meyer.

Purse in hand, she hurried to the dairy section and picked up a gallon of milk. Then she checked the aisles, finally spotting Mary Jo near the frozen food section.

"I've been meaning to come out and see you again," Elise said to Mary Jo's back. She was doubled over, her head stuck inside the ice cream freezer.

Mary Jo straightened, turned, and smiled. "I assumed with your Dad still hospitalized you'd be pretty busy. How's he doing?"

It was then Elise saw the fine purple bruise along Mary Jo's left jaw, artfully covered with make-up, but not entirely concealed. Even as her stomach did a quick flip, she forced herself to remain calm. She deliberated, wondering whether to ignore it. After all, she admitted to herself, Mary Jo was a grown woman who didn't need anyone intervening in her life and marriage. The thought of Philip Cullington and his need to hurt women struck home. The damage his fist had once done to her own face was already rising in her mind from some dark lonely spot where she had managed to keep it hidden. The pain had been nearly unbearable, and the bruises had taken weeks to heal. Before she realized it, her hand had involuntarily moved to touch her own jaw. She waited, her eyes pinned to Mary Jo's dull ones.

"Oh." Mary Jo gave her a forced, small smile. "I had some dental work done, and I bruise easily."

Elise nodded, uttering a silent but vicious mental curse. Yes, she mused, and that's why you grocery shop before sunrise so no one will see you.

"I think maybe I'd consider changing dentists," Elise said to lighten the mood.

"Yes, well..." Mary Jo struggled for something to say.

"I was talking with Cindy the other day, and she told me both Lackawanna College and Scranton University have programs in early childhood and elementary education. One of her sisters is in her third year at Lackawanna. I'm sure she'd be eager to tell you about it."

Alarm shot in Mary Jo's eyes as she chose an ice cream container and put it into the front basket of her shopping cart. Her wedding band flashed as she etched a swirl design into the frost on the lid with a fingernail. "No, I don't think it would be a good idea."

"Listen, you could start taking courses during the day when the kids are in school. I know I can help you get the money to go, even part time." Her mind flashed to Lucas Fisher. He would, if she asked him, give the money willingly and anonymously.

"It wouldn't work," Mary Jo said in low voice. "Ted and I have our problems, I'll admit, but he would never permit me to return to college."

Elise knew why he'd never agree. Because he was afraid Mary Jo might become independent and leave him. "Have you tried counseling?" she asked.

Mary Jo gave a strangled laugh. "He's a cop, Elise. He'd be the laughing stock of his peers."

"Well, that's just terrific." Elise felt her temper soar. So he protects his job even when he's incapable of protecting his own family from himself, she thought.

"You don't understand—"

"No, I don't, Mary Jo. I really don't understand how you explain all this to your children. You, who always believed in leading by example. Good Lord, how many times do you think you can tell them you've fallen down or walked into a door?" She let out a long breath and looked up at the woman's pained, defeated eyes. A woman who used to be vibrant, sparkling and full of life. "Mike Fisher knew, didn't he?" she asked.

This time the pain was replaced by fright. Sheer cold fright. Mary Jo swallowed, but didn't speak.

"Never mind, you don't have to answer." Mike Fisher knew all right, or he suspected, Elise thought. Why else would he drop Todd off for her to baby-sit? He knew Ted couldn't do anything with him lurking around.

"Tell me, Mary Jo, was Ted called out the night Mike Fisher had his accident?"

Mary Jo nodded. "Yes, he finished his shift and was glad to be in for the night. Then after midnight, he was called back out again. What are you implying? I wish you would please stop insinuating things about my husband all the time. You can ask my sister, Elaine. She was staying at the house with me that night. Ted's a good man, Elise. He's working to control his temper. He has a very difficult and stressful job. You don't understand."

"Maybe I don't," Elise admitted.

Mary Jo turned and looked up the aisle toward the cash registers. "Look, I really gotta go. Ted's watching the kids until his shift starts."

Her heart aching, Elise nodded and watched her go, pushing the half-empty cart ahead of her like her half-empty marriage.

Chapter Twenty

It was barely six o'clock the next morning when Elise rolled over in bed and heard giggles and thumping noises coming from the kitchen below. Seconds later, the smell of bacon and the rich scent of vanilla mixed with cinnamon permeated the air. It took all her willpower to drag herself out of bed and pull on a pair of running shorts and a tee-shirt to see what was causing the commotion. She found Lucas and Todd making breakfast in a kitchen that looked like it had imploded on itself. Dry pancake mix covered the counters, egg shells littered the sink, and dirty spoons, forks, measuring cups, and spatulas lay among the rubble of used but now discarded bowls. A rumpled Lucas was manning the stove and griddle while a pajama-clad Todd stood on a chair beside him. Holding a bottle of maple syrup, the little boy was covered in a fine dusting of white powdered sugar. Elise was sure there wasn't an inch on the child that wasn't sticky. Beside the chair, Bess sat contented and watchful, waiting to lap up whatever dropped onto the floor during the commotion. It took Elise a moment to realize they were making French toast.

"Wow. What's the special occasion for us to get a real homemade breakfast?" Elise took a quick peek at the cookbooks scattered on the counter to assure herself the concoction in the bowl was really a mixture of eggs and milk for dipping the bread.

"Look, look, Elise," Todd said turning away from the counter with the syrup bottle held upside down and making Bess's fondest wish come true as a stream of maple syrup flowed onto the floor. "We're making fried toast."

"French toast, little buddy," Elise said as she leaped forward and turned the bottle upright in the child's hands.

Lucas turned from the stove and smiled. "Todd and his dad used to make pancakes together on weekends. I thought we could have our own weekend ritual and make French toast."

Elise's heart did a small dive when she thought about how hard Lucas was trying to win Todd's trust and devotion and to help him make a smooth adjustment from his dad's death.

"Holy fright! How many people are you two planning to feed?" She eyed the loaf of bread, now over three-quarters gone.

Lucas looked at the bread bag sheepishly. "I guess we got a little carried away, huh?"

She shook her head cynically, smiled, and opened a cupboard to get a cup for her coffee. She poured a cup and leaned against the counter. "It does smell good."

"Then let's eat," Lucas said, turning off the stove and taking a wet cloth to scrub some of the stickiness from Todd's hands.

"Once that child picks up a fork, we'll have to pry it out of his fingers." Elise laughed and watched as Lucas scrubbed, but made little progress with the wet cloth.

"Did you know," he said while he worked, "the

earliest mention of French toast comes from Latin recipes dating back to the fourth or fifth century? During the reign of Henry V, it was known as *pain perdu,* meaning lost bread. Actually it was stale bread that might otherwise be thrown away."

"What are you, the historical guru of victuals?" Elise looked at him in dismay, then proceeded to set three plates and silverware on the table before going to the refrigerator where she found some orange juice. She motioned them to the table.

"It was just something that popped up when I was looking for the recipe. You know how I like history and trivia." He took a piece of the toast, doused it in more syrup, and took a bite.

"So how did the meeting with Mort Levinson go?"

Elise had spent all afternoon on Friday with Mort Levinson. It started with lunch at the Gourmet Café before they moved to the Radisson Lackawanna Station Hotel to meet with a group of investors. Elise thought it odd she was the only one representing Winston and Sanders, but she wasn't able to find a moment alone with Mort Levinson to ask him why Paul or Chuck wasn't present. It was only when Mort and his wife, Lucy, invited her to dine privately with them later in the evening she learned the truth. Mort Levinson very vocally and adamantly admitted he didn't want to work with anyone but her. His decision created a dilemma she didn't know how to solve. She had only two choices—make a complete break with Winston and Sanders or tell Mort Levinson she was unable to work on his projects. Sometimes, Elise thought, she was taking more steps backward than forward.

"Hello? Elise?" she heard Lucas say, breaking her

reverie.

"Fine," Elise said, coming to her senses. "Everything went fine, I guess. When we get a minute, I'd like to talk with you."

"I know what you mean. Things are moving along faster than I expected with the restoration garage. Can you watch Todd this afternoon?" he asked. "Cindy has to take her mother to the doctor and I have to meet J.B. at the showroom to meet with a client."

Elise nodded. "Actually, I was planning to take Todd, Cindy, and Bess to the cottage and check on what still needs to be done. Cindy can meet us there when she gets free." If the truth were told, she wanted to get Todd acclimated to the newness of the cottage and to look around some more. There were still boxes stacked in the shed she hadn't yet rummaged through. She wanted to get a feel for where Mike might have left more information. She was certain a good cop, as clever as he seemed to be, would leave behind valuable information just in case of his demise. Then there was the $25,000 of Lucas's money in question, a misplaced or lost will, and the undiscovered $100,000 of undercover money. All of it didn't make any sense. Something didn't add up. According to Nick, Mike Fisher was neither sloppy nor careless. Lucas described him as a stickler for detail. Elise was certain a detailed person would have a well-thought-out plan for keeping his personal information safe. But where?

"We're still going, aren't we?" Todd piped up.

"Yes." Elise smiled. "This afternoon. I have to run some errands this morning."

"And Bess, too?"

"Bess, too."

Since Todd had come to live at the farm, the dog and boy had become inseparable. Right now the dog had taken her place beside Todd's chair.

"Traitor," Elise muttered under her breath and gave Bess an evil eye. In reality, the dog was a godsend, she silently admitted. Not only did Bess keep a careful watch over Todd, but she doubled as the canine floor sweeper, snatching up all the crumbs and food that fell from Todd's plate or hands as he galloped through the house. Bess had given up sleeping in Elise's bedroom and had moved permanently to the side of Todd's bed.

"Can we look for Ranger?" he asked.

"You know, kiddo, we'll take a look in the shed and see what we can find." She nodded and watched as sheer pleasure twisted his lips into a smile. She knew they'd have no peace until they located the beanbag dog.

"Now, I can't promise you we'll find him, but we'll try," she admitted.

"I have a deal for you," Lucas said, looking over at her.

"Uh-oh, this doesn't sound good."

"Since Todd and I made breakfast, you can either clean the kitchen or clean Todd."

Elise looked around the room and winced. Then she looked over at Todd and saw every strand of his hair permanently plastered to his scalp with maple syrup. Even his little eyelashes glistened with the sticky stuff.

"I want Uncle Lucas to give me a bath," Todd said, gazing eagerly up at Lucas.

Gleefully, Elise pushed herself up from the table and started collecting plates. "Well, then, it looks like this Merry Maid has kitchen duty."

****

It wasn't errands that sent Elise to the west side of Scranton toward Dunmore, where she knew Clarisse Fisher lived in a small apartment over a small plumbing and heating business. It was a mixture of curiosity and the need to make contact with someone who might lend more insight into the affairs of Mike Fisher. There was also the need to see Clarisse in her own environment.

The borough of Dunmore comprised a little less than nine square miles. Just like Scranton, it was an old town built as far back as 1835 when interest in anthracite coal, brick, stone, and silk mills drew people to swell its meager population. She found Clarisse's apartment in a matter of minutes. It was a dilapidated two-story structure with six garbage cans lined up in front like old soldiers on guard. She took the weathered outside steps leading directly to the top apartment and knocked on the door.

From what Lucas had told her, Clarisse had spent most of her life as a waitress and barmaid, preferring nighttime bar work where tips flowed more freely with alcohol and late night inebriation.

Clarisse opened the door on the third knock. She was a tall, underweight woman with bleached platinum hair pulled into a knot at the top of her head. Dressed in skintight black leotards with a red tunic top matching her lipstick, she wore open-toed platform shoes more uncomfortable than the stilts Elise had worn when she stepped off the plane. She was also wearing more makeup than Elise had in her make-up case, and on every finger of her hands she wore some type of ring. A cheap rhinestone bracelet with a tarnished clasp twinkled from her right wrist. Clarisse obviously adored jewelry.

"My, my, now isn't this a surprise," Clarisse said in a voice capable of flash-freezing seawater. "Coming to see stepmommy?"

"May I come in?" Elise asked, ignoring the greeting. "You obviously know who I am."

"Yup, the famous architect everyone is talking about and the bitch who got Children and Youth to give you the kid." Clarisse opened the door wider and allowed Elise to step into a dull brown living room smelling like stale cigarette smoke. Clarisse gestured to a recliner across from a faded teal couch where stacks of magazines and clothes fought for room at one end.

Elise took the offered chair and decided to get straight to the point. "I was hoping you might be able to give me some insight into your ex-husband and his habits."

"Late husband." Brown raccoon-looking eyes, ringed in dark eyeliner, flashed hotly.

"Okay, late ex-husband," Elise said. "Your divorce was final. Both you and Mike signed the papers, and it was recorded."

"That doesn't mean I don't count." Clarisse's voice took on a sharp, whiney tone. "That doesn't mean Mike didn't want me to take care of Todd. That doesn't mean part of his estate doesn't belong to me-eeee."

"What it does mean," Elise said enunciating every word in a sharp tone, "is you don't have a legal leg to stand on concerning Todd or Mike's estate, unless you have proof, such as a will or mutually signed agreement."

"You mean all I get out of giving him a year of my

life was the lousy $25,000 we agreed on during the divorce?" Clarisse's voice raised an octave. "Well, ain't that a kick in my skinny backside!"

Elise stared at the woman and almost sighed in relief. Clarisse had just solved the mystery of the missing $25,000 Mike was supposed to give Lucas to invest. Elise reminded herself to choose her words carefully if she brought up the subject of Mike Fisher and his habits. The last thing she needed was to send Clarisse's temper soaring and get her own backside kicked to Scranton. The woman's temperament was anything but calm and collected.

Elise tried another approach. "You know, Clarisse, I really need some help finding Todd's health records. They weren't among Mike's belongings. Do you have any idea where he might have stashed valuable paperwork concerning family members? Did he have a safe deposit box in a local bank or a lock box or safe he kept around the house?"

Clarisse stared at her with a blank expression. Elise forged on. "Where would Mike have stored or filed insurance policies, a passport, birth certificates, or documents similar to those?"

Clarisse shrugged. "He used to keep papers in a lock box back in New Castle, but I have no idea what he did with anything once he moved to Scranton. Have you gone through all of his boxes and belongings?"

"I'm working on it," Elise lied. Technically, she decided, it wasn't a lie since she had rummaged through the boxes she had earlier taken to the farm and she planned to go to the cottage in the afternoon to dig around again. "Did Mike have any enemies?"

Clarisse laughed. "He was a cop. He probably had

lots of them, but none I knew by name or face."

Elise nodded and stood. "Well, I'd better be on my way. I'm headed to the cottage later this afternoon to check on some details." She started for the door and turned. "One more question—do you know Jack Morrison?"

Clarisse hesitated a moment too long for Elise's liking. "No, I don't believe I do."

"From Children and Youth Services?"

She shook her head. "Is he important?"

"No, not any more." She smiled. "I appreciate the time you've given me, Clarisse. If you think of anything, please give me a call."

Outside, in her car, Elise sat for a moment wearily staring at the building. She was pleased she had at least solved the mystery of the missing $25,000. However, she wondered how many of Clarisse Fisher's answers were truths and how many were lies.

****

Never in her entire harried life did Elise think she'd ever be sitting at the kitchen table with a four-year-old, sorting animal crackers into Zip lock bags as if they were gathering essential supplies for a hike up Montage Mountain. Four boxes of Barnum's Animal Crackers were spilled out into a heap before them. Juice boxes stood on the counter, waiting to be packed with a bag of toys and the crackers.

"Tell me again, Todd, why can't we take all the animals in one box of crackers to the cottage?" she asked and watched in fascination as he patiently and carefully separated the kangaroos, elephants, and polar bears and put them into individual piles.

"Because only certain ones can come," he said,

264

"and some of them don't get along. The monkeys and sheep don't like the mean lions and tigers, you know."

"But we're not taking the monkeys, sheep, lions or tigers."

The little boy looked at her with exasperated gray Fisher eyes. "But we can't leave them here all mixed up if they're not friends, Eee-lise."

Cursing Nabisco under her breath, Elise decided no one—children or adults—should ever have that many choices of animal shapes to consume in one sitting. She tried another approach. "Todd, if we don't get started soon there won't be enough daylight to play outside with Bess. How about we leave a note for Lucas and Cindy and tell them to finish sorting these? Don't forget we need to look for Ranger, too."

Beside them, Bess whined. Elise looked down at the bored canine and commiserated with her. She secretly popped a mean tiger into her mouth and then slipped a couple of lions and tigers into the dog's awaiting mouth.

There is nothing more rewarding than destroying your enemies with a couple of chews and a swallow. If only life could be so easy.

****

The late morning was getting hot and humid, but it was hotter in the beat-up old maroon Chevy pickup where Lucas sat with J.B., eating cheeseburgers and fries and watching the parking lot of Children and Youth Services a half a block away. Parked behind them, a block up the street, was Lucas's Trans Am. Across the street, the bank was doing a sporadic business through the drive-thru. Beside them, the florist shop had opened, and a worker was busy hanging colorful flowering baskets of petunias on hooks underneath a canopy over the entrance. The canopy read "Rosie's Posies."

"Man, there is nothing better than melted cheese on some meat," J.B. said between mouthfuls. He was on his second burger. "The only thing to improve this would be a beer."

"If our plan works, I'll buy you a case," Lucas said. Despite the escalating heat, he didn't want to start the truck to use the air conditioner and call needless attention to their location. He was not even fond of the idea of opening all the windows, but he knew there was no alternative. Once Elise had told him Nick found white paint chips on Mike's car, he hadn't been able to sleep, thinking sleazebag Morrison might be involved in his brother's death.

"Now tell me again how you want this to go down," J.B. asked.

"Loosely, you have to either run into the back of Morrison's car when he's coming out of the parking lot, or just hit it after it's parked. That'll give us reason to get old paint flecks from the back fenders. The police think the vehicle that ran Mike's car off the road came up on him from behind, passed, and hit him on his left front fender with its right front fender, sending him off the road. It's highly possible Morrison had his front fender, bumper, and right side panels repaired and repainted. So we need old stuff from the back side, preferably driver's side, to see if it matches the samples left on Mike's car."

"Loosely?" J.B. asked. "Now I'd call it freakin' idiotic, man. I thought you said you had this all thought out. I've no desire to up my insurance rates, ruin my perfectly stellar driving record, and possibly injure myself for a few flecks of paint!"

"Somebody's cranky."

When J.B. only glared at him, Lucas continued, "Unless you have a better idea, we are stuck with the plan."

"If you take a look ahead of you," J.B. pointed out, "you would see Morrison's white Mercedes is parked between a Lexus and a Hummer—two cars I'd hate to inflict collateral damage on using your loose plan." J.B. reached for a fistful of fries and took a sip of lemonade.

"Well, the dork always takes a late lunch, so we have some time to think this through."

"And we have to wait for what? Two hours? And sit here and fry inside this cab in this heat?" J.B. finished his burger and dropped the wrappings into the take-out bag. He reached behind the seat, grabbed a grubby baseball hat with "Wayland Construction" written on it, and rummaged around until he found an old clipboard. From his pocket he withdrew a penknife and some small plastic bags.

"You know, Lucas, when someone acts like he's guilty, he probably is. So stop acting like you're guilty and stop playing by the book. You'd put ol' Abe Lincoln to shame! Here's the new plan. You're going to drive into the parking lot like you should be there, pull perpendicular to the back of Morrison's car, stop and block any view from the opposite windows in the office building. Consider yourself part of the Wayland Construction follow-up crew who's inspecting the macadam parking lot for defects. I plan to jump out, scratch off some paint, and hop back in. It's that simple."

Lucas looked at him incredulously. "And you think *I'm* crazy? I don't even know if it's legal. What if someone recognizes me?"

J.B. shook his head and gave him a dismal look. "Legal? You're worrying about legalities *now*? For crying out loud, you make something up on the spot if you bump into someone you know." He looked over at Lucas. "Come on, boss guy, buck up. Let's do it. An adrenaline rush would do wonders for your ethics. We're trying to solve a crime here."

"Ah, bite me," Lucas grunted. With a sour look, he peered at J.B. and his battered hat. "Gawd Almighty, you look like the Jeff Foxworthy of a redneck construction company. Okay, let's get this over with." He turned the key in the ignition, and within minutes they were positioned in back of Morrison's car. J.B. jumped out with hat, clipboard, and knife.

Not even fifteen seconds elapsed before Twila Pedmo motored into the parking lot and steered her big blue Buick into a parking spot opposite and perpendicular to them, across the egress lane, and in front of the entrance to the building.

Stunned, Lucas's mouth dropped. He inched lower down in his seat and slipped his sunglasses on. "Oh, dear Lord," he muttered to himself and in earshot of J.B. "Of all the people we could have bumped into, we luck out with Twila Pedmo, Miss Manners and Protector of Small Children."

Twila Pedmo hefted her stocky frame from her car. She was wearing a floral spring dress in vibrant shades of pink, white, and yellow and her newly permed hair glistened pink in the bright sunlight. She immediately squinted at the pick-up and waved enthusiastically.

"Yoo-hoo! Lucas, Lucas Fisher, is that you?"

"Holy crap," Lucas heard J.B.'s voice grumble through the open passenger window where he was crouching on the other side of the pickup. "Now all we need is the local camera crew from WYOU-TV to document this and we can be on the late night news."

"Yeah, and we'll be watching it from jail," Lucas muttered in a hiss.

"Oh, for God's sake, Lucas," J.B spit back. "Get out of the damn truck and run some interference, will you? Now!"

Lucas threw open his door, slid out, and trotted over to where Pedmo was standing. He gave her the widest smile he could manage. "Mrs. Pedmo, so glad I could catch you. I have a quick question, if you don't mind."

Pedmo looked at him curiously then peered around him and shot another puzzled gaze at the beat-up truck. "Don't tell me you're going to restore that piece of junk?"

"Nah." He could feel the sweat trickle down his back. "Just took it in on a trade." Which, Lucas thought to himself, was the truth. "Tell me, Mrs. Pedmo, do you have any idea where Elise and I could find Todd's health records? We seem to have misplaced them along with some of Mike's other important papers."

She shook her head. "No, but I do know Mike used a pediatrician here in Scranton. I'll look up his name in our records and email Elise and you. He could probably tell you who the pediatrician was in New Castle, and you could get copies from both of them and recreate his health history."

"Thank you. It would be a big help." Lucas licked

his dry lips and smiled nervously, willing himself not to turn and look at the truck.

Pedmo peered at him with knitted eyebrows. "Lucas, are you all right? You don't look very well."

He nodded and forced himself to swallow. He was so nervous he could hear his heart wildly thumping like a war drum clear up into his ears. "This early spring heat seems to be getting to me."

"Then you need to get out of the sun right this minute, young man," she instructed him and headed for the entrance door, her sturdy shoes clopping on the pavement. He waited until she was inside, then hurried to the pickup and stood blocking the window on his side of the door until he heard J.B. open the passenger door and crawl in.

"Got it. Took samples from all four corners. See!" J.B. enthusiastically waved the plastic bags in one hand and pumped the air with his other. "I knew we could do it."

Lucas glanced at J.B. and wiped the sweat from his forehead with the back of his hand. He took a deep steadying breath. "Yeah, and I feel about five years older than when we started these shenanigans."

Chapter Twenty-One

Elise thought there was nothing more beautiful than a boy and a dog and a May afternoon warm enough so she could lower the Tahoe's windows to allow the sweet smells of spring to waft into the car. In yards and along the roadside, rhododendron bloomed in glorious shades of dark pink, purple and snow white. A soft breeze ruffled the leaves in the birch and maples, and new grass, green and rich, sprang up to crowd out winter's brown.

Elise glanced in her rearview mirror at Todd buckled in the backseat and noticed he was leafing through the dog-eared *Fox and the Hound*. In his lap were two bags of animal crackers filled with compatible animal shapes and a box of juice. Beside him, Bess eyed the bags of crackers with solemn interest, caring little, she surmised, whether the animal crackers were friends or foes.

On the drive to the cottage, she pondered what she was going to do with Winston and Sanders. To alienate them by starting her own firm could be troublesome. They had a reputation and were well-known on the West Coast. On the other hand, Mort Levinson was handing her an offer hard to refuse and she surmised he would be willing to buy her out from under her legal obligations to Winston and Sanders. As the lead architect on his projects, she stood to make a lot more money than Paul and Chuck could ever pay her. Thrown into the mix were Lucas and Todd Fisher. She was in love with Lucas. Those gray eyes and easy smile had a way of turning her inside out, and Todd was a little charmer who tugged so hard on her heart strings she was certain they were going to break if she had to leave.

She also brooded over the Mike Fisher dilemma. So far they were getting no closer to finding out how he might have died. It was the end of her two-week vacation as well, and although she had more days owed her, she didn't think it would be prudent to stay away from the San Francisco office much longer. Paul Winston had left a message on the answering machine and her cell phone yesterday asking when she planned to return to the office. She noticed there was a distinct softening of his usual terse nature, but not much.

As she and Todd drove into the cottage lane, taking the second loop of the driveway leading to the back of the cottage, she reminded Todd of the outside play rules. He was only allowed to play in the grassy yard behind the cottage and was not supposed to wander any place near the lake tucked away over a small rise on the north side.

"Can we look for Ranger?" he asked again when they stopped. He peered out the window at Cindy's car, already parked in the back driveway. "Hey, look, Cindy is here!" He unbuckled his seat belt and with Bess tagging along barreled straight for the shed.

"Wait!" Elise hurried to keep up with him. She passed the doghouse on her way to the shed and stopped for a moment to stare at it. Newly built by Mike Fisher, it was finished with charcoal gray shingles, perfectly aligned. The siding, painted a glistening white, matched the color of the cottage. So what was bothering her about the doghouse? She shook her head as if she was shaking out cobwebs from her mind and hurried along to catch up with Todd.

Cindy was already inside the shed, sitting on one box and sorting through another when Elise swung the second door open to allow more sunlight to flood inside. Elise moved to the many boxes stacked four high and marked with Mike's and Todd's names on them. Todd took the lid off a box, positioned with others on the ground to the left of her, and dug into it. It looked like it held an assortment of old baby toys. Elise watched him bite his lower lip in annoyance.

For a moment, Elise stood still, her eyes circling the shed. She stared at the junk and stacks of boxes as an eerie shiver washed over her. Her neck and scalp felt as if any army of tiny spiders was marching upward. Her sixth sense kicked in. The last time she had been in the shed, all of the boxes had been neatly stacked in tiers of four. J.B. had promised her all of Todd's boxes would be positioned within easy reach, but those labeled as Todd's were now mixed in with the rest. Someone had been in the shed. Someone had been digging though the contents of the boxes. Someone had put them back in stacks, but not in the proper order.

Frowning, Elise looked at Cindy.

"What?" Cindy asked, seeing the alarmed look on Elise's face.

Elise pulled out her phone and motioned Cindy toward her. She was just about to phone Lucas when she looked out and noticed the back door to the cottage was ajar. She pointed to the door and pushed Cindy back into the shed.

"Were you in the house?" she asked.

When Cindy shook her head, Elise whispered, "I need your help." She jerked her thumb toward the house. "I'm going inside. I want you to wait out here with Todd and Bess. It's possible the door was left unlocked by one of the contractors, but I can't take a chance that's the case. I'm going to look around to see if anyone is in there."

"I don't like this," Cindy said, her eyes growing large and worrisome.

"Stay calm and listen to me." Elise handed her phone to Cindy. "If after a few minutes you don't hear from me, call Nick and Lucas and tell them to come here. Make sure they know you're at the cottage along with Todd. Keep Todd and Bess inside the shed until you hear a familiar voice calling you, okay?"

"Okay, Elise, but let me repeat, I'm not feeling good about this. Why can't we phone them now and wait until they arrive?" Cindy's voice was now a distraught plea.

"Because if someone's inside the house, I want to find out who it is before he gets away." From her purse, Elise withdrew a small can of pepper spray, ducked outside, and crossed the distance to the back door of the house.

With her heart thumping, she stopped and stood quietly outside listening for any sounds within. Pepper spray in her right hand, she pushed the door open with the other and had a short surge of relief when the hinges didn't squeak. Silently, the door drifted open into the kitchen. On the tile floor ahead of her, she saw smudges of mud where someone had walked. She was being silly, she told herself, the dirt could easily have been from a contractor or his helper coming in and out of the cottage with tools and supplies. There was still a showerhead to be installed in the master bath, and she had asked a carpenter to build permanent bookcases for one of the walls in Todd's bedroom. She had also designed a new sunroom to expand the living area and had asked two contractors to stop by, look at the layout possibilities, and give her quotes.

Gaining more confidence, Elise eased herself into the kitchen and stood with her back flattened against the wall just inside the door. Her heart continued to thud wildly in her chest. Maybe she was just losing it, she thought. Maybe she was being silly. The place appeared empty. If an intruder had been in the house, he surely would have heard the arrival of two cars, the slamming of their doors, and the commotion outside. Surely, he would have left.

With a more purposeful stride, she started down the hallway toward the living room and bedrooms beyond and took three steps into the living room when she saw a flash of light and movement in her peripheral vision. She heard the clinking of metal before she felt the sharp, painful blow to the back of her head. The room around her faded to black as she crumpled and the floor came up to meet her.

****

Elise awoke to the fuzzy faces of four men peering down at her. She recognized the sterile, antiseptic smell of a hospital and could feel a throbbing pain at the side of her head.

"I didn't die and go to heaven. Not if you're all here with me," she mumbled. "There's no way St. Peter would allow four of you inside the pearly gates at the same time. It would be bedlam."

"No, you're at the hospital and this is a darned stupid way to visit me," her father grumbled. "What were you thinking?"

"A little sympathy would be in order," Elise said and followed her words with a painful moan. She felt her head begin to clear, and the images of the men's faces became sharper.

Beside her, Lucas only sighed and ran his hand gently up and down her arm.

Fritz grunted. "You're like a bumbling maniac when wild ideas simmer in that pea brain of yours. You could have been killed, Elise! Why did you go into the cottage without help?"

"Stop shouting." She winced, eased herself slowly up, and fingered the bandage on the side of her head.

"You have a slight concussion and a few stitches," Lucas said softly as he bent and kissed her forehead on the undamaged side of her face. "Hey, guys, cut her a break. She just woke up, for Pete's sake." He looked down at her lovingly. "How are you feeling?"

"Like someone hit me with a hammer? I'll be okay, I think."

"It was my grandmother's tarnished old candlestick."

"If you all don't mind," Nick interrupted, "I'd like a few minutes alone with Elise so I can get her statement and perhaps some information to help with our investigation. I'd like to go over some things while it's still fresh in her mind and before they give her something strong to dull the pain." He gestured to the door. "There's a waiting room at the end of the hall, guys."

As soon as the room cleared, Nick sighed. "You know, Elise, you've got yourself more deeply involved in this case than I would have liked."

Elise took a sip of water from a glass on the stand beside her. "Which means you have more information?"

"Yes. The paint chips Lucas and J.B. took from Jack Morrison's car match the paint we scraped off Mike Fisher's car after the accident." Nick ran his hand through his hair. "The problem is Jack Morrison wasn't on the road the night of Mike Fisher's death. He was seen drunk at Two Horses, got a ride home, and was there for the rest of the night, according to a neighbor. The bartender corroborates the story. Morrison picked up his car the next morning and it was already damaged."

"Did you ask the bartender who took Morrison home?"

"Yeah, it was Meyer." Nick paced in front of her bed. "Did you see or hear anything before you were hit?"

Elise shook her head. "No. Did Cindy see anything? It happened so fast. How did my attacker get out of the house?"

"Easy. Out the front door and onto the road below the cottage. Bess must have sensed someone was in the house and something was wrong because she started barking. By the time Cindy called and we arrived, the intruder was gone. We checked for tracks, but there were none. I'm sorry, Elise."

Not any more than I am, Elise thought, as she fingered the bandage on her head again.

****

Elise greeted the news that she and her father would both be released from the hospital within twenty-four hours with joy and enthusiasm, despite a pounding headache. Lucas sent a Suburban to the hospital and instructed Fritz, Cindy, and J.B. to collect them and take them back to the farm. Fritz called it the mission to gather up the misfits, but he willingly showed up to see all the insurance and hospital paperwork for both of them was completed so they could be sprung.

If Elise was happy to be home, her joy paled in comparison to Lucas and Todd, who stuck to her like burrs on Bess. Lucas refused to let her work at her computer, and after the third reading of *The Fox and the Hound* with Todd, demanded she take a rest in her room—alone.

But it didn't take long for Todd and Bess to disregard Lucas's rules and seek her out. With a silent, careful commando crawl, Todd inched his way into her room and onto the bed, where she was listening to her iPod with her eyes shut. She felt his little fingers remove one of the ear buds and his soft lips tickle her ear as he whispered, "Are you awake, Eeelise?"

Smiling, she opened her eyes, removed the other ear bud, and pulled the little boy toward her. He snuggled in close beside her and rested his head on her shoulder.

"I really missed you," he said, twisting the cord of the earbud around his little finger.

"I missed you, too," she admitted.

"Does your head hurt?"

"Not so much." She rubbed the top of his head.

"We didn't find Ranger. Cindy took me back to the

cottage, and we looked through all the boxes. It's not there."

Elise's heart hurt as he spoke. "I'm sorry, Todd. We'll just have to get you something to replace it. I know what it's like to lose something you really treasure. What do you think we can get you that would be as nice as your favorite beanbag dog?"

"A real dog?" The little boy bounced up, his face animated and his hands flying around like windmill blades. "A real dog the same color! Uncle Lucas says there's a dog called a golden tree-er. It's the same color."

"Retriever. Re...triev...er," she said slowly, smiling.

"Uncle Lucas said he'll have to check with the SP-something or with someone who raises golden tree-ers to see if we can get one."

"SPCA. Dogs are a lot of work," Elise said. "Uncle Lucas will have to see if the doghouse is finished and if it's the right size, although I don't think he'll want your puppy to stay outside. What would you name your dog?"

"Cracker," he said with a wide grin. "It's my favorite food." He stopped a moment and chewed his lip. "But the house is all done, Elise. My dad even left the tool box inside it on a shelf over the door."

Elise sat upright. "Say that again, Todd."

"I'd name him Cracker."

"No, about the tool box."

"It's inside the doghouse."

Elise grabbed the little boy and hugged him close to her. "You are a really, really smart little boy," she said. "I'm so proud of you. I think we need to go downstairs and get a box of those animal crackers to celebrate!"

"Do I have to eat the mean lions and tigers?" he asked.

"No," she laughed and patted him on his hand. "You can eat any crackers you like, kiddo."

****

Lucas, Nick, Elise, Fritz and Cindy sat at the kitchen table with Mike Fisher's toolbox and bolt cutters in front of them. Close by on the floor, Todd knelt and clutched a small golden-colored beanbag dog while he brushed Bess, who was more than willing to lie there all day and submit to the boy's ministrations. Lucas had found the beanbag dog with the tool box on a board in the rafters of the dog house.

"I think Bess needs to go outside," Elise said to Cindy. "Can you take Todd and Bess out?" They traded an unspoken look that said the group needed some time for an adult conversation.

"Sure," Cindy said. "Let's go, Todd. We need to introduce your beanbag dog to the Springer farm. I also think we need to put a collar with a carabiner clip on Ranger so we can attach him to you permanently and be sure he never gets away again. I saw some ribbon in the sewing room we can use for a collar to get started."

Fritz stood as well and checked his watch. "It's time to pack up Dad and take him to his physical therapy session."

As soon as they left, Lucas heaved a sigh. "I can't believe it was in front of our faces the entire time."

"If there's really money and Mike's papers in there, and not tools," Nick said.

Lucas picked up the box, shook it, and looked at Nick with raised eyebrows as if to say, "Does it sound

280

like metal tools?" Instead he said, "And here lies the problem, Nick. If we open this box, and there's $100,000 inside, where do you stand?"

Nick looked at him, confused.

"I don't want this reported back to the police until we nail Mike's killer." Lucas's voice was low. Hard. Unyielding.

"Lucas, I'm under obligation to report it to headquarters."

"Then take a hike, Nick. Walk out of here now."

Nick flushed red. "What are you implying?"

"I'm implying there's a leak somewhere in your department." This time he didn't try to hide his irritation. "And I don't think we need to advertise drug money was found...if it's really in this toolbox. It might stop whoever knows it exists from searching any longer, and maybe he is also the one who killed Mike. Mrs. Pedmo knew about the money, so did Jack Morrison, and it wouldn't be a giant leap to think Meyer knew all the details as well. Hell, I thought undercover cops were supposed to be protected."

Nick looked at him warily. "What do you want me to do?"

"Put a lid on it for a while," Lucas admitted gruffly. "Let's nail the killer."

Nick heaved a sigh and picked up the bolt cutters. "This could get me in a lot of trouble with the department. Whatever is in here, you have twenty-four hours before I say anything about this box being found, agreed?"

"Agreed," Lucas and Elise said in unison.

Chapter Twenty-Two

It was just as Elise had hoped. She sat at the table with Lucas beside her and surveyed the contents of the toolbox spread out on the kitchen table: valuable papers, insurance policies, Todd's health records, a will, banking information, and $50,000 of police money with a note stating the remaining $50,000 was in a Scranton bank in a safe deposit box. She peered at Lucas beside her. The only emotion she saw was one of relief as he stared at all the paper laid out before them. "This is good news, Lucas. Your brother's name is finally cleared." She patted him on the back. "I wonder why he separated the money."

Nick, who had just phoned the bank to verify the whereabouts of the other $50,000, put his phone back in his pocket. "It's at the bank, all right. Agents often separate large amounts of money. They can have easy access to it and be assured it won't walk away. There are a lot of sticky fingers when working undercover. A cop can't be shaken down for any more money during a deal other than what's on them, either." He looked at Lucas with a serious expression. "I never doubted Mike Fisher was anything but an honest, clean cop."

Lucas nodded. "Twenty-four hours, right?"

"You have twenty-four hours, correct," Nick replied. After a perusal of the papers, he excused himself to take a shift for someone at the barracks who had called in sick.

Elise sat silently for a few minutes, thinking Nick had been right. The toolbox had been hidden in a conspicuous place, just waiting for discovery. How many times had they walked past the doghouse? The only reason Mike hid Todd's scruffy beanbag dog with the toolbox was because he knew his precocious son would hound them until they looked harder and located it.

Elise unfolded the will and scanned it. It gave all of Mike's belongings to Lucas, willed all of his money and property to him, and gave him legal guardianship of Todd.

"Well, it should be pretty clear to everyone Todd is now your child to raise," Elise said and watched Lucas's sober face light up like a cookie at Eat 'N Park.

"Yes, all I need is one more thing," he said, and took her hand, caressing the top of it. There was a devilish look on his face.

She stared at those smoke-colored Fisher eyes. "What?"

"You, of course. We're two lonely men in desperate need of a very special person to make us two very happy men."

"Oh, Lucas, things are so complica—" she said when the ringing of the phone interrupted her. She picked it up to hear Chuck Sanders' voice on the other end.

"Ready to come back to work?" he asked.

"Well, hello to you, too, Chuck. And no, not yet. Although I hardly think you called to ask that question." By the tone of his voice, she knew something was not quite right.

"Actually, yes. It looks like Mort Levinson is trying to cut us out of the five-hotel deal. I understand he wants only you as the lead architect on his projects."

A set of alarm bells started ringing in her head. "He'll change his mind once we get the first building started, and he sees all the work that needs to be done."

"Maybe, but with Lucas giving him a hefty sum as an investor, I'm guessing it won't happen, at least with the Wilkes-Barre endeavor."

"Surely you're kidding?" The warning bells pealed even louder in her head. She rubbed the back of her neck, feeling tension starting to rise between her shoulder blades.

"No, Lucas Fisher's money might have come into the project through a third party, but it's Fisher Enterprises money, there's no doubt. Paul is livid. Absolutely livid."

"I would imagine so." She looked over to where Lucas was reading through Todd's health records. "Listen, Chuck, can I call you back?"

She pushed the button to end the call and heaved a weary sigh. "What's this about Fisher Enterprises investing in Mort Levinson's new venture?"

"I was meaning to tell you." Lucas's face turned crimson. "J.B. told me we needed to invest some company money so I suggested he contact Mort Levinson. You said his idea was brilliant, right?"

Elise shook her head. It was a brilliant idea, all right. It was a spectacular idea, in fact. However, the last thing she needed was for Lucas to get involved and make it look like his investments were sealing the deal, assuring she would be lead architect on the project.

"Lucas, I can take care of myself. I don't need

intervention from Fisher Enterprises. Do you know how this looks? It looks like you bought me the position! How could you do this to me?" She stood up, irritated, disgusted, and unhappy with him.

"Liz, please, listen to me." He stepped toward her.

She held up a hand to ward him away. "No, not now, Lucas. I need to take some time to think this through. I'm going for a drive and to finish some errands. I need to clear my head. Just stay away from me." She whirled and almost ran out the front door.

"Okay," was the only response she heard as she bolted outside, the screen door banging shut behind her. She met Fritz and her father arriving just as she put her car into drive and checked the rearview mirror. Turning off the engine, she slipped out and walked back to Fritz's car to help get their father out of the passenger seat and into the house. Anton Springer looked tired, but there was still a lot of gumption in the old man as he grumbled at Fritz, who was trying to persuade him to use his walker.

"Get that blasted piece of metal junk out of my sight and get me my crutches!" Anton waved his spidery hand in the air. He turned to Elise. "And where do you think you're going, Missy, with a look on your face like you just sucked on a bucket of lemons?"

Elise sighed. "It's a long story, Dad."

Her father squinted up at her and snorted. "Since I had to cancel my salsa lesson for today, I've got a lot of time for sitting and listening." He pointed to the side of the house and twirled his index finger. "Grab a couple of those old lawn chairs under the oak tree around back and let's sit outside, right here on the front lawn. A man should at least be able to enjoy the outdoors and his own farm even if he's an old cripple."

Fritz and Elise started for the chairs together.

"Is he always this ornery after therapy?" she asked her brother.

"I can hear you," Anton called out. "I have a busted ankle and leg. My ears are fine!"

Fritz rolled his eyes, and they grinned at each other. When they returned with the chairs and had positioned Anton Springer safely in his seat, Fritz dropped them both like hot potatoes.

"I've done my duty with this cranky old coot. He's all yours," he said and, with a wave, hightailed it to his car to go back to his office in town. Together, Elise and her father watched Fritz's car until it disappeared down the driveway.

"Okay, Lizzie, my girl, tell me what's eating you." Anton winced, stretched out his injured leg, and laid the crutches beside his chair.

Elise flung her hands in despair and jerked her head toward the house. "I just found out Lucas invested in Mort Levinson's new project here in Wilkes-Barre. It looks to Winston and Sanders like he tried to buy me the lead architect position and cut them out."

"Oh, for the love of God! That's a problem? Those two clowns in California should be happy the firm's name is even associated with Levinson's project."

Elise pursed her lips. "I think I need to fly back there, Dad, and see if I can straighten it out before my career gets pushed off a cliff and nosedives into a slimy pit."

"I'll say you do," Anton agreed. When she looked at him surprised, he continued, "And I'd tell those two buffoons exactly what you want. By the way, tell me, what is it you want?"

"I'm in love with Lucas and Todd, but I'm also in love with my job," she admitted, "and they're separated by about twenty-eight hundred miles."

"Oh, Lizzie, don't you know love can conquer the impossible?" He parted his arms and raised them toward the sky. "Love is the master key that opens the gates of happiness."

She looked at her dad, surprised again. "Oh my, that's so sweet and poetic, Dad."

Anton grunted. "Yeah, Oliver Wendell Holmes thought so, too." He resettled himself in the chair again. "Lizzie, you're an accomplished professional. If you have to go back to California, do it. Get the next plane out. Tell those idiots you want both love and your job. Why don't you offer to set up a satellite office on the East Coast here? You use their name to expand. After all, they've been using you, mind you, for the last seven years—and not in the right way!"

She stared at her dad. When her father got on a tear, there was no stopping him, but she had to admit, the idea wasn't so far-fetched. She could take occasional trips back to San Francisco when need be or do face-to-face meetings with video conferencing.

"It might work," she said. "You are amazing." She leaned over and brushed a gentle kiss on his weathered cheek. "Please don't say anything to Lucas until I can call Winston and Sanders and try to sort this out."

She stood up. "Oh, and to make matters worse, we're still no closer to solving Mike Fisher's murder even though we found the department's money safely stashed along with all Mike Fisher's important papers. Something just doesn't jive. Somehow, I think Jack

Morrison is involved, even if he has an alibi."

Anton pursed his lips and drew his eyebrows into a puzzled look before he spoke. "So nose around. Talk to some of the staff who are close to him. Someone knows something, Liz. No one is asking the right person the right questions. Throw your rope farther out and see what it catches."

Elise stood. "I guess I'll have to. Do you need help getting into the house?"

'Nah, I'm going to sit out here a while and listen to the birds and feel the sunshine on my face." He pulled out a cell phone. It looked like one of the new models everyone was buying for the elderly at large discount department stores. "This is Lucas's new gift to me." He flipped it open to show her the keypad. "They must think all old people are blind or have big fingers. Take a gander at these gigantic numbers, will you? Won't Lucas be thrilled when I make my first call to him from the front lawn of my own house and ask him to come out and help me inside?" The old man chortled and slapped his knee.

Elise sighed and shook her head. Without another word, she headed for her car.

Rosie's Posies was doing a brisk business when Elise entered the shop an hour later. A tall thin girl wearing a green logo apron was working the counter, and a lanky boy in cargo pants and a green tee-shirt with the same logo was stocking coolers with flowers from a recent bulk delivery. The shop smelled heavenly of roses, gardenias, and moist moss and earth.

Elise approached the girl, whose nametag said "Amy." "I need some help," she said. "One of my friends in Atlanta wants a bouquet just like the one

Monique DuBois received a few days ago. Could you look it up?"

The girl punched the keys of her computer for a few moments, stared at the screen, then looked up at her. "It was a mixture of pastel roses, lilies and wild flowers," she said. "It's called Springtime Medley."

"Can you tell me the name of the person who sent the bouquet?"

The girl looked at her warily, but admitted, "It was paid for in cash."

Elise decided her only option was to lie. "Do you know what the person who paid for the flowers looked like? It seems the card was misplaced when they were delivered to Monique in Atlanta, and she has no way of thanking her admirer."

"Oh, I'm so sorry," the girl said.

"It was a woman," the boy said with his head still in the cooler. "I remember her well. A tall, thin woman with lots of rings on her fingers and flashy bracelets on her wrists. She smelled like she had just smoked a carton of cigarettes. She wore bright red lipstick, too."

Clarisse Fisher. Elise made the connection without much thought. Why would Clarisse be sending Monique flowers with Lucas's name on them? Unless she wanted to get rid of Lucas by hoping Monique would lure him back to Atlanta? Unless she was involved with something that warranted keeping Lucas at a distance. Was she somehow involved in Mike's murder? Elise headed for the door with more questions tumbling around in her head than she when she entered the shop.

"Would you like to place an order?" the girl at the counter called after her.

Elise shook her head. "No, thank you, maybe next week." She tugged on the door handle. Outside she paused on the street and felt warm sunlight on her back. It cast shadows cutting the sidewalk in two. Farther up the street, the sweet smell of cinnamon, sugar, and yeast drifted from a bakery shop.

Throw your rope out farther echoed in her ears as Elise opened her car door and realized her windshield was decorated with a parking ticket. She groaned, snatched it from underneath the wiper blade, slapped it on the dashboard inside her car, and turned the ignition. She needed to find someone to give her a better insight into Jack Morrison, and the only person she knew was Linda Cook at Child and Youth Services. She put the car into drive, maneuvered it through a coffee kiosk, and headed for the agency. She was glad to see Morrison's car was not in the parking lot when she arrived. She called Nick from her cell phone before she went into the building.

He picked up on the first ring. "Got good news?" he asked.

"Can you tell me if there were any connections between Jack Morrison and Mike Fisher?"

She could hear Nick rustling papers on his desk. "Fisher had Morrison in his sights. He thought maybe Morrison was selling marijuana, but could never pin anything on him. Mike was actually interested in bigger guys than an occasional pot smoker, but Morrison and he didn't see eye-to-eye about foster care, as you well know, so Morrison was on his radar."

"Do you think Ted Meyer knew Morrison might be involved with illegal substances?"

"I really don't know, Elise."

"Okay, it's a start, Nick. We have a connection. One more thing—we've checked Mike's outgoing calls for that day, but did you check his incoming calls? I'm wondering if anyone of interest called him the day he died, either Morrison, Clarisse, or Meyer?"

"I'll look at the printout again. I'll get back to you if I find anything."

"Okay, call me on my cell." Elise punched the end button and slid out of her car.

Linda Cook looked up suspiciously from her computer when Elise entered the office minutes later and slumped down into a chair beside the desk, holding two cups of coffee.

"Did you have an appointment with someone?" Linda asked and nervously scanned her appointment calendar, the pencil in her hand tapping away on her desk blotter like a nervous woodpecker. "I don't have your name anywhere here."

Elise shook her head and set a cup of coffee on the desk in front of Linda. "You look like a cream and sugar gal, right?"

Linda curled her hand around the offered coffee and waited.

"I need some information about Jack Morrison," Elise admitted. "I figured since you worked with him, you might help me." She had Linda's attention now and she knew it.

"I don't want to jeopardize my job," Linda said, looking at her suspiciously.

"You're right, so I'll ask the questions, and you can decide whether you want to answer or not." Elise removed the cover on her coffee and blew on it. "You dated Jack at one time, didn't you?"

Linda nodded.

"And didn't you think it might jeopardize your job?"

When Linda only stared at her with a raised eyebrow, Elise realized her mistake and quickly relented. "Never mind, you don't have to answer." She took a sip of coffee. "Do you know whether Jack owed any money?"

"Probably," Linda admitted with another nod of her head. "Jack was a big gambler. Gamblers lose money. Gamblers don't always have money to cover their habit or their debts."

"Any big amounts?"

Linda Cook shook her head. "I wouldn't know about the amount."

"Did Jack know Mike Fisher?"

Linda snorted. "Know? More like knew and disliked. Jack always had a gripe about Mike Fisher. Mike was the champion of the underdog. If there was a domestic dispute, Mike tried to get it worked out between the husband and wife, girlfriend and boyfriend, especially if children were involved. He wasn't big on removing children from the home, being a foster kid himself. Jack said Mike Fisher was naïve and interfered with his ability to do his job."

"Why did you and Jack break off your relationship?" Elise was sure that Linda Cook was a straight shooter. The woman was the type to count the office pencils to verify they weren't misplaced or stolen on her watch.

Linda shrugged. "It just didn't work out."

"Did you know Jack used pot?" she asked.

Linda looked down at her appointment calendar

without speaking.

"Okay. Let's forget that. Did Clarisse know Jack Morrison?"

"I believe they knew each other, yes."

Elise stood. "One more thing, Linda. Did Ted Meyer know about any of this?"

This time Linda looked up and laughed a soft, cynical laugh. "There's nothing around this town Ted Meyer doesn't know. Are we finished? I have work to do." She turned back to her computer, signaling the discussion was ended, and added, "Thanks for the coffee."

Chapter Twenty-Three

Outside, Elise checked her watch and paused to think things over. Having a confrontation with Clarisse Fisher was not on her list of favorite things to do, but it couldn't be avoided. On her way over to Clarisse's apartment, she stopped at the Bank of America on Linden Street, used her ATM card at the drive-thru, and pulled into an empty parking space in the bank's parking lot. She cut the engine. The wind had kicked up and a food wrapper and paper cup tumbled about, dumped out by an uncaring litterbug.

She called home to check on her dad. Cindy answered on the first ring and told her Chuck Sanders had called, but hadn't left a message, and an hour later, Paul Winston had also called, but didn't bother to leave a message either. She was not surprised to hear her father was happily engaged in teaching Todd how to play checkers. The man loved children. Better yet, she was pleased to know dinner was taken care of. Cindy was busy making a pan of lasagna and homemade bread.

"Where's Lucas?" Elise asked.

"He's at the showroom, checking on the construction crew. He said to tell you to stop by. He needs to talk to you. It's important," Cindy said.

Elise felt sorry for leaving so abruptly. She knew she had stomped on his feelings. She was in love with him, and he was the last person she ever wanted to hurt. He was a businessman, plain and simple. The more she thought about it, the more she realized he wouldn't have invested to hurt her. He was not a man to do damage of any kind to anyone. She rubbed her eyes with her hands. Why was she feeling so edgy? She was tired, she decided. She had been living on adrenaline for days now. Her head hurt and her body ached from the fall at the cottage, and Mike Fisher's murder was scratching at her inner thoughts with a vengeance. She had hoped all her efforts would have unearthed one clue or made one connection to what really happened the night of his death. To make matters worse, she had less than twenty-four hours until Nick Peters reported the missing drug money was found.

"Okay," she told Cindy, "I'll swing by the garage." She was about to start her car and back out of the parking spot when Nick phoned.

"Yeah?" she asked shutting down the engine again.

"Frightfully polite, Ms. Springer."

"Well, pal, I've hit a brick wall. I'm too weary and disgruntled to be polite. What do you have?"

"I rechecked the phone records," Nick said. She could hear him moving papers around again on his desk of disaster. "I've got it right here. An hour before he left his shift at 11 p.m., Mike got a call from the Meyer home. However, Ted was on duty as well, so it must have been a call from Mary Jo about Todd because he returned it before he left the barracks at the end of his shift."

"Any others?"

"None relating to anything other than routine work."

"Okay, well, it was a shot," she said and heaved a sigh.

"Hey, stay merry, keep the chin up, don't get discouraged yet," Nick said. "Eventually, something will pop up or something will shake loose to give us the lead we need. All we need is one spark, one clue, one thought or one thread that starts to unravel, and then everything falls into place like a jigsaw puzzle."

She sighed again. "Yeah, thanks, Nick, but if this day gets any merrier, I'll have to hire clowns to spread the joy around." She heard him chuckle as she disconnected her cell phone.

Minutes later, as Elise arrived at Clarisse's apartment, she pondered all the things she'd like to tell the woman before she went inside, reached out, and choked her scrawny neck. It was obvious Clarisse had a hand in trying to get Lucas out of Scranton and back to Atlanta. But why?

Elise pulled her car into a spot in front of the building, which looked even more tired and run-down than last week. Besides the garbage cans, recycling bins of cans, glass, and plastics now stood with their contents overflowing onto the weed-lined walk leading to the stairs. Someone had even abandoned a ratty-looking blue lounge chair in the center of the sidewalk, and Elise had to step around it to reach the first step.

Clarisse answered on the first knock.

"You again?" she asked. "This is an unexpected pleasure. Keep it up and someone might start thinking we're friends." Clarisse laughed her high-pitched laugh.

"We need to talk," Elise said, not trying to hide her irritation as she pushed past Clarisse. The inside of the apartment was worse than the last time she was there.

More blouses, slacks, and sweaters were discarded over the chairs and sofa, and it looked like a shoe store had exploded over the worn shag carpet. Dirty dishes and empty wine bottles littered the kitchen counter top. Clarisse scooped up a load of jackets from the same chair Elise used before and dumped them on the couch.

As usual, Clarisse was wearing her signature bright red lipstick and red nails, and she wore at least three cheap bracelets on her wrist to accessorize her black leggings and a white shirt tunic with a green turtleneck sweater underneath. She looked like a stork.

"I'm tired, I have a headache, and my patience is worn thin," Elise admitted with a scowl and sat down. "So let's not concoct any more misinformation. I already know you sent Monique a bouquet of flowers and signed it from Lucas Fisher. Just tell me why."

Clarisse quipped back, "My, my, testy, aren't we?"

"Why, Clarisse? Don't make me hurt you. My tank of compassion is on empty."

Clarisse gave a flippant shrug. "I wanted him out of the picture. I thought if he got back with Monique, he would give up the idea of staying in Scranton. The undercover money was never found. I wanted it."

"Did you want it enough to kill Mike Fisher?"

Clarisse laughed heartily, a high-pitched tone that rippled out and cackled like a witch. "Would I tell you if I did?" She shook her head. "No, I didn't kill Mike. Our relationship was over with the divorce. It was a mistake from the start and both of us knew it."

"How does Jack Morrison fit into the picture? And don't tell me you don't know him."

"I figured you'd eventually catch me on that little white lie," Clarisse admitted. "People saw us together at

Two Horses and around town before we split."

"Get to the point, Clarisse."

"We were just friends. We dated a few times. I loved to motor around in Jack's white Mercedes, and he sure knew how to show a girl a good time. We went to the best restaurants in the area and gambled at all the casinos in the state. Do you have any idea how nice it was to have someone else serving the best booze to me for a change? So when I found out Lucas was back in town and trying to get custody of Todd, I pressured Jack to send Todd back to New Castle. I was hoping to get Lucas to leave." She grew more heated as she spoke. "After all, there was a rumor the drug money was somewhere near $100,000. I figured Mike had to have stashed it somewhere close. I figured I could buy me some time so I could find the will, too. I should be the one to get Mike's money and property since I was his wife."

"Was." Elise looked at Clarisse, who was pacing the room now, flinging her hands into the air as she spoke. Elise saw flashes of light as the sunlight from a window caught the rhinestones in her bracelet. Her eyes widened. Fear and uneasiness washed over her as scenes from the cottage tumbled wildly in her brain. It all came flying back. She was certain she was having a déjà-vu moment. She gritted her teeth, holding her raw emotions in check while she fought back an urge to leap up and throttle Clarisse with her bare hands. She remembered being hit at the cottage, and the last thing she saw before she felt the blow were flashes of sparkling light. It was the rhinestones or the bright metal of Clarisse's bracelet reflecting sunlight from the cottage window.

Elise sucked in a lengthy breath of air and let it out slowly. "So it was you who dug through the boxes in the shed and later hit me over the head." She shook her head and didn't even try to hide her irritation or disgust. "Wow, I'm afraid to ask what your next idea would have been if you didn't knock me completely out. I have stitches and a concussion for your moment of insanity."

"You can't prove anything!" Clarisse snapped and glowered at her.

"If I have the police lift fingerprints off the boxes in the shed, none will match yours, right? Be reasonable, it's only a matter of time before you become a suspect in Mike's murder."

"I didn't kill Mike!" Clarisse was near hysterical now. "Okay, I snooped through a few boxes. If you hadn't been so nosey and surprised me, you wouldn't have been hurt."

Elise looked at her now with open disdain. Clarisse had just confessed to the assault. Elise took another deep breath and tried another tactic. "The night Mike died, where were you, Clarisse?"

"I was working at Two Horses. You can ask anyone. Even the bartender. Hell, ask Ted Meyer, he was there. He took Jack home that night. The poor schmuck was so plastered he could barely stand up. He was so drunk Meyer used Jack's car instead of the squad car for fear Jack was going to get sick and muck it up. Word around the bar was Jack owed over twenty five grand for weed stolen from the trunk of his car before he was even able to distribute it and collect his money. Talk about getting on the wrong side of bad people. Yeah, I think I'd get pretty slammed too if I owed money to a drug ring."

Elise opened her mouth to speak, but Clarisse cut her off, pointing to the door. "Now get out of here! I'm tired of your insinuations I had anything to do with Mike's death. Did you ever consider the fact it just might have been an accident? I'm tired of your high and mighty attitude. Get out."

Elise rose and returned her hostile stare. She was beyond intimidation at this point. "Just a friendly warning, Clarisse. I wouldn't consider going anywhere in next few days. I don't know yet whether Lucas wants to press charges for breaking and entering, and I haven't decided what I plan to do about assault charges. If you take off, I promise you, I'll have the police hunt you down and drag you back by your ugly, bleached blonde hair!"

Back in the parking lot, Elise slid into the driver's seat and leaned her head against the headrest. She let out an exhausted breath of air. She touched the stitches in her hairline and winced. Thoughts from her conversation with Clarisse were tangled like a big ball of yarn. This was one of those unlucky days, Elise decided, when jumping out of a plane with a parachute would be a bad idea. The chute probably wouldn't open and she'd bet the bank the back-up chute wouldn't either.

As she threaded her way back through Dunmore toward Interstate 81 and the on-ramp at Exit 188, she pulled off along the road and scrolled through her contact list to find the airline's number to book a flight back to San Francisco on Sunday. Before she could find the number, her phone rang. "Dang," she said aloud, when she realized it was Paul Winston calling. "Good-bye, back-up chute." Disappointed she couldn't speak with Chuck Sanders first, she put Paul on speakerphone, laid the phone on the console between the seats, and pulled back onto the highway.

"Hello, Paul," she said.

"I've tried to get you for the last four hours, Elise! Where on earth are you?"

"Yeah, well, I was just about to book a flight for Sunday to see you when your call interrupted me," she shot back.

His demeanor instantly changed. "This is good news! Real good news. Chuck will be so delighted to hear you're coming back."

Elise stopped for a red light and watched a mother with a little boy cross in front of her. The child skipped gaily along, chattering away to his mom who seemed delighted to be engaged in conversation with him. That's what I want, she thought, staring at them as she waited for the light to change. That's exactly what I want with Todd. I want a cheerful, fun-filled, and solid loving relationship with both a man and a child I've come to adore. She watched them for a second longer until the light turned and someone behind beeped his horn. Elise blinked, forcing herself back to reality.

"Are you still there, Elise?" Paul asked.

"Yes."

"Elise, is something the matter?"

Elise smiled. "No, nothing is the matter. Everything is perfectly fine. I was going to talk to you about working here on the East Coast, but I've changed my mind."

"Excellent. That's even better news," she heard Paul Winston say.

"Do me a favor, Paul, tell Chuck I quit. He can call me if he'd like when he gets a few minutes. I've decided I'm flying back long enough to collect my personal things from the office and to have my belongings from my apartment shipped back East. I've finally realized the people and things I love are right here. I'm setting up my own office in Scranton. Tell Chuck I appreciate everything he has done for me. Naturally, I appreciate all you've done."

"Wait! What? Quit?" Paul Winston's voice rose another octave. "You're going to ruin your career! You haven't thought this through, Elise. You're going to regret an impetuous move like this. Why do you want to destroy everything we've built over the years? What will I tell our clients? You're only thinking of yourself again, as always. You're so selfish. You can't be serious—"

Elise picked up the phone and looked at it. Paul was yelling so loud now she didn't need the speakerphone. She shook her head in dismay, clicked the end button, and tossed it on the passenger seat. Then she let out a cleansing breath of air and laughed—a gentle laugh that rippled out into the interior of her car.

Taking the ramp onto I-81, she lowered both windows and let the soft spring winds come streaming in steady soothing waves. *Love truly is the master key that opens the gates of happiness*, she thought. She pressed the gas pedal to the floor, enjoying the surge of speed as the engine eagerly responded. Grinning, flying down the interstate, she had never felt so free, so focused, and so in love in her entire life.

Chapter Twenty-Four

Lucas was sitting on the doorway stoop when she arrived minutes later, squealing the tires as the car came to a stop in the parking lot out front. She opened the door and, with a determined gait, she walked up to him.

"I screwed up big time, didn't I?" he asked, rising and looking at her warily.

"Oh, just shut up and kiss me, will you? I just quit my job because of you...you...you big lug nut!"

"You quit?" he asked incredulously.

"Yeah, you know the song with the lyrics 'give me a reason to stay'?"

He nodded.

"Well, I realized there were more important people I want to be with than the Smothers Brothers of California. I love Todd. I love you. I'll find a way to set up an office here and start all over if I have to. Being tied to those two dimwits was like lumbering around with old tires slung around my neck." She smiled and stood on tiptoe to kiss him.

"You're serious?" he whispered against her lips. "You'll marry me?" He barely let her head bob when he scooped her up and kissed her with intense hunger and passion. He lifted her off her feet and spun her around, and then set her back down and rained kisses down her neck before lifting her off her feet again.

"Lucas," she broke the embrace and pushed at his

chest, "I'm getting dizzy. Put me down this instant!"

When she was on solid ground, he laughed. "I'm the happiest man alive! You are going to make Todd the happiest kid in the state. Your dad will be thrilled, too. Let's go home and tell them." His gaze flitted between the two cars. "We'll take my car and leave yours here. J.B. left a spare car at the farm for Cindy to use. When I come back here to do some paperwork later tonight I can drive it back here and trade it for yours. Come on, let's go!"

He grabbed her hand and started to pull her toward his car.

"Wait, Lucas," she said, laughing. "I have to get my purse and my phone." She walked to her car, reached in through the open passenger window, grabbed her phone and purse from the seat, and was hurrying across the parking lot when a sudden thought came crashing down on her. She stopped. Her face paled, her heart thumped wildly in her chest, and she felt sick. Her purse slipped from her hands and thudded onto the macadam. She took a deep breath, trying to steady her nerves as she stared out across the horizon where clouds with gray underbellies were beginning to scud across the sky. There would be rain by nightfall. She had always liked the smell of rain. It washed the ugly dust from the trees and grass. *Too bad rain couldn't wash away the ugliness of murder, too,* she thought. The spinning in her head slowed and all the pieces surrounding the murder of Mike Fisher fell into place like a row of dominoes falling on each other.

"What's the matter?" Lucas called from across the lot. He walked quickly to stand beside her and put a hand on her shoulder. "Are you all right? You look like you just saw a ghost. Please tell me I didn't hurt you when I spun you around. I forgot all about your head. Honey, I'm so sorry."

Still deep in thought, she shook her head and held up a hand to silence him. "No, no, I'm fine. You have to help me. Please call Nick," she said, handing him her phone, still staring at the sky as she took a deep breath of air. "Tell him to meet us at Ted Meyer's house." She looked up at him, but her eyes had a frightening faraway look in them. "Lucas, I know who killed your brother."

****

It was almost dinnertime when Elise and Lucas arrived at Ted Meyer's house. Elise slammed her car door and went up the front walk before Lucas could shut down the engine and get out. She noticed Ted's cruiser was parked in the driveway. She knocked on the door and was greeted by Mary Jo.

"Elise. Come in. We were just talking about you, wondering why you haven't stopped in lately," Mary Jo said. "Oh, and Lucas is with you. Come into the kitchen."

"Where are the children?" Elise asked, frowning and following her to the back of the house.

"Oh, I fed them early and sent them outside to play so Ted can eat his dinner in peace. You know what it's like with three noisy kids underfoot."

Elise knew all right. She knew how Ted Meyer had a temper and no tolerance for children. The kids were downright scared to be around their own father and weren't even allowed to eat with him.

"Where's Ted?" Elise said.

"Here," he said behind her. "What's this

unexpected visit about?"

Elise wasted no time and no words. "The night of Mike Fisher's murder, where were you, Ted?" She could feel Lucas beside her, radiating strength and reassurance.

"You know where I was. I finished my shift and came home."

"After you dropped Jack off from Two Horses, right?"

"That's right." Ted Meyer's lips thinned in anger. "Just what are you trying to prove here? I've been over this a dozen times with the local and state police. I resent—"

"Answer my question!" Elise shouted. She threw the words at him like stones. She wanted answers and was determined she would not be put down by this brute. She lifted her chin, refusing to cower. "You drove Jack home in his car and then you drove his car home. Here, to the house, didn't you?"

"I did no such thing." Ted Meyer looked warily at Mary Jo. "Isn't that right, Mary Jo?"

She nodded and averted her eyes.

Elise persisted. "No, the car that hit Mike Fisher was Jack Morrison's. You came home from your shift in Jack's car."

She turned to Mary Jo. "I would never have figured it out, if it wasn't for the phone call you made earlier to Mike at work. At first, I was confused when we spoke in the supermarket about why you would tell me your sister was staying with *you*, not *us*, the night of Mike's murder. Your sister was coming to stay with *you* because Ted was on one of his tyrannical rants again, and you were afraid of what might happen when he came home from work and you were alone with him."

Ted interrupted her. "If you think you can accuse me of murder or abuse, you little bitch, think again!"

Behind her, Lucas lurched forward, but Elise blocked his move with her arm.

"No." She shook her head at Ted, swallowed hard, and boldly met his gaze. "No, I'm accusing you of being an accessory to the murder."

She took a deep breath and turned to Mary Jo. "You called Mike before his shift ended to tell him Ted was on one of his rages again. Your sister came over, hoping to help put the lid on it and save you from another beating. Mike arrived shortly after Ted came home and threatened to expose him and his violent temper. Mike knew what was going on inside your house. He was a savvy cop." She looked at Ted Meyer. "When Mike left, you threatened Mary Jo and told her if anything got out about being a wife beater, you'd be washed up with the local force and your character would be tarnished. It was going to be her fault if it happened, right? Tell me, Ted, isn't that loosely the way it all went down?"

Elise met Mary Jo's angered eyes without flinching. "So as soon as Mike left, you took Morrison's car and tried to stop him, didn't you?"

"It was an accident!" Mary Jo cried out. "I only wanted to talk to him. To stop him!" She buried her face in her hands and wept.

"Shut up, Mary Jo," Ted shouted at her. His nostrils flared with fury.

Elise shook her head sadly. A cold knot formed in her stomach. "You ran him off the road, didn't you, Mary Jo? And when you stopped and determined he was dead, you took Jack's car back to the bar, picked up Ted's cruiser and drove it home. No need to report it. Problem solved."

She turned to Ted. "When you found out Jack Morrison needed money to pay off his debt for the marijuana stolen from his car, you lent it to him." She turned to Mary Jo. "The money you said you and Ted were saving for your cabin in the woods."

Elise rounded on Ted again, her voice curt and full of contempt. "You needed to be good buddies with Jack. You wanted the Mike Fisher incident to go away. What you never planned was someone getting paint samples from Jack's car and matching them to the chips taken from Mike's, so you lent him the money he needed to make good on his mishap with the stolen marijuana from his trunk."

Ted Meyer lurched and started toward her with an upraised hand. "You meddling little bitch. You just wouldn't give up, would you? You had to keep digging, and digging and *digging*!"

"I wouldn't touch her," Lucas said, stepping between Ted and Elise. "Give me a reason to knock your block off, Ted. Right here. Right now."

From behind Ted, Nick and two other state troopers entered the kitchen from the living room. "Well, I've heard enough of the conversation, Meyer. The party's over. You and Mary Jo are under arrest."

Elise glanced at Mary Jo. Her own eyes filled with tears as she looked at a person who she thought was her friend. She wondered whether she really knew her at all.

"Call your sister, Mary Jo," Elise said sadly. "You'll need a babysitter for your children tonight."

She swiped at her eyes with the back of her hand.

Lucas put a reassuring hand on her shoulder and pulled her close. "It's all right, Elise. It's over now. Let's go home," he said softly.

He signaled to Nick to take over as they walked silently out to the car.

The ride to the farm was a quiet one, broken only by the sound of the windshield wipers scraping against the window. When they reached home, the rain continued, harder, like tears falling from above. They sat together and listened to it drumming on the roof of the car.

"When did you figure it out?" Lucas finally asked in an exhausted voice.

Elise sighed. "When you told me you'd take the spare car at the farmhouse and pick up mine later. Clarisse had told me Ted dropped Jack Morrison off at his house using Jack's own car, instead of a cruiser. All along I figured only one person drove Jack's car and he would be the person who killed Mike. I suspected Ted. Then it dawned on me it could easily have been two people and when Mike didn't immediately return Mary Jo's call to him at the barracks on the night he was killed, I figured the call couldn't have been about Todd. Mike would have returned that call immediately, as any responsible worried parent would. Suddenly all the pieces started to fall into place."

Lucas nodded. "I'm sorry it had to be one of your friends." He leaned over and kissed her on her forehead and then on her cheek. "But I'm not sorry you solved the mystery surrounding Mike's death. I'm not sorry you're here with me, Elise Springer, and I'm not sorry you're going to stay and marry me. You're going to make me the happiest man in Scranton."

He smiled and peered out the window. "Let's make a run for it. Come on. Let's tell everyone some good news for a change."

Chapter Twenty-Five

It was the perfect spring morning to sit on the Springers' front porch with a cup of coffee and watch the sky bloom in shades of rose and gold. Elise and Lucas sat on the old wicker swing, and at their feet Todd and Cindy were leafing through a stack of bridal magazines. One big square diamond twinkled from Elise's hand.

The wedding plans were driving her crazy. She and Lucas had decided upon the last Saturday in July for the big day. However, everyone was needling her. Fritz wanted a big splash at a huge reception hall in Scranton. Her dad wanted a church wedding with a reception under a huge white tent on the front lawn of the farm. Lucas said a destination wedding would suit him just fine, which could be a short trip to city hall if she so chose.

What Elise hadn't told anyone yet was she finally decided upon a church wedding, followed by a reception by the lake at the cottage. She wanted three tents—one with a band for dancing, one with food and drink, and one especially for the children to play in. She had already spoken privately with Cindy, who had agreed to be her personal wedding planner and who would take care of all the details, including organizing games for the kids. Cindy was researching a few honeymoon destination packages for Lucas as well.

For his wedding present to her, Lucas had bought an office building in downtown Scranton and had helped her with all the legal startup procedures and paperwork for her new firm, called Springer Architectural Designs. Lucas had insisted she use her maiden name for the company's business, even if she decided to use his once they were married. Mort Levinson was her first client, but with his recommendations and circle of friends and investors, she was certain more clients were on their way.

Todd looked up at her. Beside him was a large basket with a small Golden Retriever puppy sleeping soundly on a blanket, and beside the basket, Bess lay quiet, but alert, protecting both boy and puppy. "I like the idea of blowing bubbles after the ceremony," he said, "and I think the favors for the wedding reception should be animal crackers. But no lions and tigers allowed, okay, Elise?"

"Only if I don't have to sort them, buddy," she said and followed her words with a smile and a wink.

With Cindy's urging, the little boy scrambled up. He approached Elise cautiously, one hand behind his back. Earlier in the morning he had acted unusually withdrawn and quiet. Elise thought there had been too much commotion for the child to absorb everything that had happened during the last few days. She had been away from the farm, frantically trying to solve Mike's murder before the twenty-four hours elapsed and the police disclosed the drug money had been located. Even though her father had tried to keep everyone on an even keel, she thought the child might have been affected by the high emotions surrounding the last few days.

He looked at her almost shyly now with those big,

dusty gray Fisher eyes. "I have an early wedding present for you, Eeeelise," he said in a solemn voice, and handed her a card he had made. On the outside of it he had drawn a barrel-like brown dog with floppy ears and long legs, and beside him, a bouquet of brilliant red, yellow, and blue flowers.

Elise opened the card. Inside were only five simple words. He had written them in an uneven, childlike script, obviously coached by Lucas or Cindy. She thought her heart would burst with delight. Leaping off the swing, she scooped up the little boy in her arms and crushed him to her.

"Yes, yes, yes," she squealed, hugging him to her and ruffling his hair. "Yes, Todd, my answer is yes. Oh, yes!" In her exuberance, she dropped the opened card onto the porch floor, revealing the five little words that formed her key to love.

"Will you be my mom?"

A word about the author...

Judy Ann Davis began her career in writing as a copy and continuity writer for radio and television in Scranton, PA. She holds a degree in Journalism and Communications from Point Park University in Pittsburgh, PA.

Throughout her career, Judy Ann has written news articles and features for newspapers, advertising copy for businesses, and curricula and grants for various educational institutions.

Over a dozen of her short stories have appeared in various literary and small magazines, and anthologies. *Up on the Roof and Other Short Stories*, a collection of nineteen short stories, will be published this year.

Her first novel, *RED FOX WOMAN*, published in 2010, is a western, mystery, and romance and was a finalist in the International Book Awards and USA Book News Best Book Awards.

When Judy Ann is not behind her computer, you can find her looking for anything humorous to make her laugh or swinging a golf club where the chuckles are few. She is a member of Pennwriters, Inc. and lives with her husband in Clearfield, PA.

Visit her at: www.judyanndavis.com and www.judyanndavis.blogspot.com.

You can find her on Facebook: Judy Ann Davis and on Twitter: @judyanndavis4